continued . . .

"Fans of Dr. Mark Sloan will not be disappointed. If anything, *The Shooting Script* is an even more compelling showcase for the good doctor than the television series."
—Rick Riordan, Edgar Award–winning
author of *Southtown*

"Rx for fun! Lee Goldberg's *Diagnosis Murder* series is the perfect prescription for readers looking for thrills, chills, and laughs. I know I'll be standing in line for my refill!"
—Meg Cabot, author of *The Princess Diaries*
and *Boy Meets Girl*

The Death Merchant

"Dr. Mark Sloan returns in a crime story that seamlessly interweaves two radically different story lines while taking the reader on a roller-coaster ride through the delights—and dangers—of Hawaii. If you liked the broadcast episodes, you'll love *The Death Merchant*."
—Jeremiah Healy, author of the John Cuddy mysteries

"This novel begins with tension and ends with surprise. Throughout, it is filled with gentle humor and a sure hand. *Diagnosis Murder,* the television series, could always be counted on for originality and a strong sense of humor, particularly when Lee Goldberg's name was on the scripts. This is not just a novel for fans of the television series."
—Stuart M. Kaminsky, Edgar Award–winning
author of *Not Quite Kosher*

The Silent Partner

"A whodunit thrill-ride that captures all the charm, mystery and fun of the TV series . . . and then some. . . . Goldberg wrote the very best *Diagnosis Murder* episodes, so it's no surprise that this book delivers everything you'd expect from the show . . . a clever, high-octane mystery that moves like a bullet-train. Dr. Mark Sloan, the deceptively eccentric deductive genius, is destined to join the pantheon of great literary sleuths. . . . You'll finish this book breathless. Don't blink or you'll miss a clue. A brilliant debut for a brilliant detective. Long live Dr. Mark Sloan!"
—*New York Times* bestselling author Janet Evanovich

"An exciting and completely satisfying read for all *Diagnosis Murder* fans. We were hooked . . . Goldberg's skill in bringing our favorite characters to the printed page left us begging for more."
—Aimée and David Thurlo, authors of the Ella Clah, Sister Agatha, and Lee Nez Mysteries

"For those who have, as I do, an addiction to Mark Sloan, Lee Goldberg provides a terrific fix . . . will cure any *Diagnosis Murder* withdrawal symptoms you might have had."
—S. J. Rozan, author of *Winter and Night*

DIAGNOSIS MURDER

THE WAKING NIGHTMARE

Lee Goldberg

BASED ON THE TELEVISION SERIES CREATED BY
Joyce Burditt

A SIGNET BOOK

SIGNET
Published by New American Library, a division of
Penguin Group (USA) Inc., 375 Hudson Street,
New York, New York 10014, USA
Penguin Group (Canada), 10 Alcorn Avenue, Toronto,
Ontario M4V 3B2, Canada (a division of Pearson Penguin Canada Inc.)
Penguin Books Ltd., 80 Strand, London WC2R 0RL, England
Penguin Ireland, 25 St. Stephen's Green, Dublin 2,
Ireland (a division of Penguin Books Ltd.)
Penguin Group (Australia), 250 Camberwell Road, Camberwell, Victoria 3124,
Australia (a division of Pearson Australia Group Pty. Ltd.)
Penguin Books India Pvt. Ltd., 11 Community Centre, Panchsheel Park,
New Delhi - 110 017, India
Penguin Group (NZ), cnr Airborne and Rosedale Roads, Albany,
Auckland 1310, New Zealand (a division of Pearson New Zealand Ltd.)
Penguin Books (South Africa) (Pty.) Ltd., 24 Sturdee Avenue,
Rosebank, Johannesburg 2196, South Africa

Penguin Books Ltd., Registered Offices:
80 Strand, London WC2R 0RL, England

First published by Signet, an imprint of New American Library,
a division of Penguin Group (USA) Inc.

First Printing, February 2005
10 9 8 7 6 5 4 3 2 1

ACKNOWLEDGMENTS

As always, I am deeply indebted to Dr. D. P. Lyle for his medical advice and hearty laughter. I'd also like to thank William Rabkin, Tod Goldberg, Paul Bishop, Twist Phelan, Bill Dinino, and Joel Goldman for their wise counsel.

In the midst of writing this book, I had an accident and broke both of my arms, one of them quite severely. It was a situation that required far more than the usual patience, understanding, and support that my wife Valerie and my daughter Madison bless me with every day. During those weeks, writing was a daily struggle . . . actually, *everything* was . . . and I couldn't have done it without their love.

I'm also grateful to the hundreds of *Diagnosis Murder* fans who inundated me with encouraging get well cards, e-mails, and letters. This book is for you.

CHAPTER ONE

The woman sitting in front of Dr. Mark Sloan was determined to die and there was nothing he could do about it. He'd brought her into this world over forty years ago and, more than likely, he'd see her out of it, too.

Although Mark was Chief of Internal Medicine at Community General Hospital, he still acted as Lenore Barber's family physician. Despite all his dire warnings, she'd taken up smoking as a teenager and never gave it up. Seven years ago, she was diagnosed with lung cancer. She smoked on the morning of her lung surgery and during the five months of chemotherapy that followed.

It made Mark furious, but he understood her flawed, fatalistic thinking. She was dead already. What difference would it make if she kept smoking now if it gave her some comfort through the ordeal?

But luck was on her side. After six chemotherapy sessions, and the weeks of crushing fatigue, complete hair loss, and constant nausea that followed, all signs of the cancer were eradicated.

She'd survived.

He was certain the harrowing, near-death experience would have a profound effect on Lenore's life. The mere thought of another cigarette would surely repulse her. But if it didn't, all she had to do was look at herself naked to be dissuaded from having a smoke.

Lenore spent a small fortune on breast implants, a nose job, and elaborate orthodonture to make herself more competitively attractive to casting directors, eligible bachelors, and people she was trying to sell real estate to. The surgical scars on her body would be a constant, undeniable reminder of the fate she'd narrowly escaped. Mark believed that would be enough to guarantee that she'd never smoke again.

He was wrong.

She shrugged off the experience as if it was just a bad bout with the flu and fell right back into her old life as an aspiring actress, real estate agent, single mother, and heavy smoker. If anything, she smoked even more than she had before, as if losing a chunk of her lung and being bombarded with radiation had given her some kind of immunity from disease.

Over the ensuing years, Mark reminded her of the hell she'd been through. Did she want to endure it all over again? He urged her to try the nicotine patch, to enroll in smoking cessation classes, to do whatever it took to kick her deadly addiction to cigarettes. But she blithely ignored his admonitions.

A few months ago, she came in to see Mark for a routine follow-up exam, which revealed a tiny growth on her liver. Mark ordered a biopsy and the results confirmed his worst fears. The cancer was back, only now it had migrated to her liver. Lenore immediately began a new, aggressive regimen of chemotherapy.

Now she sat in an exam room with Mark, who reviewed the latest PET scan results and blood work analysis from the hospital's Chief of Oncology.

It was good news. The growth was gone and her hematology was all normal. No more treatment was necessary, no surgery would be required.

She'd cheated death again.

"Wow," she said, scratching under the wig she wore to cover her radiation-induced baldness. "Just like that? It's gone?"

"That's right," Mark said.

"I don't believe it," she said. "I thought you were going to tell me it was time to start looking for a good surgeon."

"You were very lucky. I can't recall seeing results this positive after only three chemotherapy treatments," Mark said. "But if you keep smoking, I can guarantee you that the cancer will return."

"Can't you give me even a minute to enjoy the good news before lecturing me?"

"I know you've kept smoking throughout the chemo," Mark said.

"And the cancer is gone, isn't it?" she said with a casual shrug. "Obviously, it didn't make a difference."

Mark looked her in the eye. "You can't keep smoking, Lenore."

"I'm not smoking nearly as much as I used to," she said. "Give me a break."

"You just got your break," he said. "You're still alive."

"I didn't smoke at all yesterday and I didn't have a single cigarette the whole week I was in the Bahamas," she said, flashing a smile that showed her unnaturally bright teeth. "Maybe I should move there. Prescribe that."

"You shouldn't be smoking at all, anywhere," he said. "Think about your kids."

"I never smoke around them."

"You know what I meant," Mark said. "Who is going to raise them when you're gone?"

"Don't be so dramatic, Mark." Lenore got up from her seat and grabbed her purse. "So I had an itsy-bitsy smudge on the x-ray. If it comes back, we'll just zap it again. In the meantime, I'm going to celebrate. With a drink and a cigarette!"

And with that, Lenore kissed Mark on the cheek and quickly left the exam room, closing the door behind her.

Mark stared at the door for a long time, angry and frustrated. It wasn't like him to be so heavy-handed. He knew it was counterproductive. But he couldn't help himself. There were so many cancer patients who never got the second chance that Lenore had been given and she didn't seem to care.

Why couldn't she see how lucky she was?

Her self-destructive behavior infuriated him, more so because he felt a special responsibility to her. He was the one who delivered her, cut her umbilical cord, and laid her in her mother's arms. Mark couldn't help feeling that her good health had been in his hands ever since. It was the way he felt about any of the children he delivered who, as adults, still were his patients today.

Intellectually, Mark understood Lenore's addiction. She was unable to control her need for nicotine and would sacrifice anything to satisfy it. But emotionally, he just couldn't accept it. After what she'd suffered, how could she light another cigarette ever again? Didn't she want to live? Didn't she want to be there for her children?

It was a deplorable and unnecessary tragedy. But unless she acknowledged her addiction and was willing to do something about it, he was utterly powerless to save her.

His frustration with the situation was a cancer, too. Malignant and spreading with each encounter with her. He could feel it gnawing at his bones, eating him alive from inside.

Mark had felt that frustration with patients before and knew there was only one cure for his affliction: to distract himself with another insurmountable problem.

He thought of the murders he'd solved over the years as

a consultant to the Los Angeles Police Department and wondered if one reason he did it was to compensate for all the times he couldn't help the living.

Why was it that the problems of the dead were so much easier to solve?

Mark got up and wandered down the hall to the doctors' lounge, where Dr. Jesse Travis was sitting at one of the chipped Formica tables catching up on his paperwork, a stack of bulging medical files teetering in front of him.

"You ever have one of those days you wish you weren't a doctor?" the young doctor asked, peeking around the corner of the pile at Mark, who was helping himself to a cup of coffee.

"As a matter of fact," Mark replied, "this happens to be one of them."

"Where's the excitement in paperwork?" Jesse said. "Where's the intimacy? Where's the human drama?"

"Today I wouldn't mind a little less human drama and a lot more paperwork." Mark took a seat at the table beside him and stirred some sugar into his coffee cup.

"You want to talk about it?" Jesse asked, not really expecting Mark to unburden himself. After all, what knowledge or experience could the young doctor possibly have to offer his mentor, a man he tried to emulate as a doctor and even as a detective.

"Thanks," Mark said. "I could use your advice."

"You *could?*" Jesse asked in disbelief. Mark Sloan was actually turning to him for counsel. Like they were equals.

But Jesse's excitement quickly morphed into fear. What if he didn't have the answers? What if his advice was wrong? What would Mark think of him then?

Jesse didn't get the chance to find out.

Just as Mark was about to speak, he happened to take a casual glance out the window at the office building across the street. At first, Mark didn't quite register what he was seeing.

There was a woman sitting outside on the sill of her fifth-floor window, as calm and relaxed as if she were on the edge of a swimming pool, gently kicking her feet in the water.

She was pretty, in her mid-twenties, wearing a loose-fitting white blouse and a navy blue jacket that befitted a professional woman. She had pale skin and bright green eyes that met his gaze as she pushed herself into the air.

Mark bolted up from his seat, spilling his coffee onto the floor.

"No!" he yelled, horrified.

Her jacket flared behind her like wings as she plummeted silently to the ground below. She smacked into a tree limb, snapping it in half, then dropped onto the awning that stretched over the street-level coffeehouse. She bounced off the awning and landed on top of an old Buick Skylark parked at the curb. The roof crumpled and the car windows exploded under the impact, spraying glass onto the street.

Mark dashed for the stairs.

Jesse glanced out the window, saw the woman's body splayed on top of the car, and ran after Mark. They scrambled down the stairs together, taking them two at a time. There was no need to speak. They both knew what they had to do.

They burst out of the stairwell into the busy emergency room, the doors smacking into the walls with an explosive bang that caught everyone's attention.

Mark ran out the lobby doors into the street while Jesse started gathering supplies and yelling orders to the nurses.

"I need a crash cart, cervical collar, and a stretcher, stat!" he hollered.

Mark raced across the street, weaving through the traffic that had already stalled to gape at the bloodied body and the damaged car. Several people gathered on the street around the car, staring at the woman, uncertain of what to do. He pushed through them, jumped up onto the hood and leaned over the woman, who was on her back, her head lolling on the shattered windshield. Blood seeped out of her nose and mouth and dripped from under her hair. One of her legs was twisted grotesquely underneath her.

He felt for her pulse and found one. She was still alive. He lifted her eyelids and checked her pupils, which were reactive and equal, indicating that there was no bleeding in the brain. Mark took out his stethoscope and pressed it to her chest, listening. Her breathing wasn't good. Hitting the tree and the awning on her way down had broken her fall and saved her life, at least for the moment.

Jesse barged through the crowd, carrying an emergency medical kit and leading two orderlies with a stretcher and three nurses wheeling a battery-powered crash cart.

"She's alive," Mark said. "We have to get her into the ER."

He took a cervical collar from one of the nurses and secured the woman's neck and head, while Jesse leaped up on the trunk so he was positioned at her feet. Mark and Jesse helped the orderlies ease the stretcher under the woman; then the four men carefully lifted her off the car. The orderlies rushed her across the street to the hospital, Mark and Jesse running alongside.

Mark could hear sirens wailing in the distance, getting louder as they drew near. Somebody must have called 911. By the time the paramedics got there, all they'd find was the damage and the blood. The woman would already be receiving treatment in the ER.

The orderlies carried the woman into the first vacant trauma room, where Jesse's girlfriend, Nurse Susan Hilliard, was already standing by with her team, ready to assist the doctors.

Mark started shouting out orders, but stopped when he

couldn't catch his breath. He let Jesse take over and went outside into the hallway, where he found a chair and sat down, breathing hard, holding a hand to his chest. His heart was pounding. Sweat ran down his cheeks. After running as fast as he could down five flights of stairs, across the street, and back again, he was lucky he wasn't on the table in the trauma room himself.

He wasn't a young man anymore. He should have stayed behind at the hospital and let Jesse, who was more than capable, treat the woman in the street.

What was he thinking?

Mark wasn't thinking. He was reacting, going on pure impulse. He closed his eyes for a moment and saw the woman sitting on the windowsill, staring right at him. One instant she was there, the next she was falling . . .

"Are you okay, Mark?"

"I'll be fine," he said, his eyes flashing open to see Jesse standing in front of him, looking concerned. He glanced up at the wall clock and was surprised to see that forty minutes had passed.

Mark gestured to the trauma room. "More importantly, how is she?"

"Lucky she fell outside a hospital," Jesse said.

"She didn't fall," Mark said. "She jumped. I saw her do it. She looked right at me."

"Did you know her?"

"I never saw her face until today," Mark said.

"Well, you're never going to forget it now," Jesse said. "She's comatose. She's got a fractured humerus, fibula, and tibia, but no broken bones that appear to require surgery. There are no cervical or skull fractures, but her chest x-ray shows three broken ribs on her left side and a small pneumothorax."

"I'll have to watch that," Mark said.

"*I'll* watch that," Jesse said. "Your shift is over and after what you've just been through, you could use the rest."

"What about her lab work?"

"Still waiting on it, but I don't think she was high, if that's what you're getting at," Jesse said. "I've ordered a CT scan and then I'll send her up to the ICU. There's nothing more you can do here. Go home."

"Something made her desperate enough to want to kill herself," Mark said.

"It's too late to do anything about that now," Jesse said, and went back into the trauma room.

Mark wasn't so sure. Today he'd encountered two women who faced a choice between living and dying. Both of the women looked him in the eye and chose death. Perhaps he could still save one of them.

CHAPTER TWO

Still wearing his lab coat and hospital ID, Mark walked back across the street to the office building. The paramedics had left but several uniformed policemen remained behind, taking statements from witnesses. He doubted any of them saw what he saw. The cold look in her eyes. The grim, almost casual acceptance of her fate.

Those facts weren't important. All the police were interested in was whether or not she was pushed. She wasn't; they'd know that by now. So the police were just filling in blanks on a routine report that wouldn't matter much to anybody but the insurance companies covering the policies on the building, the Buick, and, perhaps, the young woman's life.

His statement could wait.

The building directory in the lobby listed only one tenant on the fifth floor: Funville Toys. Mark took the elevator up. It moved very slowly. There was a tiny video screen mounted in the wall that showed commercials for recently released DVDs and a new low-carb cookie. Until that moment, Mark never thought he'd miss elevator music.

The doors opened to a reception area that could have been a pediatrician's waiting room. The chairs and coffee tables were overflowing with toys. Fuzzy toy creatures covered the receptionist's wide desk, climbed her lamp, clung to her telephone receiver, and dangled joyfully from drawer handles.

The gaiety expressed by the frolicking toys wasn't reflected by the sole occupant of the room, a thin receptionist with a stud in her lower lip and a half-dozen earrings dangling from each ear. She sat shell-shocked, staring at nothing as Mark approached.

"Excuse me," Mark said quietly.

The receptionist looked up, teary-eyed, and Mark noticed the tissue balled up in her hand.

"I'm Dr. Mark Sloan, from Community General," he said. "We're treating the woman who jumped."

"Rebecca Jordan," she mumbled.

Now he had a name to go with the face, with the glance across an expanse that seemed to him both vast and intimate all at once.

"Is there someone here I can talk to about her? We need to contact her family."

"You'd better talk to Morrie Gelman, our boss," she said. "Down the hall, corner office."

Mark smiled politely and headed down the hall. People were gathered in their offices and outside their cubicles talking, crying, hugging. They all had the same, shell-shocked look as the receptionist.

The door to the corner office was slightly ajar. Behind it, Mark could hear a man's gravelly voice.

"Die, foul Gorpine fiend from hell!"

Mark peered through the opening and saw Morrie Gelman, a paunchy, gray-haired man in his fifties, wearing a jacket and tie, on his knees beside his coffee table, which was a battlefield filled with robot soldiers wielding ray guns, futuristic tanks, and flying saucers covered with cannons. Gelman was holding one of the robot soldiers, challenging an alien that looked like a lizard crossed with a polar bear.

"You'll never take Umgluck, not while we still breathe its sweet air," Gelman said.

Mark knocked lightly on the door and eased it open. "Mr. Gelman? Your receptionist sent me down."

Gelman got to his feet, not the least bit embarrassed to have been caught playing with toys. Mark didn't see any reason why he should be. It was a healthier way to handle stress than the methods most of the people he'd just seen would try tonight.

"What can I do for you?" Gelman asked.

"I'm Dr. Mark Sloan. I'm Rebecca Jordan's doctor. We've got her in the intensive care unit across the street."

"So she's alive," Gelman said, sighing with relief. "Thank God."

"She's in a coma and in critical condition," Mark said. "But I think she's going to make it. I'd like to contact her family."

Gelman regarded Mark suspiciously. "That's why you came here? Surely you could have asked the police for that information."

"You're right," Mark said. "To be honest, I was hoping you could tell me more about her as a person."

"Why?" Gelman asked.

It was a fair question, one Mark hadn't even bothered to ask himself yet. He didn't know the answer. There was only one thing he could think of to say.

"I saw her sitting in her window. We looked at each other. There was a connection. Before I could say or do anything, she jumped," Mark said. "So here I am."

Gelman studied Mark for a long moment, then seemed to come to a decision. He picked up one of the robot soldiers from the coffee table and held it out to Mark.

"See this? Everybody in the toy business is making them. We're working on a ray gun that a kid can fiddle with and turn into a robot ship," Gelman said. "Mechanical heroes and spatial-manipulation games are what kids want today. So what does Rebecca come up with? Let me show you."

Gelman led Mark two doors down the hall to another office. From the way everybody was looking at them, Mark knew it belonged to Rebecca. It was clean and sparse. The window was wide open and he could see straight across the street to the fifth-floor window of the doctors' lounge. The walls were covered with sketches, which fluttered in the breeze. Each sketch was a rough, yet strangely animated, depiction of the giant stuffed bear that sat in the guest chair in front of Rebecca's orderly desk.

It was the biggest, fluffiest, most lovable-looking stuffed animal Mark had ever seen, with outstretched, broad arms, a goofy smile, wide eyes, and a round little belly that demanded patting. Mark gave the belly a pat and was surprised by how soft it was.

"This is Cuddle Bear. Just an enormous stuffed animal. It should have bombed, but it's the biggest hit in the fifty-year history of this company." Gelman shook his head. "It took off immediately. We can't keep up with the demand and the publicity has been amazing."

Gelman pointed to a framed newspaper clipping on the wall. It was a wire-service story, dated a month earlier, about the surprising success of the stuffed animal. There were two photos with the article. One of the pictures was of a little child hugging the Cuddle Bear, snuggling up against its comfy belly, practically lost inside its big arms. The other picture was a candid photo taken of Rebecca in the Community General pediatric cancer center, a huge swarm of kids gathered around the stuffed animal, looks of pure joy on their faces.

She'd been in the hospital before, Mark thought. Perhaps they'd even passed in the halls or stood beside one another in the elevator. Perhaps she knew who she was looking at when their eyes met. Perhaps she was hoping for a spark of recognition and empathy in that instant before she jumped.

Mark shifted his attention to the newspaper article, reading a portion of it out loud. " 'Ms. Jordan describes the Cuddle Bear as a friend you can tell everything to, a friend who is always there for you.' "

"She could have been describing herself," Gelman said. "You start talking to her and before you know it, you've told her things you'd never tell anybody. She's a great listener. Everybody comes to her with their problems."

"Where does she go with hers?" Mark asked.

"I don't know." Gelman gave Mark a sad, guilty look. "We didn't realize until today that maybe she came up with the Cuddle Bear because she needed one herself."

Mark's cell phone trilled.

"Pardon me," Mark said, taking the phone from the pocket of his lab coat and bringing it to his ear. "Mark Sloan."

"Hey Dad," replied Steve, his voice even and businesslike, indicating he was not alone. "I need your help."

"What's the problem?" Mark asked.

"It will be obvious as soon as you see the corpse."

Lt. Steve Sloan knew his conversation with his dad was overheard by the police officers and forensic techs working around him that afternoon in the middle of a vast expanse of dry scrub land.

It didn't really matter. As soon as his father arrived at the scene, on the northernmost edge of Los Angeles, the usual derisive whispers about Steve's competence as a homicide detective would start up again.

He didn't have to hear a word of it to know. He'd see it on their faces. He'd see it in the way they looked at him without looking at him. He'd see it in the judgmental smirk of his superiors, even though they'd often called on his father's deductive expertise.

But they held Steve to a different standard than the one against which they measured themselves. He was the forty-year-old son of a legendary detective, one who didn't even have a badge and yet managed to solve an astonishing number of perplexing, high-profile cases. If not for that, Steve's impressive solve rate would certainly have earned him the unqualified respect and admiration of his peers. Instead, the assumption was that whenever he closed a difficult case, his father must have helped. The widespread belief within the department was that Steve Sloan was a mediocre detective with a brilliant father.

Steve couldn't blame his colleagues for their opinion of him. His father *was* brilliant and he showed up frequently with him at crime scenes, which only confirmed the speculation. If that wasn't enough, Steve lived on the first floor of his father's Malibu beach house, making it easy to consult with him on cases. Mark often offered his unsolicited advice, sometimes leaving his thoughts behind on little Post-it notes stuck in the case files that Steve brought home. More than once, Steve forgot to remove a Post-it or two, and they were discovered by other detectives, who immediately told others what they'd found.

On top of all that, his father often intruded on homicide investigations, whether they were Steve's or not. That was partly because the county's adjunct medical examiner, Dr. Amanda Bentley, worked out of the morgue at Community General Hospital, giving Mark plenty of opportunity to stumble in on an intriguing autopsy and offer his insights.

Steve didn't mind living under his father's shadow. He'd made peace with it a long time ago. He loved his father and respected him. Steve was good at his job, but he knew his father had a gift, a natural affinity for solving mysteries. Together, they made a great team. How many sons had that kind of relationship with their fathers? Too damn few, as far as Steve was concerned.

He cherished it.

Even so, he knew this time his professional reputation would take a bigger hit than usual. This time he was openly and directly asking for his father's help and he didn't care who knew it. He couldn't solve this murder without his father. Nobody could. And he wasn't going to let his pride get in the way of capturing a killer.

"You did the right thing calling Mark," Dr. Amanda Bentley said, crouching over the corpse that lay on the parched earth at Steve's feet. The beautiful African American woman knew exactly what Steve was thinking. She'd be a fool if she didn't.

She glanced down at the hunting knife buried to the hilt in Winston Brant's chest, his parachute spread out behind him, dancing in the desert wind.

"If anybody can figure this out," Amanda said, "Mark can."

CHAPTER THREE

By the time Mark Sloan arrived at the scene, a large white tent had been erected over the corpse to protect it from getting ripe in the sun.

Two Range Rovers, a Lincoln Navigator, and a Jeep Cherokee with the words AIRVENTURES SKYDIVING written on the side were lined up in a neat row facing the tent a hundred yards away, like patrons at a drive-in movie angling for the best view of the screen. Several patrol cars and Steve's police-issue Crown Vic were parked at haphazard angles behind the SUVs.

Four men wearing blue Airventures jumpsuits milled around talking in hushed tones to family and friends, all under the watchful eyes of five uniformed cops sweating in the hot sun. Everyone but the cops seemed to have the same stunned expression on their faces as the employees at Funville Toys. The cops were trying hard to show no expression at all, their eyes hidden behind reflective sunglasses.

Mark drove past them, his Saab convertible bumping and lurching across the rough terrain, and continued on to the tent, where the morgue van was parked, the engine idling to keep the air conditioner running and the interior cool for passengers living and dead.

He got out of the car, nodded at the bored morgue assistants in the van, and stepped into the tent, where Steve and Amanda were waiting, holding bottles of water and standing on either side of the body. The first thing Mark noticed was the knife in the guy's chest. The second thing he noticed was the bright blue parachute, gathered up into a bundle, its lines still attached to the backpack that was strapped to the victim.

Steve was surprised by the instant relief he felt when he saw his father, despite the misery he knew would soon be coming his way from within the department. It was one thing to call his dad for help; it was another to keep the witnesses around and put up a tent to protect the body until he arrived. He could already hear the Chief yelling in his ear: *Why didn't you just put up a billboard on Sunset Boulevard announcing that the LAPD is full of morons who can't solve a murder on their own?*

"Thanks for coming all the way out here, Dad," Steve said.

"How could I resist?" Mark said with a smile. "It's not often I get an invitation."

Besides, he was grateful to have something to distract him from the haunting image that kept replaying in his mind, of Rebecca Jordan calmly looking at him and hurling herself out her window.

Steve explained that the victim was Winston Brant, the forty-two-year-old publisher and editor of *Thrill Seeker* magazine, a publication that celebrated the American man's pursuit of excitement and adventure. Brant tried to personify the ideals of his magazine, like Hef did with *Playboy*.

Brant was always making news, whether it was running in the Iditarod, swimming across the English Channel, or bungee jumping off the Eiffel Tower. Each year, he'd shame his board of directors into joining him in an "adventure weekend" before the annual shareholders' meeting. One year it was white-water rafting, another year it was rock climbing, this year it was skydiving.

Although these annual events weren't nearly as extreme as the activities Brant did on his own and wrote about in his magazine, they were often terrifying for his fellow board members, most of whom limited their thrills to playing the stock market.

That afternoon, the board of directors of Brant Publications flew out of Van Nuys Airport in a Cessna that was owned and operated by the skydiving company. The plan was they'd jump, be picked up at the drop zone by their waiting family and friends, and then meet that night for a private dinner at Spago in advance of the shareholders' meeting the next day.

Brant, his three fellow board members, and one dive instructor jumped from a Cessna at twelve thousand feet above the drop zone. Everyone landed safely except for Brant, who landed dead.

"It's not often a murder this bizarre comes along," Steve said, motioning to Brant. "I've never seen anything like it."

"If you need to know how it was done, yeah, it's baffling. But from my standpoint, it's nothing special," Amanda said. "It looks like a simple stabbing to me."

"'Simple' is not a word anybody would use to describe what happened here," Steve said.

"I see a great big knife in his heart," Amanda said. "That's about all I need to know."

Mark looked down at the dead skydiver. Brant was wearing the same jumpsuit as the skydivers outside, presumably his fellow board members. In addition to his parachute pack, Brant wore gloves, an open-faced helmet, and a pair of tinted, streamlined goggles that didn't look any different than the kind swimmers wore.

"If you don't need to know any more," Steve asked Amanda, "why are you still here?"

"I like to see Mark work," she said. "And it also happens to be my responsibility as adjunct county medical examiner to take possession of the body and transport it to the morgue for autopsy. I can't just leave it here unattended."

"And you enjoy watching me fumble around," Steve said.

Amanda shrugged.

Steve shifted his attention to his father. "So what's your take on what happened?"

"It's pretty obvious," Mark said, rising to his feet with a sigh. "He was stabbed."

Amanda looked at Steve. "Told you."

"It's a little more complicated than that," Steve told her, then turned back to Mark. "Isn't it?"

"He was stabbed in midair," Mark said. "Sometime between the moment he jumped out of the plane and the instant he hit the ground."

Saying that, the image of Rebecca Jordan, slamming into the parked car, flashed across Mark's mind again. He blinked it away and tried to concentrate on the matter at hand.

"How do you know he wasn't stabbed and then pushed out of the plane?" Amanda asked.

"I thought you knew all you need to know," Steve said to her.

"I'm naturally curious," she replied, then faced Mark. "How do you know he wasn't stabbed when he landed?"

"For one thing, this is a flat, wide-open space and the family and friends of the skydivers were waiting here," Mark said. "If Winston Brant was murdered after he hit the ground, everyone would have seen it."

"Maybe they *did* see it," Steve said. "Maybe they lied when they told me he was already dead when he landed."

"There must be a dozen people out there," Amanda said. "You think they were all in on it?"

"Did you ever see *Murder on the Orient Express*?" Steve asked.

"No," Amanda replied. "And now I never will. Thanks for ruining it for me."

"I knew whodunit in the first five minutes," Steve said.

"How?" she asked.

"Dad told me," Steve said.

"The witnesses aren't important in this case," Mark said.

"They aren't?" Steve said.

"At least not to determine when this man was killed. I'd know he was stabbed in midair even if there were no witnesses at all and he jumped in pitch darkness," Mark said. "The evidence right here in front of us says it all."

"What evidence?" Amanda asked.

Mark crouched beside the body. Steve and Amanda joined him.

"There's specks of blood on his chin, his goggles, and his helmet. There's also traces of blood on the risers, the lines, and the chutes, but there's hardly any blood pooling around the body," Mark observed. "All of which proves Brant did most of his bleeding out as he fell, the blood blown upward by the force of his descent."

"Didn't any of the other skydivers see anything?" Amanda asked Steve.

"Everybody on board the plane, including the instructors, insist there wasn't a knife in his chest when he jumped," Steve said. "And they have the video to prove it."

"A video?" Mark asked.

"Their jump was filmed by the skydiving instructor as a souvenir of their experience," Steve said. "During the minute of free fall, they all joined hands, waved at the camera, all the usual hey-look-at-me-I'm-skydiving stuff."

"And none of the hey-look-at-me-I'm-being-murdered stuff," Amanda said.

"You never know. Where there's video, there's hope,"

Mark said, remembering a murder investigation of his own not so long ago where the crucial clue was hidden in the video. "I'd like to see that tape."

"I'm having copies made," Steve said, then gestured to the body. "So, how do you think he was murdered in midair?"

"I have no idea," Mark said. "I suppose I'll have to find out more about skydiving."

"The crime scene mice are scurrying over every inch of the plane," Steve said, referring to the techs from the LAPD's Scientific Investigation Division. "When they're done with that, I'm going to bring in an FAA-certified rigger to help them go over Brant's equipment. In the meantime, I'm getting a bunch of uniforms and some cadets from the police academy bussed out here to walk the drop zone, looking for any evidence that might have fallen from the sky with the corpse."

"That's going to make you real popular with the rank and file," Amanda said. "What are you hoping to find?"

"I'm thinking maybe the knife was in Brant's parachute pack," Steve said. "Maybe it was rigged to spring out somehow when he pulled the rip cord or when his automatic activation device released the chute."

"Then it seems to me he'd be stabbed in the back, where the pack is, and not the chest," Mark said. "Don't you think?"

"I think maybe it was a very clever device and the cadets will find pieces of it scattered over the drop zone," Steve said. "And then we'll know how it could have been designed to stab him in the chest."

"Uh-huh," Amanda said.

Steve glared at her. "I have to explore every avenue of investigation. That's my job."

"I didn't say anything," Amanda said.

"You said 'uh-huh,'" Steve said. "It was a very critical 'uh-huh.'"

"It was a nonjudgmental, I'm-paying-attention 'uh-huh,'" she said.

"I don't think you'll find anything unusual about the parachute rigging," Mark said. "Someone on that plane knows how this man was killed."

"You mean one of the skydivers did it," Steve said.

"Maybe all four of them did it," Amanda said, earning another glare from Steve. "And the instructor was in on it, too."

"If we can find out *who*," Mark said, "we'll figure out *how*."

"Uh-huh," Amanda said.

"That was definitely not the same 'uh-huh' you gave me," Steve said. "That was a very supportive, I-agree-with-you 'uh-huh.'"

"Uh-huh," she said again.

"*That's* exactly what I mean," Steve said, pointing as if the words were written in the air and still floating between them. "That was a patronizing, you're-crazy 'uh-huh.'"

"Can I remove the body now?" she said. "We're going to hit rush hour getting back to Community General as it is."

Steve glanced at his dad. "You need to see any more?"

"Just the autopsy report," Mark said.

"Should be ready first thing in the morning," Amanda said. "I'm not expecting any surprises. From my standpoint, this is an easy one."

"Stop rubbing it in," Steve said.

Amanda hid her smile as she walked out. Teasing Steve was almost as much fun and almost as easy as provoking Jesse. She figured Mark must enjoy it, too, because he never acknowledged what she was doing or leapt to their defense.

While she and her morgue assistants put the corpse in a body bag and carried it out to the van, Steve and Mark ambled outside, walking a little way out into the desert for some privacy.

"There are a lot of easier ways to kill a guy," Steve said. "I don't understand why the murderer went to so much trouble."

"Whoever did this was showing off. The whole point was to attract attention. He wants us to know how intelligent he is," Mark said. "And how dangerous."

CHAPTER FOUR

"Everybody is still here except for Brant's wife and two kids," Steve said as he and his father approached the on-lookers, among them the three skydivers and one instructor who were on the plane with Brant. "I sent them home. They were devastated. I figured we could ask them questions later. Besides, I think she'll be more at ease with you around."

"Because of my wonderful bedside manner?"

"Because you might know her," Steve said. "Dr. Sara Everden."

Mark looked surprised. "I had no idea Sara was married to Winston Brant."

"Then I guess you didn't know her very well," Steve said.

"She's a general practitioner with a modest practice down in Newport Beach," Mark said. "I've only met her on a few occasions when she's had patients at Community General or when we've bumped into each other at medical conferences."

"I wonder why she didn't tell you about her husband," Steve said.

"Possibly for the same reason she kept her maiden name. My guess is that she wanted to maintain her own professional identity and not have it completely overwhelmed by her husband's," Mark said. "Winston Brant was larger-than-life."

"He isn't larger-than-dead."

"We'll see," Mark said.

Steve motioned to the four skydivers in their matching suits. "The kid with the ponytail and the sunburned nose is Justin Darbo, the skydiving instructor. The other three are the Brant Publications board of directors, Dean Perrow, Clifton Hemphill, and Virgil Nyby."

He was about to tell Mark more about them, when the chubbiest of the four skydivers marched up angrily to meet them. He had a puffy, pockmarked face and a deep, even tan that looked applied rather than sun-baked.

"That's Hemphill huffing towards us," Steve whispered.

Although Clifton Hemphill was in his early fifties, what struck Mark was how clearly he could see the petulant child this man once was underneath the jowls, the creases, and the tan-in-a-can.

"We've been stuck out here for hours," Hemphill said, directing his anger at Steve and ignoring Mark. "What the hell is going on?"

"A murder, Mr. Hemphill," Steve said.

"You've already questioned all of us," Hemphill said. "So what are we waiting around here for?"

"Him," Steve said, cocking his head towards his father.

Mark smiled amiably at Hemphill.

"We already told you everything we know, which is squat," Hemphill said. "Why do we need to say it all over again to another cop?"

"I'm not a police officer, Mr. Hemphill," Mark said. "I'm Chief of Internal Medicine at Community General Hospital."

"You're a little late, Doc, the patient has been dead for

hours," Hemphill said, turning to confront Steve again. "What kind of investigation are you running?"

Steve expected to hear that question a lot over the next few days.

"Dr. Sloan is being disingenuous, Clifton." Dean Perrow stepped forward, a broad smile on his face, greeting Mark as if they were bumping into each other at a garden party instead of a crime scene. He had the body language of a salesman, the well-defined features of a male model and, Mark thought, the practiced sincerity of a television evangelist.

"You know this guy?" Hemphill asked.

"Of course I do. This is Dr. Mark Sloan," Perrow said, his skydiving goggles dangling around his neck more for style than for the convenience. "He's a self-taught master of criminology, a legend in law enforcement circles."

Perrow shook Mark's hand with a firm grip and introduced himself, saying his name as if it should mean something to Mark, too. It didn't.

"I'm a fool for not making the connection the moment Lieutenant Sloan identified himself," Perrow said. "Everybody knows Mark Sloan's son is an LAPD homicide detective."

"You're like Buffy," said Justin Darbo, the skydiving instructor, with the drowsy vocal inflections of a pothead, which, Mark thought, should have made anybody think twice about jumping out of an airplane with him.

"Buffy?" Mark asked.

"The Vampire Slayer," Justin said, absently picking at the dry skin on the bridge of his peeling nose. "You've got your own mythology. I bet your car is part of it, too."

Mark glanced at his Saab convertible. It didn't look very mythic to him.

"Glad to have you on board, Dr. Sloan," intoned Virgil Nyby with the authority of a man who should be in judges' robes instead of a skydiver's jumpsuit. He was barrel-chested, with broad shoulders and arms the width of tree trunks. "It means we'll get to the bottom of this horrific tragedy that much faster."

"That's certainly my intent," Mark said. "Though you are under no obligation to talk to me."

"You can talk to my dad, or you can talk to me in a tiny little interrogation room downtown," Steve said. "Your choice."

"We aren't a bunch of street thugs, so you can save the tough guy routine," Hemphill said. "There isn't a man standing here who isn't worth millions."

Justin raised his hand. "I'm carrying three thousand dollars in debt on my Visa card."

"I think I speak for all of us," Virgil Nyby said, like someone accustomed to speaking for everybody, "when I say we'll cooperate in any way we can. Winston was the heart and soul of this company and, more importantly, a dear friend. We want his killer brought swiftly to justice."

Mark couldn't think of anything to ask that Steve wouldn't have asked already. Besides, he'd rather hear what Steve found out, go over the autopsy report, and perhaps do a little research on skydiving before facing these men again.

"You've had a long, traumatic day, so I won't keep you any longer," Mark said. "We can talk another time."

He had started back towards his car, Steve at his side, when Dean Perrow called out to him. "Surely you must have some idea what happened, Dr. Sloan."

Mark stopped and turned to look at Perrow, who was standing with his arms open wide, hands up, palms towards him, as if to say *go ahead, take your best shot.*

"You are a genius at this sort of thing," Perrow said. "Aren't you?"

"Actually, Mr. Perrow, there is one thing I'm certain of

already," Mark said, letting his gaze pass over each of the four men. "The murderer is right here."

As if on cue, the medical examiner's van passed behind them, carrying the corpse of Winston Brant to the morgue, kicking up a thick plume of dust in its wake. All four of the skydivers turned to watch in grave silence as the van drove away, as if it was the hearse in a funeral procession.

When the dust settled, they turned around and were surprised to see that Dr. Mark Sloan was gone.

Rebecca Jordan lay comatose in the Community General intensive care unit, her right arm and leg splinted, elevated, and immobilized. She was surrounded by complex machines that monitored all the activity in her body. The machines were supposed to provide Mark Sloan with essential information that would help him restore her to perfect health. But none of those machines could tell him what he really needed to know—none of them could track the fear, chart the sadness, or measure the desperation that drove Rebecca Jordan to hurl herself out a window.

Mark didn't need to see a readout to know those demons were still there, waiting to torment her again when she awoke from her coma. Examining her chart, he didn't see any obvious physical indications that she'd been suicidal before. There were no scars on her wrists nor old needle marks elsewhere on her body. There were no drugs in her system nor any signs in the x-rays of serious injuries in the past.

It was pointless, of course, to try and make any assumptions about her mental state from what he could see in an x-ray or determine from a tox screen. What afflicted Rebecca Jordan wouldn't show up in any medical chart.

There was nothing more he could do to help her now. There might not be anything he could do to help her at all.

Mark suddenly realized how tired and hungry he was. It

was after eight p.m. He left the ICU and went to the elevator, pushed the DOWN button, and idly glanced around.

There was only one person sitting in the waiting area. The man occupied one chair, his Stetson occupied another. He wore a corduroy jacket, crisp white shirt, faded jeans, and sharp-toed leather boots. The man seemed engrossed in the *Ladies' Home Journal* he was reading. The headline on the cover read: TEN BEAUTY SECRETS EVERY WOMAN SHOULD KNOW.

It struck Mark as a great photograph. The Marlboro Man catching up on beauty and skin care tips.

The Marlboro Man.

An old, outdated advertising icon. What made him think of *that?*

Clearly, it was the guy in the chair, who was just a man with a weather-beaten face wearing a cowboy hat. There were a thousand other cowboy images that could have come to mind.

Why the Marlboro Man?

And then it hit Mark. It was so obvious.

Marlboro cigarettes.

His visit to see Rebecca Jordan had reminded him of Lenore Barber, the other suicidal woman he'd encountered today. His subconscious was graciously reminding him that he hadn't been able to save either one of them.

Hurrah for Mark Sloan.

The elevator arrived and Mark stepped inside, irritable now as well as tired and hungry. What a lousy day. As the doors closed, he glanced again at the cowboy, who was setting aside the *Ladies' Home Journal* for the latest issue of *Cosmopolitan.*

CHAPTER FIVE

Mark met Steve for dinner at BBQ Bob's, the restaurant his son and Dr. Jesse Travis bought a few years ago when the original owner retired. Steve and Jesse arranged their lives so that most of the time one of them was there to run the place while the other pursued his day job.

It was a charming dive with loyal customers who didn't mind wearing bibs when they ate. For years, most of the customers looked like long-haul truckers, construction workers, and professional wrestlers. While business wasn't bad, customers could always count on finding plenty of open tables and empty stools at the counter.

But lately, at lunch and dinner, the tables filled up fast and often there was a line out the door, thanks to Jesse's shrewd reworking of the menu to capitalize on the low-carb craze. In addition to the usual fare, slathered in barbeque sauce, Jesse introduced a menu of smoked-only meats and carb-conscious side dishes.

Now the place was filled with fresh-faced, carb-counting carnivores ready to feast on the wide selection of meat and a leaf or two of lettuce.

Mark almost felt guilty occupying a booth, taking it away from a paying customer. As the principal investor in BBQ Bob's, he enjoyed the privilege of never paying for a meal. But he was costing them double if, by taking the only available seat, he was simultaneously denying them the opportunity to serve someone else.

If Steve resented Mark taking a booth, he didn't say anything about it; he was too busy thinking about "The Case of the Dropped Dead Skydiver," which was what one local TV station was already calling the homicide on their early evening newscast.

"When they put it like that, it sounds like Encyclopedia Brown should be investigating the murder," Steve said, wiping some barbeque sauce from his chin. "He'd probably have a lot better luck."

"Give yourself a break, Steve," Mark said, washing down his last bite of brisket with some draft root beer. "You've only been on the case for a few hours."

"Usually I've at least got something to go on," Steve said. "Or you do." He looked hopefully at his dad.

"Sorry, Steve," Mark said. "But nothing jumps out at me yet, no pun intended."

"Uh-huh," Steve said.

"I see you've learned a few things from Amanda," Mark said.

"It was a nonjudgmental 'uh-huh,'" Steve said.

"Uh-huh." He waved over a waitress and asked for a thick slice of apple pie and a cup of coffee. Steve asked for the same and Mark thought about Rebecca Jordan, lying in the ICU, being fed her dinner through an IV.

"It might help if I knew more about the suspects," Mark said, forcing the image out of his head.

"As you can tell from the short time you spent with the board of directors of Brant Publications, they are a swell bunch of guys," Steve said. "Each one of them is a multimillionaire, as Clifton Hemphill was so quick to point out—once to you and twice to me before you got there."

"Clearly Mr. Hemphill derives his identity from his

money," Mark said. "It's like you saying you're a cop or me introducing myself as a doctor."

"But neither one of us whips out our bank statement when we do it," Steve said. "He could've said he's in the construction business and that he bought a big chunk of Brant Publications when Winston took the company public."

"When did Brant do that?" Mark asked.

"About five years ago," Steve said. "The magazine industry was in a slump and he'd expanded too fast, putting out other magazines that strayed too far from the corporate identity established by *Thrill Seeker*. He had to go public to generate the capital to keep his company afloat."

"Who told you all that?"

"Dean Perrow," Steve said. "A professional investor, likes to swoop in and gobble up companies when they're the most vulnerable. He's got his hand in all kinds of enterprises."

"Where do his millions come from?" Mark asked.

"Other people's millions," Steve said. "He used to be an investment banker, specializing in hostile takeovers, before he decided to go solo."

"And what's Virgil Nyby's story?" Mark asked.

"You mean besides bringing down the Ten Commandments and parting the Red Sea?"

"He does project a tremendous amount of authority," Mark agreed.

"He has the voice, which makes sense, since he owns a bunch of radio stations," Steve said. "Mostly talk-radio and all-news in the major markets, and country-western stations in the smaller ones. His father was a radio preacher and built his station group to spread the gospel."

"I bet you won't hear Winston Brant's murder referred to as 'The Case of the Dropped Dead Skydiver' on any of the newscasts on Nyby's stations."

"Don't be so sure," Steve said. "Despite his Charlton Heston voice and commanding demeanor, his broadcast philosophy has changed quite a bit since his father's day. His stations have been slapped by the FCC with some of the largest indecency fines on record. His LA and Chicago stations run *Mike and Ken*."

"The guys who once broadcast naked from a vat of pig excrement?"

"It beats listening to Dr. Laura," Steve said. "Though I think she gets her advice from the same vat."

"You listen to Dr. Laura?"

"You've got to do something on an eight-hour stakeout to relieve the boredom," Steve said. "And distract you from your bladder."

"Good to know," Mark said. "What did the skydivers tell you about what happened today?"

"Besides how rich they are and how much they wanted to go home? Basically they told me what you already know," Steve said, pausing while the waitress set down their pies and coffee. "They met at the Airventures hangar at the Van Nuys Airport. Nothing unusual happened during the ten-minute flight to the drop zone. They engaged in some small talk that no one remembers, then jumped out of the plane."

What was important to Mark now was the chronology and choreography. He needed to know who did what, when, and where, before he could even begin to figure out who killed Brant and how they managed to do it.

"Who jumped first?" Mark asked.

"Brant, of course, followed by the dive instructor, Justin Darbo, and then the three others," Steve said. "They met in midair during their free fall, joined hands to form a circle for forty-five seconds, then let go. A few seconds later, they pulled their rip cords."

"Did anyone see a skydiver close enough to Brant to stab him before he opened his chute?"

"If they did, no one is admitting it," Steve said.

"Leading to your theory that they all did it," Mark said.

"No," Steve said. "It's desperation that led to that theory."

So far, chronology and choreography weren't helping Mark much. Perhaps it was time to consider what happened before they even got on the plane.

"Who packed Brant's chute?" he asked.

"There's a guy at Airventures who does nothing but that," Steve said. "He didn't keep the packs under constant supervision. It's possible that someone could have gone in and sabotaged Brant's pack. There's just one problem."

"Just one?"

"SID says there's nothing hinky with Brant's pack," Steve said.

"Hinky?"

Steve shrugged. "I watched a lot of seventies cop shows."

"It explains your hair," Mark said.

"I see you've learned a few things from Amanda, too," Steve said.

"Amanda couldn't be here tonight," Mark said. "She's stuck doing the Brant autopsy, so she asked me to pinch-hit for her."

"You can tell her my hair looks great. Retro is in," Steve said. "The way things are going, pretty soon it will be cool again to have your shirt unbuttoned to show off all your chest hair."

"You don't have any chest hair."

"Neither do you," Steve said.

"I'm not the one wondering when it'll be stylish to walk around with his shirt open to his navel," Mark said.

"I didn't say I wanted to do that," Steve said. "You want to know about the chute or make fun of my hair?"

"Can't I do both?"

"The chute and all the other equipment appear to be in perfect shape, nothing out of the ordinary. Except for Winston Brant getting stabbed to death ten thousand feet in the air." Steve shook his head and frowned. "How the hell did the killer pull that off?"

They sat in silence for a few minutes, thinking about the case, sipping their coffees, and enjoying their pie. Mark mentally reexamined Brant's corpse and went over every detail Steve told him. He visualized the entire jump in his mind and tried to see who had the best opportunity to stab Winston Brant in the chest.

"I think they all did it," Mark said.

"Really?" Steve asked.

"Nope," Mark sighed. "I'm desperate."

"Like father, like son," Steve said.

When they got back to the beach house, Mark and Steve watched the video that the skydiving instructor shot of the jump. The camera work was shaky, but that was to be expected when the photographer is falling at 125 miles per hour and the camera is mounted in his helmet.

Events played out exactly as Hemphill, Perrow, Nyby, and Justin Darbo said they did. The five men jumped out of the plane, joined hands to form a rough, free-falling circle, and then let go, flying out of frame.

Justin Darbo tracked a few of them with his camera, but since they were all wearing identical helmets, goggles, and jumpsuits, it was virtually impossible to tell who was who. Perhaps, Mark thought, that was significant. Whether the confusion was intentional or not, it could be the first clue towards unraveling the mystery. Or it could mean nothing at all.

None of the four men were caught on camera when they pulled their rip cords, and when Justin pulled his, the camera jerked wildly. The camera tilted up as Justin examined his own chute and rigging before he bothered looking around again to find the other skydivers. What the camera captured was four colorful parachutes and not much, if anything, of the skydivers suspended beneath the canopies. Two of the parachutes seemed to drift close together, but Mark couldn't be certain if they actually were near one another. He knew the camera's perspective could be playing tricks on the eye, making the genuine distance of objects relative to one another hard to gauge. Considering the camera, and the skydivers it was filming, were all in motion, it was hard for him to judge the speed, distance, or the true size of anything they saw.

The rest of the footage wasn't much more helpful and probably would have been edited out before the video was given as a souvenir to the skydivers. There was a fascinating shot of Darbo's shoes, a couple of riveting close-ups of Justin Darbo's altimeter, and a few quick views of the drop zone below, desolate except for the row of neatly parked SUVs.

Steve clicked off the TV and tossed the remote onto the coffee table. The screen was empty, but Mark could still see a picture. Rebecca Jordan sitting on her window ledge, staring at him.

"Our last case had much more interesting video," Steve said, referring to the infamous Lacey McClure sex tapes. "There ought to be a rule. If there's going to be video involved in a homicide investigation, there should at least be some sex, explosions, or martial arts to watch."

Mark groaned and rose from his recliner, not an easy task considering how plush and soft the cushions were. It was about eleven thirty, but felt much later. He was exhausted, his eyes stinging.

"I'm going to bed," Mark said, trudging towards his bedroom. "Wake me when the case is solved."

CHAPTER SIX

The case wasn't solved, but Mark was awake nonetheless. He lay in bed, unable to sleep. As soon as he closed his eyes, he'd see Rebecca Jordan in her window, staring across the street at him for what seemed like hours.

Help me.

And then she'd jump—only in his mind, she managed to hold her stare with him as she fell. The instant she hit the tree branch, Mark's eyes would flash open and he'd find himself looking at the electric clock on his nightstand.

The fourth time it happened, around three a.m., Mark gave up. Despite his exhaustion, he got out of bed, put on his clothes, and went to his car.

Mark drove along the dark, deserted streets to the nearly empty parking structure at Community General. He took the pedestrian bridge from the parking structure to the hospital, pausing midway to look across the street at Rebecca's building. It was a dark night, and the building was lit only by the glow of some streetlamps, but it looked to him like her window was still open. And for a moment, he could almost see her sitting on the windowsill.

Help me.

He blinked away the image and continued quickly on

his way to the hospital, taking the elevator to the intensive care unit.

The first thing he noticed as he stepped out of the elevator was that the Marlboro Man was still there, reading *Highlights for Children*. Mark wondered if the cowboy was looking for the hidden objects in the illustrations. As far as Mark knew that's all anybody who opened the magazine ever did. He also wondered what the big man was still doing there.

Mark went directly to Rebecca's bed and checked her chart. Nothing had changed, not that he was expecting anything. He wasn't quite sure why he was there, except that he couldn't sleep, that he couldn't close his eyes without seeing her looking back at him.

She wasn't looking at him now.

He took a seat beside her bed, glanced at the monitors, then studied her face.

She seemed at peace. Tranquil. Of course, she also looked that way when she jumped.

It occurred to Mark that he'd encountered two jumpers yesterday. One who wasn't wearing a parachute and one who was. One who wanted to die and one who didn't.

The irony might have amused Mark if it wasn't so tragic and if, in some way, he didn't feel responsible for making sense out of what happened to them both.

Usually when he embarked on an investigation, there was at least something that didn't fit, some inconsistency or incongruity he could focus on, a clue trail to get him started.

Not this time. Not with either situation.

For one thing, Rebecca Jordan's case wasn't a murder. It was an attempted suicide. He'd never investigated anything like that before, which forced Mark to ask himself some basic questions.

If he started looking into her life, what mystery did he hope to solve?

Why did she want to die?

If that was truly his motivation, was the answer to that question any of his business?

That never stopped me before.

But in all those cases, there had always been a higher purpose besides indulging his curiosity. He was seeking justice for the dead.

What higher purpose was there than saving a human life?

It was a nice, and sanctimonious, rationalization but he wasn't sure he bought it. Even if he wanted to help Rebecca, he had to face some facts. Her problems were probably emotional. He was a doctor and a police consultant, but he wasn't a psychologist. And even if he was, he couldn't do anything for her unless she opened up to him about her troubles. She was in no condition to do that now, and even if she was, he wasn't sure that she would. A woman willing to talk about her problems doesn't hurl herself out a window.

So where would he start? What was he looking for?

Those questions were easier to answer in the Winston Brant case. Of course, Mark had much more experience dealing with murders, even ones as perplexing as Brant's.

Killing a man in midair was quite a magic trick. Although Mark was an amateur magician himself, he didn't have the slightest idea how the killer pulled it off.

So rather than trying to figure it out, Mark decided to follow the advice he gave Steve. He'd learn as much as he could about Brant and his three fellow board members: Clifton Hemphill, Dean Perrow, and Virgil Nyby. He'd also need to know more about Justin Darbo, the skydiving instructor.

The easiest place to start was with Brant's wife, Dr. Sara Everden. She knew all the people in the plane that day, which meant she already knew who her husband's killer

was; she just didn't realize it yet. It was up to Mark to figure that out for her.

A shrill alarm from one of the monitors intruded on his
thoughts. It was the O2 monitor. Rebecca's oxygen saturation had dropped below 92 percent, triggering the alarm.

Mark didn't have his stethoscope, so he pressed his ear to
her chest. There were good breath sounds on the right, none
on the left. Her left lung had collapsed. He glanced again at
her monitor. Her oxygen level had dropped to 88 percent.

Dr. Jesse Travis rushed in, trailed by two nurses. He was
stunned to see Mark standing there. But before Jesse could
say anything, Mark spoke.

"She's got a pneumothorax," he said. "I need to do a
chest thoracotomy."

"I'll do it," Jesse said. "She's my patient and I'm the doctor on call."

There was no argument there. Mark stepped aside and let
Jesse go to work reexpanding her collapsed lung. Both doctors slipped on rubber gloves. The nurses quickly brought in
a surgical tray, from which Jesse selected a scalpel, which he
used to make an incision in the space between two ribs on
her left side.

Mark handed him a pair of scissors, which Jesse slid into
the incision until he felt them pierce the pleura, the lining of
the chest cavity.

"I'm in," Jesse said, carefully spreading open the scissors
and pulling them back, giving himself a wide opening into
the chest cavity. He eased a finger inside, feeling around to
see if the collapsed lung was stuck to the pleura.

"Is there any lung adhesion?" Mark asked.

"No," Jesse said, removing his finger.

Mark handed him a chest tube, which Jesse slid into the
opening, snaking it up to the top of her chest. The other end
of the tube was attached to a suction bottle. The procedure
would allow the air trapped in her chest cavity to escape, re-

lieving the pressure on the lung that had caused it to collapse.

Jesse taped the tube in place and glanced at the oxygen monitor. Mark was already watching it and seeing immediate improvement. Her oxygen saturation levels were increasing.

"Get me a chest x-ray and update me on her O2 until it gets to 95 percent," Jesse said to one of the nurses; then he turned to Mark. "You're going to tell me what you're doing here."

"I am?" Mark asked.

"Right after you buy me a cup of coffee," Jesse said.

CHAPTER SEVEN

Mark and Jesse sat at a table in the center of the empty cafeteria. Jesse was on his fourth cup of coffee, listening as Mark finished telling him what little he'd learned about Rebecca Jordan and what little he knew about Winston Brant's murder. As little as all that was, it still took Mark an hour to tell it. Mark didn't bother telling Jesse about his problems sleeping or the disturbing dreams that kept waking him up.

During that hour, Jesse left briefly to examine Rebecca's chest x-ray and her O2 levels and reported back to Mark that her chest tube was in proper position and her lung was reinflated.

When Mark finished his story, they sat quietly for a moment; then Jesse nodded.

"I think I've got it," Jesse said.

"Got what?" Mark asked.

"I know how Winston Brant was murdered."

Mark leaned forward. "So tell me."

"You know those things that hunters use to shoot arrows?"

"Bows?"

"No, the cool thing that assassins use," Jesse said. "What do you call 'em? There was a girl holding one in a James

Bond poster. You see her standing from behind and James Bond creeping by between her legs."

"A crossbow."

"You know the poster?"

"I know the weapon," Mark said.

"What if somebody modified a crossbow to shoot a knife?" Jesse mimed holding a crossbow and aiming it up at a target. "Somebody hiding at the drop zone could have shot Winston Brant right out of the sky."

"You're saying the killer was one of the people on the ground waiting for the skydivers."

"Using a crossbow that shoots knives," Jesse said. "It's the only explanation."

"It's *one* possible explanation," Mark said. "But to be honest, it seems a little far-fetched."

"What could be more far-fetched than a skydiver getting stabbed in midair?"

"I can't argue with that," Mark said. "But even if we accept for the moment the possibility that someone could modify a crossbow to shoot a knife, and that he could fire it unseen by the others on the ground, there are still some major flaws in your theory."

"Like what?" Jesse asked.

"The killer would be shooting from a great distance at a moving target hundreds of feet up in the air. It's an impossible shot, unless the knife is propelled by some kind of explosive force, the way bullets and missiles are," Mark said. "Even if no one saw it, they would have heard it."

"That's why I called it a *modified* crossbow," Jesse said. "Coming up with a way to shoot a knife with enough velocity and keep it quiet would have been part of the modifications."

"It seems like an awful lot of effort to kill just one man."

"That's true no matter how the killer did it," Jesse said.

Mark sighed, suddenly feeling every minute of every

hour of sleep that he'd missed. "There has to be a simple explanation."

"Why does it have to be simple?"

"Because if it's hard," Mark said, "it's just too hard."

Jesse looked at him. "All this stuff about Winston Brant is very interesting, Mark, but you still haven't answered the question I asked you an hour ago in the ICU. What were you doing here at four thirty in the morning?"

"I was checking on Rebecca Jordan," Mark said.

"I know," Jesse said. "Why were you doing that?"

"I couldn't sleep."

"That's what TVs were invented for. Why do you think there are *Gunsmoke* reruns on three different cable networks every night?" Jesse said. "You're supposed to watch Matt Dillon and Chester and Festus and Doc and Miss Kitty until you're unconscious. You don't get in your car and go to work. So why did you?"

Mark shook his head and sighed. "I don't know."

"I think I do," Jesse said.

"I hope this doesn't involve a modified crossbow," Mark said.

"What was that problem you wanted my advice on yesterday?"

"Just something with a patient," Mark said.

"What something?" Jesse prodded. "What patient?"

Mark sighed again and told him about Lenore Barber, her two brushes with lung cancer, and her continued smoking.

"I can't get her to quit," Mark said. "She's going to kill herself."

"Uh-huh," Jesse said.

"That's really catching on," Mark said.

"What is?" Jesse asked.

"Nothing," Mark said. "Forget it."

"I'm no shrink, but I think Lenore Barber and Rebecca Jordan are connected," Jesse said. "Both women are trying to kill themselves. You can't save one, so you glom on to the other."

"*Glom?*" Mark asked.

"You can't save Lenore, so it's imperative that you save Rebecca," Jesse said. "She is your surrogate Lenore Barber!"

Jesse smiled, clearly quite pleased with himself. Mark glowered, which was something Jesse had never seen him do before. He'd seen Steve glower plenty of times and now he knew where his friend picked it up.

"I saw a woman try to kill herself and I'm concerned about her health and well-being," Mark said. "The way I am about all my patients."

"When was the last time you came in to check on a patient at four a.m.?"

Mark's glower got much more glowerful. Before he could respond to Jesse's question, Steve strode up to their table. Steve looked tired and irritable and was working on a good glower of his own.

"You could have left a note for me or at least turned your cell phone on," Steve said. "I woke up and you were gone."

"And you deduced I was here," Mark said.

"I didn't deduce anything," Steve said.

"Why start now?" Jesse muttered.

Steve shot him a look, though he was tempted to shoot him with a bullet, then turned his attention back to his dad. "I'm here because I'm supposed to get Amanda's autopsy report. What are you doing here?"

"That seems to be the question of the day," Jesse said.

Mark told Steve all about how he'd witnessed Rebecca Jordan's suicide attempt and brought him up-to-date on her current condition.

"So you had two jumpers in one day, Rebecca Jordan and Winston Brant," Steve said. "That has to be some kind of record."

"I forgot about that other connection," Jesse said. "It's fascinating how everything that happened to Mark yesterday is thematically and emotionally connected. No wonder he can't sleep."

"There's more?" Steve asked. "What else happened to you?"

"Earlier in the day I met with a patient who, you could say, is killing herself and I haven't been able to stop her," Mark said. "Jesse believes I'm focusing on Rebecca's case because I couldn't save my other suicidal patient."

Steve glanced at Jesse. "I see what you mean."

"You do?" Mark said.

"You don't have to be a detective, or a doctor, to see what's going on here," Steve said, shaking his head. "It's obvious. You're in deep trouble, Dad."

"Thanks," Mark said.

"But I think I can help solve your problem," Steve said.

"Do tell," Mark said.

"Forget about Lenore, let Jesse deal with Rebecca, and you concentrate your attention on the compelling mystery surrounding Winston Brant's murder," Steve said. "Narrow your focus, and you eliminate two-thirds of your troubles."

"Which, coincidentally, means I'd be focused entirely on helping you with your case," Mark said.

"I bet you feel better already," Steve replied.

"Ordinarily, you'd be telling me to do the opposite," Mark said.

"Then it proves I really am looking out for your best interests," Steve said.

Amanda didn't usually open for business so early in the morning, but now that the murder of Winston Brant had become "the Case of the Dropped Dead Skydiver" on every TV station in town, she was feeling some pressure to move fast. She met with Mark, Steve, and Jesse in the pathology lab, which doubled as the adjunct county medical examiner's morgue.

"Here's my autopsy report," she said, handing a file to Steve and a copy to Mark.

"Where's my copy?" Jesse asked.

"All you need are the headlines," she said, "which I'm about to tell you."

"You all have reports," Jesse said. "It's not fair. I should have a report."

"Fine." Amanda snatched a file from her desk and slapped it into his hands before continuing. "The cause of Winston Brant's death was a knife stabbed directly into his heart. There were no other wounds or injuries, unless you want to count the nick on his chin from shaving."

"Wait a minute," Jesse said, flipping through his file. "This isn't Winston Brant's autopsy. This is a report of your office supply expenditures."

Amanda ignored Jesse and continued. "From what I can tell, Brant was in great shape. He was obviously a man who led an active, athletic life."

"Did you find anything unusual at all?" Steve asked.

She shook her head. "I checked his stomach contents and ran a full tox screen. He had eggs Benedict and a little Prozac for breakfast, well within therapeutic levels."

"The eggs or the Prozac?" Steve asked.

"Both," Amanda said.

"You go through an incredible amount of paper clips," Jesse said, studying his file. "Have you considered stapling papers instead? It's a lot cheaper."

Amanda acted as if Jesse wasn't even there. "It may seem like a complex case to you, but that's if you're looking at how the murder was accomplished. If you look at what actually killed Winston Brant, this is a no-brainer. He was stabbed in the heart. My job is done."

"Want to switch jobs?" Steve asked.

"Sure." Amanda motioned to a gigantic body bag on a gurney across the room. "You can start with the autopsy on the three hundred and twenty-two–pound guy found dead in his bathtub this morning. He's only been in the tub for a few days."

Steve grimaced. "Never mind."

Mark closed the report and handed it back to Amanda. "Thanks, Amanda."

"You've been awfully quiet this morning," she said. "Anything wrong?"

"Everything's fine," Mark said. "I didn't ask any questions because your autopsy found exactly what I expected you to find."

"Nothing," Amanda said.

"Nothing," Mark repeated.

"So where do we go from here?" Steve asked. "We don't know any more about this murder than we did when we found the body."

"I'll make you a deal," Mark said. "I'll talk to Brant's wife if you'll do a little checking on Rebecca Jordan."

"Rebecca Jordan hasn't committed any crime," Steve said.

"She tried to take her own life," Mark said. "I want to find out why."

"To satisfy your curiosity?" Steve asked.

"To stop her from trying again," Mark said. "Maybe I can if I know why she wanted to die."

Steve sighed. He knew if he didn't do it, his father would just do it himself, taking time away from investigating Brant's murder.

"Okay," Steve said. "You've got a deal."

"I've got to get back home, shower, shave, and put on some fresh clothes," Mark said. "Let's talk again around lunch."

And with that, Mark and Steve left the lab. Amanda glanced at Jesse, who was still standing there, looking at her.

"Can I help you with something?" she asked.

"I have a plan," he said. "And I'm going to need your help."

CHAPTER EIGHT

Before leaving the hospital, Steve decided it would probably be a good idea to visit Rebecca Jordan. Maybe she'd be awake from her coma and could answer all his questions, saving him the trouble of investigating something that didn't merit any investigation in the first place. And if she wasn't awake, at least he'd know what the woman looked like.

When he walked into the ICU, he found a short man in suspenders sitting sadly beside her bed, holding four pink bakery boxes and a couple of wax paper bags.

The little man looked like an overgrown hobbit, only without the hairy feet. Startled, he jumped up from his seat the instant he saw Steve standing at the end of the bed.

"I didn't know she already had a visitor," the man said, rising from his seat. "I'll come back later. I brought some day-olds. I'll just leave them."

The man set the boxes on a tabletop.

"My name is Steve Sloan, I'm—"

The man interrupted Steve with a nervous rush of words. "The name's Tucker Mellish and believe me, you don't have to explain anything. I always knew Rebecca must have someone special. I'll just be a moment longer."

Mellish gave Steve a quick glance, then busied himself

with the bakery boxes, opening them and arranging the pastries on paper plates.

"I don't really know Rebecca, I'm—"

Mellish didn't let him finish. "You don't have to explain anything to me. If she wanted me to know about you, she would have told me. Of course, she hasn't really told me anything about herself."

He looked at Steve with puppy eyes. "Does she ever mention me?"

Steve shrugged. Why bother trying to get a word in? He figured he'd let Mellish keep talking. Maybe the guy would finally spit out whatever was making him so nervous.

"I knew she didn't," Mellish said. "Why should she? We're just buddies. Hardly that, acquaintances really. She comes into my bakery every morning when I open up. I don't even know why I came here today. I just thought she might like something sweet. She likes sweet things. Want a pastry?"

"Sure," Steve said, taking a bear claw. Now that he thought of it, he was hungry. He'd skipped breakfast that morning.

"Listen," Mellish said. "Don't tell her I was here, okay? I'm not anybody, really."

Steve's mouth was full of bear claw, so he just nodded.

"And you, well, you're the better man," Mellish said, going towards the door. "Take care of her."

Steve swallowed what he was eating. "I've never met Rebecca Jordan."

Mellish stopped, a confused look on his face. "You haven't?"

"This is the first time I've ever laid eyes on her," Steve said, licking some frosting from his lips.

For a moment, Mellish looked relieved, even hopeful. But only until Steve flashed his badge.

"I'm LAPD," Steve said, holding up his ID in one hand and taking another bite of the bear claw he held in the other.

Mellish narrowed his eyes at him and took a protective stance beside Rebecca's bed, drawing Steve's attention to the woman for the first time. She looked pretty good to him for a woman who'd fallen five stories.

"She hasn't done anything wrong," Mellish said.

"I know," Steve said. "My father is her doctor. He thought maybe if we knew why she wanted to kill herself, we could prevent her from trying again. Did you make this bear claw?"

"Yeah," Mellish said.

"It's tasty," Steve said. "I could eat a bunch of them."

Steve was trying to put Mellish at ease. He was also trying to get another bear claw. His strategy worked on both fronts. Mellish picked up another pastry, put it on a napkin, and offered it to him.

"Have another one, while they are still warm," Mellish said. "They're not really day-old. I just said that when I thought you were her boyfriend."

Steve waved it off, snatched another bear claw, and took a bite. After chewing for a moment, he asked, "Do you have any idea why she jumped?"

"We don't talk about her personal life. Her choice. She wants to talk about ideas. She picks out a book and we buy two copies. Then we talk about it in the mornings."

"It sounds nice," Steve said, but he was really thinking about how good his bear claw was. So warm, so satisfying, so sweet.

"Last night, I had a theory on who killed old Karamazov. I couldn't wait to tell her. When she didn't show up, I called her office and they told me what happened."

Steve didn't know who Karamazov was, but perhaps she was so distraught over his murder, she leaped out a window. If that was her reason, then this was definitely a problem his father could solve for her—*after* he figured out who stabbed Winston Brant in midair.

"What was her relationship to Karamazov?" Steve asked. "Was she hit hard by his death?"

Mellish stared at Steve. "It's *The Brothers Karamazov*."

Steve stared back at him, finished the bear claw and was contemplating a third, when Mellish finally spoke again.

"He's a character in a book, written by Fyodor Dostoyevsky, in 1880," Mellish said.

"Right, I knew that," Steve said, trying to hide his embarrassment by wiping his face with a napkin. "I was wondering if maybe she was one of those really intense readers who gets emotionally involved in what she reads."

"You mean someone who'd read *Anna Karenina* and then leap in front of a train?" Mellish said.

"Yeah," Steve said. "It happens."

"I don't think it happened this time," Mellish said. "But I don't know what was bothering her. She didn't tell me."

"Do you know anyone she might have told?"

"She mentioned her roommate Lissy sometimes," Mellish said. "Lissy works the graveyard shift as a telephone customer support technician for a software company. They don't see each other much, but they did live in the same apartment."

"Thanks," Steve said, picking up another bear claw. "This is my third one. I can't keep my hands off them."

"I noticed," Mellish said.

"You only sell these out of your bakery?"

"Yeah," Mellish said.

"I think they'd make a great breakfast item on a restaurant menu," Steve said. "And I know just the place."

After making a deal with Tucker Mellish to provide breakfast pastries to BBQ Bob's, Steve drove out to Rebecca Jordan's apartment in Culver City. He figured if her roommate Lissy worked the graveyard shift, she was likely to just be getting home and they could have a quick chat. Steve brought a few of Mellish's pastries for her, to get things off to a friendly start, but ended up eating them all on his way.

By the time he arrived outside the one-story courtyard apartment building, he had the mother of all sugar headaches. The first question he was going to ask Lissy was if she had some Advil.

Steve parked, got out, and walked across the dry crabgrass lawn and into the building's courtyard, a brick-ribboned cement patio cluttered with rusted garden furniture and sickly potted plants. He had an immediate sense of déjà vu, but he didn't give the feeling much credence. Los Angeles was paved with thousands of charmless apartment blocks just like this one and his work took him to two or three of them a day. They became a blur, though today he wasn't sure if it was from weary familiarity or his sugar hangover.

He was nearly at Rebecca's apartment door when he heard a woman's unmistakable cry of pain from inside and the sounds of a major scuffle. Glass breaking, furniture sliding, fists against flesh.

Steve tried the knob and shoved his shoulder against the door. It was locked. The sounds of a struggle intensified from inside, a man's growls intermingled with a woman's furious shrieks. He supposed it could be lovemaking that he was hearing, but he instinctively knew it wasn't. He could almost feel the violence.

"Open up," Steve said, drawing his gun. "This is the police."

There was a huge crash, the sound of something heavy falling, followed by the woman's yelp of pain and surprise.

He stepped back and kicked open the door, the thin wood splintering at the doorjamb. He sprang low into the apartment in a firing stance and, in a split second, took in the scene. It looked like the aftermath of an earthquake. The apartment was trashed. A woman was sprawled on the floor. A man was racing out the back door.

Steve went to the woman first, who was already struggling to her feet. "Are you okay?"

She nodded, so Steve charged through the small apartment, jumping over all the upended furniture and broken glass, and out the back door. He burst out into the alley, but there was no sign of the attacker anywhere.

Steve holstered his gun and trudged back into the apartment. His head was splitting with pain. He told himself this was the last time he'd eat half a dozen pastries before chasing an assailant.

Lissy was already on her feet, wiping off the blood from her forehead with the back of her wrist. He got a good look at her now. She was a stocky, strong-boned woman in jeans and an oversized sweatshirt. Strong and tough but still very feminine, the way he imagined frontier women must have been like in the Old West. If she was afraid, she didn't show it. All Steve saw was anger.

"You get the bastard?" she asked.

"He got away," Steve said. "What happened here?"

"I work nights," she said. "I walked in and saw some guy trashing the place. So I hit him with a chair and we danced."

"You're lucky he didn't kill you," Steve said.

"He's lucky I buy cheap furniture."

Steve liked her already. She went to the kitchen sink, wet a rag under the faucet, and dabbed the cut on her forehead.

"You're pretty tough," he said.

"I had five older brothers," she said. "I can handle myself. It's your fault he got away."

"My fault?"

"I got distracted when you yelled. He caught me off-balance and smacked me headfirst into the coffee table." She gave him a smile. "You owe me a new coffee table."

"Then I'm lucky you buy cheap furniture, too," he said.

"Usually people who are being attacked are glad when the cops show up."

"It's that guy who should be glad, because he was two seconds away from losing his ability to procreate."

"No wonder he was running so fast," Steve said. "Any idea who he was or what he wanted?"

She shook her head. "Probably the same guy who tried breaking in a couple days ago while I was sleeping. I scared him off."

"How did you do that?"

"I threw a meat cleaver at him." She pointed to the back door. There was a meat cleaver stuck into the wall beside the door frame.

Steve hadn't noticed it before. He wondered how he missed it and decided he was distracted by the meat cleaver in his skull.

"You got any aspirin?" he asked.

"I really don't need it," she said.

"I do."

She gave him a look. "Hurt yourself breaking down my door?"

"I had six bear claws on the way over," he said.

Lissy opened a cabinet near the sink, found a bottle of Bayer, and tossed Steve the bottle. He shook out two pills and dry-swallowed them.

"Who called the cops?" she asked.

"No one," Steve said.

"You were just strolling by eating bear claws?"

"I came to ask you about Rebecca."

"Why?" she asked. "Is something wrong?"

He would have slapped himself on the forehead if his head wasn't already hurting. Of course, Lissy didn't know about what happened. She'd been working all night. Besides, who would have called to tell her?

"Your roommate tried to commit suicide yesterday," Steve said. "She jumped out of a window at work."

Lissy caught her breath. "Oh, hell."

Steve gave her a moment to absorb the news and for him to absorb the aspirin.

She leaned against the counter, her shoulders sagging with fatigue. "How is she?"

"Lucky," Steve said. "She's in the ICU with a concussion and some broken bones, but she's going to make it. Any idea what might have been bothering her?"

"We rarely saw one another, she'd be coming in as I was leaving," Lissy said. "But the attempted break-in the other day really spooked her. Rebecca said something about being afraid her past was going to walk through the door someday real soon."

"Was she running from something?"

Lissy shrugged. "She moved in a year ago. She pays her rent on time. Does her dishes. Keeps her stuff in her room. That's about all I can tell you."

"Mind if I look at her stuff?"

"Go ahead," Lissy said. "Second room on the left."

Steve carefully negotiated a path through the trashed apartment to the hallway, then opened the door to Rebecca's room. It was as clean and orderly as a motel room and about as personal. He couldn't tell anything about her from what he found. Some inexpensive jewelry, off-the-rack clothes, a bathroom full of the expected personal hygiene products. There were a couple of paperback romances on the night-stand and the most recent issue of *People* magazine. The only thing that struck him as unusual was the enormous teddy bear on the bed.

That's when he heard a shriek from the living room. He ran out to find Lissy holding up one end of a fallen bookcase and staring in horror at something on the floor.

"I think I found what she was running from," Lissy said. "I'm thinking of running myself."

He stepped up beside her and followed her gaze.

There was a dead man on the floor, his head caved in, his lifeless eyes staring up at them. The man wore soiled clothes and had a sick, pasty look that had more to do with his previous lifestyle than his current circumstances as a corpse. On his left hand, two fingers were taped together and braced with Popsicle sticks.

Steve glanced at Lissy. "Recognize him?"

She nodded. "He's a homeless guy. I've seen him around the neighborhood the last few days."

Steve tipped the bookcase aside, crouched over the body, and checked the man's pockets for ID. He found a thin wallet and opened it up. There was no driver's license or credit cards, just six dollars, a hotel room key for room 17 at the Paradise Hotel, and a newspaper clipping folded into a tight square.

He unfolded the clipping. It was a picture of Rebecca Jordan and the huge stuffed bear.

"I've been home ten minutes and already I've fought off a burglar, I've learned my roommate tried to kill herself, and I've found a corpse in my living room." Lissy sat down on the couch and sighed. "I've had better mornings."

CHAPTER NINE

The living room of Winston Brant's Spanish-Mediterranean mansion in Newport Beach was two stories tall. The walls were adorned with several large paintings, smatterings of vivid color reminiscent of Jackson Pollock. Perhaps they were Pollocks, for all Mark knew. Marble sculptures filled individually lighted niches near the ceiling. One of the sculptures was of a jaguar, poised to spring on its prey below which, in this case, was Brant's widow, Dr. Sara Everden, and her guest, Dr. Mark Sloan.

Sara sat very straight on the edge of a white couch covered with little pillows of various colors and fabrics. She was tall, blond-haired, with the gently muscled physique of a casual athlete, the kind who kept in shape with occasional visits to the tennis court or golf course. She deftly balanced elegance and relaxed charm. Her white silk blouse hung loosely on her fine-boned shoulders, a strand of pearls around her long, slender neck, a stark contrast to the faded jeans and Reeboks she was also wearing.

Mark sat across from her in an extremely uncomfortable antique French chair and tried not to squirm too much while they spoke, their voices echoing off the high, steepled ceiling. He wondered what kind of home Rebecca Jordan came from, what kind of art was on the walls, and if the chairs were cushy and comfortable.

"I'm glad you're here, Mark. If your son hadn't asked you to look into my husband's murder, I would have," Sara said. "What happened to him was an abomination."

"Murder always is," Mark said.

"This was worse," she said. "Whoever did it not only killed Win, but cruelly mocked everything he lived for."

"Win?"

"That's what my husband liked to be called," Sara said. "He thought 'Winston' sounded prissy and aristocratic. He felt that 'Win' embodied his approach to everything."

"He was competitive?"

"It wasn't about beating somebody else but succeeding against adversity, overcoming an obstacle on his own terms. Win never felt more alive than when he was tackling a physical challenge, particularly if it was dangerous. That's where the thrill came in. To him, feeling that exhilaration was life itself."

"And he only felt that alive when he was cheating death?"

"He found exhilaration in other things," she said, a sad look passing over her face. "In his family, of course. Watching his children grow up. But it wasn't the same kind of thrill. It wasn't enough."

"That didn't bother you?"

"I knew what kind of man he was when I married him," she said, her eyes becoming moist. "It was part of the attraction. I've always been so practical, so 'down-to-earth.'"

"You aren't a thrill seeker, too?"

Sara shook her head. "I'm a doctor. I can't take those kinds of physical risks. I know all too well what happens when you lose. It's not worth it to me. I can't even get on a roller coaster."

Mark knew how she felt. He was the same way and

couldn't understand how Steve could enjoy surfing and dirt biking and any other sport that could leave him paralyzed for life. His son was probably the target audience for Brant's magazine.

"You didn't try to change him?" Mark asked, thinking of all the times he tried to talk Steve out of dangerous pursuits.

"I always knew to stay vibrant and alive, Win needed a wave to tame, a mountain to climb, to know the only thing between him and death was his ability to master himself and the world around him."

Mark saw her face redden, her cheek muscles tighten. Her tears came now, not with sadness, but with anger.

"To murder him while he was doing something inherently death-defying ridiculed him, the man that he was, and the magazine he published," she said. "It was an act of utter contempt and pure hatred."

"Do you know anyone who hated him enough to go to such lengths?"

"You don't have to look any further than the people who were on the plane with him," she said, wiping the tears from her cheeks with the back of her hand.

"I wasn't planning to," Mark said. "But my decision was based on opportunity, not the motive. You'll have to help me there."

"Greed," she said. "Win should never have gone public and let those sharks into our lives."

"Then why did he?"

"Win was ambitious," she said. "As if you couldn't tell by the name he picked for himself."

It was the first time she revealed any resentment towards her husband. Mark made mental note of it.

"At least he was up front about it," Mark said. "How did Brant Publications come about?"

She explained that it was a family business, started by Brant's grandfather. They published small, regional newspapers in farming communities all over California. After Winston's father died, he sold off the newspapers and launched *Thrill Seeker* with the proceeds. The magazine caught on and became not just a publication, but a lifestyle. Brant wanted to capitalize on that with spin-off publications and branded items, like clothing, athletic equipment, even cologne. He needed capital and took the company public to get it, which brought Clifton Hemphill, Dean Perrow, and Virgil Nyby into the fold.

"They're strictly businessmen, they have no passion for anything but making money. They didn't care about *Thrill Seeker* or the lifestyle it stood for," she said. "I told him going public was a mistake, that he would end up losing control of the company to them. But Win couldn't imagine losing anything to anyone. His answer to everything was 'They don't call me Win for nothing.'"

"Were you right?"

"I wish I wasn't," she said. "The three of them formed a voting block on the board against him. They thwarted all of his projects and pushed forward their agenda. Let me show you what that was."

She got up and walked through a side door into the next room. Mark followed stiffly, his back sore from the antique chair. If Winston Brant wanted a real physical challenge, Mark thought, he should have tried sitting on some of his living room furniture.

Stepping into the library was like walking into an entirely different house. It was full of dark wood and supple leather, the bookshelves overflowing with hardcovers and paperbacks. The room had a warm, lived-in look, far from the formality of the living room. The leather chairs were creased from use, the shelves cluttered with mementos, the coffee tables covered with well-thumbed magazines.

Sara picked up one of the magazines and held it up for Mark to see. It was an issue of *Thrill Seeker*, the cover featuring a rugged-looking, incredibly fit man free-climbing up the face of a jagged peak over a deep canyon.

"This is what the magazine used to look like before the company went public," she said, then picked up another from the table and held the two issues up side by side. "This is what it looks like now."

The magazine was retitled *Maximum Thrill Seeker*, the word "Maximum" written in a font that looked like it had been seared into the old masthead with a blowtorch. The cover of the new issue featured a young woman in a low-cut, skintight jumpsuit hang gliding into the lens, her massive, surgically enhanced breasts rocketing towards the reader like blazing cannonballs.

"They felt covers like this would appeal to a wider audience and increase circulation," she said. "To the groin. Win was mortified."

"Wasn't there anything your husband could do to stop it?"

"Besides walk away from the magazine and watch it all go crashing down? He'd never walked away from anything in his life," she said. "So he found another way to fight back. The last thing he said to me before he got on the plane was that he'd finally beaten them, that 'they don't call me Win for nothing.'"

"What was he going to do?"

"He was going to announce at the shareholders' meeting today that he'd discovered that Hemphill, Perrow, and Nyby were embezzling money from the company through all kinds of illegal schemes," she said. "They killed him to keep him from revealing what he knew."

"The evidence must still be there," Mark said. "Did he tell you what he found?"

"No," she said, dropping the magazines back on the table. "He wanted it to be a big surprise to me, too. I got a big surprise all right. So did the kids. We watched him fall . . ."

Sara started to cry. Mark stepped forward and gave her a hug. She pressed her face to his chest and all her grief seemed to escape at once, her entire body heaving, her tears dampening his shirt. He patted her back and gently rocked on his heels, comforting her as if she were a baby.

He wanted to tell her the usual platitudes, that everything was going to be all right and that he would make it all better. But he knew that would be a lie.

All he could do was try to get her some measure of justice.

That would have to do.

Lenore Barber left her house off Laurel Canyon at about nine a.m. and drove in her Lexus sedan down to the Starbucks on traffic-clogged Ventura Boulevard, flicking ashes from her cigarette out her window the whole way. She parked in the handicapped space, ran inside the Starbucks, and emerged a few minutes later with a cup of coffee. She then drove a half block west on the boulevard to Exclusive Properties Real Estate, parked beside the five other Lexuses in the narrow lot, and went inside.

She stayed in her office for about an hour, came back outside to smoke a cigarette, then went back inside for another hour, before emerging again and driving off, lighting a cigarette at the first stoplight.

Her destination was a sprawling, ranch-style estate nestled in the low-lying hills south of Ventura Boulevard in Encino. There was an Exclusive Properties FOR SALE sign in the freshly laid lawn. Lenore was met by a young couple who looked as though they'd stepped out of a Ralph Lauren billboard, grabbed the first Range Rover they saw passing by, and drove right over.

She led them up to the house, unlocked the key safe, and took them on a tour of the home.

Lenore Barber never even noticed the Toyota Prius parked across the street. Perhaps if she had, she would have remembered also seeing it outside her house and parked across the street from her real estate office.

Susan Hilliard waited until Lenore Barber closed the front door before she nudged Jesse, who was sleeping in the passenger seat, which he'd reclined into almost a flat position.

"What?" he blubbered, bleary-eyed, his hair askew. He was still wearing his surgical scrubs and had been asleep since she picked him up at the hospital a few hours ago.

"She's showing a couple a house," Susan said.

"Okay," Jesse said, rolling over to face the door, curling into a fetal position as if he was in bed.

She nudged him again. "I thought you'd be interested."

"Why?" he mumbled.

"Because you asked me to follow her, remember?" Susan said. "This is your stakeout."

"I've been up for over thirty hours, I'm too tired to drive," Jesse said. "It wouldn't be safe."

"I know," Susan said. "But I'm not sure what I'm supposed to be looking for."

"Exactly what you're seeing. Take lots of notes," Jesse said, and went back to sleep.

So Susan sighed, turned on the radio, and listened to an unbelievable story about a skydiver who somehow got stabbed to death in midair.

CHAPTER TEN

It was a couple of hours before Steve was able to leave the crime scene at Rebecca Jordan's apartment. First he had to report the homicide, then call in the SID techs to gather forensic evidence, and then wait for the arrival of the medical examiner to gather the body. In the meantime, he took Lissy's statement and sent out uniformed officers to question the neighbors.

Steve had hoped to keep the favor he was doing for his father quiet. He figured that he'd take care of it on his way to work and nobody would have to know about it.

Fat chance of that now.

He left the apartment a few minutes after Amanda arrived and drove straight out to Hollywood, to the Paradise Hotel and the door that would fit the key he found in the dead man's pocket.

During the drive, Steve tried to figure out the best way to explain to his captain how he happened to discover a corpse in an apartment in Culver City. No matter how Steve looked at it, he was in trouble.

But now he was no longer doing a favor for his dad; he was investigating a murder, and this next stop was official business. He wanted to know who the dead guy was and what he had to do with the attack on Lissy and, perhaps, the suicide attempt by Rebecca Jordan.

The Paradise Hotel was on a grimy side street off Hollywood Boulevard. If the hotel was somebody's idea of paradise, Steve couldn't imagine what their vision of hell was like.

The building was a rotting tenement, strewn with trash and reeking of urine. And that was just the impression Steve got from the street. It got worse once he went inside. Hookers, drunks, and junkies were draped over soiled furniture like discarded garments. The desk clerk was asleep or unconscious, facedown on his scribble-covered desk blotter, four cigarette butts floating in the filthy cup of murky coffee that he still gripped in his hand.

Steve walked past him, taking the stairs up to room 17. He pressed his ear to the door and heard someone moving around quietly behind it. He drew his gun and tested the doorknob with his other hand. The door was unlocked.

He threw open the door and burst into the room, training his gun on the biggest rat he'd ever seen, scurrying across the floor and disappearing into a hole in the cracked, water-stained wall.

Steve holstered his gun and took in the empty room. He saw the lopsided bureau and its uneven drawers. He saw the sagging bed and its thin, soiled mattress. He saw the curl of smoke coming from a cigarette dropped hastily on the floor. And just as he was realizing what it meant, she came at him, springing from her hiding place behind the door, a table knife in her fist. He sidestepped her, almost by reflex, grabbing her wrist, wrenching the knife free and using her momentum to slam her face-first against the wall.

He glanced down at the knife on the floor. It wasn't sharp enough to cut a slice of bread. He kicked it under the bed anyway and another rat scurried out, disappearing into the same hole as the other one.

"Paradise," he muttered to himself, then glanced at the woman, who was facing him now, feral anger in her eyes, her nose bleeding, thin rivulets of blood rolling over her lips and dripping onto her faded denim shirt.

She looked a lot like the guy he'd just seen in a body bag, only she was still breathing. She had pale, sunken cheeks and oily, matted hair that hung on her shoulders in tangled clumps. Besides the shirt, which reeked of body odor, she wore only a pair of panties. Her bony legs were blotched and bruised, her thighs covered with scratches and needle marks.

She was either a junkie or a reanimated corpse, not that there was much of a difference.

Even though she'd attacked him with a dull knife, he felt guilty for hurting her. He did, after all, bust into her room unannounced with a gun in his hand. It was only natural that she'd tried to defend herself.

He leaned towards her, offering her his hand. "I'm sorry I crashed in here like that, I'm—"

She flung herself at him with a primal yelp, fingers bared like claws, her mouth open wide as if revealing fangs instead of her yellow, crooked teeth. He pinned her easily against the wall, her arm twisted behind her back, and let her thrash until she ran out of energy.

Steve dragged her limp body to the edge of the bed and sat her down. He moved back to the center of the room, a safe distance away. Her face was smeared with blood from her nose. He took out his handkerchief, ran some brownish water over it in the sink, and gave it to her.

"Wipe your face," he said.

"So I can be clean when you kill me?" She balled up the handkerchief in her hand. "Go to hell."

She threw the handkerchief at him. He easily dodged it and let it hit the wall with a wet smack.

"We aren't running, you sonofabitch," she hissed. "We're getting Maurice Balcore his damn money. Deke is getting it from his sister, okay? You going to break some of my fingers now, too?"

Steve took out the newspaper clipping and held it up to her. "Is this Deke's sister?"

The woman stared at the paper as if he was dangling Deke's decapitated head in front of her.

"That's from Deke's pocket," she said, almost in a whisper. "You killed him already, didn't you?"

"He's dead, but I didn't kill him." Steve opened his coat so she could see the badge clipped to his belt. "Lieutenant Steve Sloan, LAPD homicide."

"Oh hell." She flopped back on the bed, her legs still dangling over the side.

"You want to tell me what's going on?"

"No."

"I could arrest you for assaulting a police officer with a deadly weapon," he said. "Or I can forget about it."

"You want to make it with me?" She tugged at the waistband of her panties. "Is that what you'd like?"

"No," Steve said, disgusted. "I want some answers. Let's start with your name."

"Your momma," she said.

Steve sighed. His morning wasn't turning out much better than Lissy's.

"Deke said if we came down here, we'd have all the money we'd need." She yanked up the sheet from the mattress and used the corner to wipe the blood off her face. "Now what am I supposed to do? Huh?"

"You could answer my questions before I lose my temper," Steve said.

"Or what? You gonna beat me up some more?" she asked, examining the bloody sheet. "Is that what gets you off? Throw in a twenty, I'll let you kiss me, too."

"Is this who was going to give him the money?" Steve dangled the clipping over the woman's face.

"His big sister Rachel, though he used to say she was dead," she said. "Wouldn't be the first lie he's told me."

"You sure he said *Rachel?*"

"That's all he talked about all the way down from Spokane," she said. "He saw her picture in the paper. Said she'd give us money to pay off Balcore and get his goons off our backs for what we owe. Deke said she'd help us for sure."

"Right now, she can't help anybody," Steve said. "She tried to kill herself yesterday. She's in a coma."

The woman propped herself up on her elbows and looked at Steve with genuine interest. "Is that so?"

"Yeah, it is."

"Deke was the only family she had left," she said. "We got hitched in Vegas one time, which makes me her sister-in-law."

"You want to send her flowers?"

"I'm just thinking." She licked her chapped lips. "If she dies, don't I get her stuff?"

Mark Sloan believed that the best way to learn about a man was to talk to his wife or his secretary and not necessarily in that order.

Grace Wozniak was not at all what Mark expected her to be. For one thing, she was nearly Mark's age. She was a stout woman, with a big, bold head of gray hair that had been puffed, sprayed, and cemented into a dandelion that could withstand hurricane-force winds. Her eyeglasses dangled from a chain around her neck and rested on her formidable bosom, just one of the barriers she'd established in front of Brant's corner office.

The first thing anybody saw when they entered was Grace, facing them from behind a massive desk she manned like a military fortification. There was no way to reach his door without getting past her desk first.

Behind her was a window overlooking the John Wayne Airport. Mark doubted it was a coincidence that the offices just happened to overlook a tribute to an enduring cultural icon of rugged American individuality and courage, everything *Thrill Seeker* was supposed to stand for.

Mark was surprised that Grace was manning her post the day after Brant's murder. The stockholders' meeting, originally scheduled for today, had been postponed for a week, so he couldn't imagine what business needed to be done that couldn't wait for a few days.

"This is where I belong," she'd said flatly, explaining it was a job she'd held first for Winston's father, Gaylord Brant, during "the great man's later years."

The way Grace talked about Gaylord Brant, it was clear the woman not only admired him, but loved him. She'd also worked on the day of his death. In fact, she proudly declared that she'd only missed one "non-vacation day" in thirty-five years, and that was to attend the funeral of her beloved poodle Starchy, the dog who was now stuffed and positioned beside her desk.

Grace told Mark that she'd babysat Winston when he was a child and had continued, throughout his life, to "protect him as if he was one of my own bear cubs."

Her comment gave Mark, who was practically dozing off in his guest chair after more than a day without sleep, a natural segue into the questions he'd come to ask.

"Did he still need your protection?" Mark asked.

"More now than ever before," Grace said.

"From whom?"

"His so-called partners," she said. "Every day was war. Win took the company public because he wanted to expand the brand, but his new investors had other ideas."

"What kind of ideas?" he asked.

"Like buying this building, changing the name of the magazine, and spending a fortune on advertising," she said.

"They said they were focusing on maximizing profits rather than speculative spending."

"Speculative spending," Mark repeated. "I don't think I've ever heard that phrase before."

"They came up with it as a way to reject every idea Win had," she said. "They felt his ideas were too risky. All they wanted to do was tout the surge in circulation since they 'freshened the concept' of the magazine."

"You mean when they changed the name of the magazine and started putting women on the cover."

"Half-naked women," Grace said, scowling. "Win prided himself on only using real people on the cover, doing the activities they genuinely excelled at. No touch-ups, no trickery, and no pandering to prurient interests."

To illustrate her point, Grace held up the same issue Sara had showed Mark before, the one with the woman hang gliding in her skintight jumpsuit.

"This woman hang glides as much as I do. This photograph was shot in a Van Nuys studio against a green screen. Everything else was added and enhanced on a computer, including her bust." She tossed the magazine into the trash can. "It made us all sick, especially Win."

"Even though the magazine's circulation was up?"

"He was convinced they were cooking the numbers somehow. He had lots of anecdotal evidence that the core audience of the magazine, the folks who'd stuck with us since the beginning, were leaving in droves," she said. "Even if they were right, and we had two hundred thousand new readers, Win said to me, 'Grace, I'd rather have fewer subscribers and a magazine I can be proud of.' God, it was powerful. In that moment, he was truly channeling his father, may he rest in peace."

"Then why didn't he order an audit?" Mark asked.

"Because he felt a responsibility to the shareholders and to the reputation of the magazine," she replied. "He didn't want to appear bitter and vindictive or create a scandal. It would hurt the magazine too much."

Grace reached down and petted Starchy, who stared at Mark with his glass eyes. "It really got to Win over the last few months. He'd lost his spirit. He didn't seem to care anymore."

"So what changed Win's mind?"

"What do you mean?"

"Sara told me he was preparing to fight back," Mark said. "She said he was going to announce at the shareholders' meeting that he had evidence that Hemphill, Perrow, and Nyby had been stealing from the company."

Grace shook her head. "If he was, I didn't know about it."

Mark stared at her. "You've been sitting right outside his door for years. No one gets to him without getting through you first. If he was building a case against his partners, you had to know about it."

"Perhaps he said that because it was what Sara wanted to hear. She hated what the partners were doing to the magazine even more than Win did," she said. "But even if he had the evidence, he never would have made it public, because it would have destroyed this magazine. Win was *Thrill Seeker*. It would have been like destroying a part of himself. He wouldn't have been able to live with it."

"Somebody on that plane wasn't willing to take that chance," Mark said.

Grace picked up her stuffed dog and hugged it to herself. "Then they killed him for nothing."

Mark was on his way out of Brant's office when he was intercepted in the corridor by Dean Perrow, a broad smile on the man's face.

"Don't tell me you were going to leave without saying hello to me." Perrow gave Mark a firm, businesslike handshake. "I'm still a suspect, aren't I?"

"Absolutely," Mark said, smiling right back at him.

"So how come you didn't stop by my office to play cat and mouse?"

"I need more evidence against you first."

"Does that mean you have some?"

Mark shrugged. Perrow wagged a finger at him. "There you go, playing me already. You're good at this."

Perrow tilted his head toward Brant's office. "I suppose the pit bull told you I'm the root of all evil."

"She mentioned that you and Brant didn't get along," Mark said. "I'm sure it's not much of a secret."

"I don't always get along with my wife either, but we love each other deeply," Perrow said. "I admired Winston Brant. The man, the adventurer, and the publisher. *Thrill Seeker* was Winston Brant, we knew that when we bought into it. I don't know what kind of future this magazine will have now without him."

"If that's the way you felt, why did you infuriate Brant with your changes to the magazine and ignore his new business initiatives?"

"We were looking out for his best interests," Perrow said. "The magazine had stagnated creatively. Circulation was down. Ad rates were plunging. We couldn't risk expansion until we shored up the core asset, *Thrill Seeker*. All we wanted to do was revitalize the magazine and we succeeded, amazingly well."

"That's apparently not the way Winston Brant saw it," Mark said.

"Let me ask you something, Mark. How would a woman feel if you went up to her and said 'I love you, honey, but you need bigger boobs, a nose job, a face-lift, and a tummy tuck if you want to be a knockout again.' "

"She'd be offended and deeply hurt."

"That's what happened here. *Thrill Seeker* was Winston's public face and we said it needed work. Of course he was upset. But when all was said and done, he forgot his anger as soon as he saw his profits." Perrow winked at him. "Same way my wife appreciates that guys are checking her out again when she walks down the street."

"You told your wife she needed plastic surgery?" Mark asked incredulously.

"Tough love is the truest love," Perrow said.

CHAPTER ELEVEN

Mark was stuck in the crawl of traffic north on the San Diego Freeway, trying not to fall asleep at the wheel. If traffic had been moving any faster than three miles an hour, for safety's sake he would have pulled off the road for a cup of coffee. But at this speed, the only danger he posed was a gentle nudge to the car in front of him.

He used the unwelcome downtime to think about his conversations with Sara Everden and Grace Wozniak. Beyond learning a bit more about the kind of man Winston Brant had been and the history of Brant Publications, he was no closer to learning who the killer was or how the murder was committed.

Winston still wasn't out of danger. If his body wasn't placed under guard, Mark thought, Grace might have him stuffed and mounted right next to Starchy.

The only thing that puzzled Mark was the odd discrepancy between what Sara and Grace had to say about Winston's state of mind on the day of his murder. Sara believed her husband was going on the offensive and was intending to expose Hemphill, Perrow, and Nyby's dirty dealings at the stockholders' meeting. Grace believed he was a beaten man, unwilling to do anything that might involve the magazine in a scandal. How could these two women, who knew

Brant better than anyone, have such contradictory accounts? What was Brant really up to, and did it lead to his murder?

Even if Mark could determine that, it didn't narrow the field of suspects down any further than the three men he was already considering.

Was he overlooking anyone?

There were at least two other people in the plane with Brant that day. The airplane pilot and the skydiving instructor.

Mark could safely scratch the pilot off his list. There was no way the pilot could have left the controls of the plane, stabbed Brant in midair, and returned to the cockpit, unless he was also hiding his secret identity as Superman.

That left the skydiving instructor, Justin Darbo. What possible motive could Darbo have for killing Brant? And if he did do it, wouldn't the act have been caught on tape by the video camera mounted on his helmet?

If Mark assumed Darbo was the killer, and that the video itself hadn't been altered, what explanation could there be for the murder not being captured on tape?

He considered that for a moment as traffic inched forward. All the skydivers looked alike. What if the video wasn't shot that day? Mark remembered it was virtually impossible to tell the skydivers apart. What if the video he saw was actually shot earlier using other people dressed in the same helmets, goggles, and jumpsuits as Brant and the others?

It was possible, but it meant that Justin Darbo would have needed at least four willing accomplices. That seemed unlikely.

Mark reconsidered his theory. What if it was a genuine video of Brant and the others, only shot on a previous day? That would eliminate the need for accomplices.

There was also another possibility. What if Darbo was an innocent dupe and his camera was sabotaged in some way?

What if he was unaware that he wasn't actually recording anything on the day of the murder? What if what he thought was a blank tape already contained footage that was nearly identical to what he thought he was shooting?

It was a long shot at best, but Mark made a note to himself on the stick-it pad on the dashboard, which he kept just for moments like this. He'd ask Steve to check out if Brant and his board of directors ever took a practice jump together and if Darbo filmed it. He'd also recommend that Steve dig deep into Darbo's past to make sure the skydiving instructor didn't have some grudge against Brant.

Mark's cell phone rang, breaking him out of his fatigued stupor. It was Amanda, calling from the path lab.

"I just wanted to let you know I'll have the autopsy report on Deke Swicord ready for you around three," Amanda said. "I know you're probably in a hurry for it, though it's hardly a mystery what happened to him."

"It is to me," Mark said. "I've never heard of him."

"He's the dead guy Steve found when he went to talk to Lissy Dearborn."

"Lissy Dearborn?"

"Rebecca Jordan's roommate," Amanda said. "She's lucky she wasn't killed, too. Odds are it was the murderer she was fighting off when Steve got there."

"Got where?"

"Rebecca Jordan's apartment," Amanda said. "Though I suppose we can stop calling her that now."

"What should we call her?" Mark was thoroughly confused, chalking it up as another symptom of his sleep deprivation.

"Rachel Swicord," Amanda said. "That's assuming that Deke is really her brother, and we only have Darla's word for that."

"Darla?"

"You can't trust a junkie's word on anything," Amanda said.

"I suppose not," Mark said, replying to what seemed to him like a non sequitur.

"Darla says she's Deke's wife, which entitles her to whatever Rachel has if she dies," Amanda said. "Can you believe it?"

"I honestly can't understand any of it," Mark said.

"That makes two of us."

"It certainly sounds like it to me," Mark said. "Where can I find Steve?"

"He's at the station, getting chewed out by his captain, who has a lot of questions about how Steve stumbled into this murder when he was supposed to be working the Brant case."

"I've got a few questions to ask him myself," Mark said. "I'll see you at three."

He flipped his phone shut and tossed it on the passenger seat beside him. Now there was another murder for him to solve. Some days, he thought, the killing just never stops.

Traffic let up north of LAX, so Mark managed to get to Community General Hospital in West LA at two. He stopped in the cafeteria for a hamburger, fries, and a Coke, which he devoured, surprised by how hungry he was. Sated by his meal, and feeling more alert, he decided to stop by the ICU to check on Rebecca Jordan before meeting Amanda and Steve in the path lab.

He emerged from the elevator and immediately looked to the waiting area on his left, and wasn't surprised to see the Marlboro Man still there, though he'd managed to freshen up his reading material. The man was now immersed in an issue of *Allure*, which promised to reveal THE 12 AWESOME JUICY FRUITY LIP SHADES OF SPRING.

Rebecca Jordan's corner of the ICU was now filled with

flowers and boxes of pastries. There was a man who reminded Mark of a garden gnome asleep in one of the guest chairs. Somehow, the gnomish fellow managed to make the stiff-backed plastic chair seem comfortable. Mark envied him his nap.

Mark made a quick check of Rebecca's chart, saw that her condition was unchanged, and took the elevator back down to the path lab.

Steve was already standing with Amanda on either side of the autopsy table, where a body was covered with a white sheet.

"I understand you've had a busy morning," Mark said to Steve, then glanced at the toe tag on the body. The tag read DEKE SWICORD.

"Why is it when I do you a favor one of two things always happens," Steve said. "I either find a corpse or one of my superiors threatens to fire me. Come to think of it, *both* things always happen."

"Then you should be used to it and not complaining," Mark said.

Steve and Amanda both looked at Mark. It wasn't like him to be so harsh and he knew it.

"Sorry," he said. "I haven't had much sleep and I'm running on caffeine."

"That's me every day," Amanda said.

"You're a single parent working two jobs," Mark said. "You have an excuse."

"So do you," Amanda said. "You're also a single parent with two jobs."

"Excuse me," Steve said. "I'm an adult."

"Who still lives at home," Amanda said, then turned to Mark. "When was the last time he cleaned his room?"

"1978," Mark said, grateful to Amanda for lightening up the conversation, though he doubted Steve shared his appreciation. "So, does anybody want to tell me about this gentleman?"

"Meet Mr. Deke Swicord, thirty-two, of Spokane, Washington," Steve said. "He's got a history of priors for petty theft, public drunkenness, and possession of controlled substances."

"Which he didn't possess more than mere seconds before injecting, snorting, or swallowing them," Amanda said. "His cadaver could be used as a teaching aid in medical school to illustrate the damaging effects of chronic drug abuse on the human body."

"In other words, the guy was a junkie," Steve said. "But that's not what killed him, not directly anyway."

"What was the cause of death?" Mark asked Amanda.

"Having his head slammed against the floor of Rebecca Jordan's apartment a half dozen times," she said.

"That's where things get murky," Steve said.

Mark sighed. "Things have been murky for me since I left the house this morning."

"Deke came down to Spokane with his wife Darla, another drug addict," Steve said. "They're running from a loan shark named Maurice Balcore."

"Who, I presume, is responsible for this." Amanda lifted the sheet to show them Deke's two broken fingers, no longer taped and splinted with Popsicle sticks. The fingers were swollen and dark purple. "Someone smashed his fingers with a mallet. I'd say it was about a week ago."

"Which nearly coincides with the publication of this picture in the *Spokesman-Review*." Steve handed Mark the newspaper clipping he found in Deke's wallet.

"I saw this wire story in Rebecca Jordan's office," Mark said.

"Her name isn't Rebecca," Steve said. "She's Deke's sister, Rachel Swicord. When he saw her picture in the paper, he hitched his way down here as fast as he could to hit her up for money."

"If he showed up at my door," Amanda said, "I might jump out a window, too."

"Rachel's roommate Lissy Dearborn saw him hanging around the neighborhood," Steve said. "She also said somebody tried to break in the other day, but she scared him off with a meat cleaver."

"A meat cleaver?" Amanda said. "Who keeps a meat cleaver under their bed?"

"When this case is closed, I think I'm going to ask her out."

"Because she keeps a meat cleaver under the bed?" Amanda said incredulously. "That would send a very different message to most men. Then again, it's been a while since you had a date."

"Have you confirmed yet that Rebecca Jordan really is Rachel Swicord?" Mark asked before Steve could reply to Amanda's dig.

"I just took her prints," Steve said. "I'll run them through AFIS when I get back to the station."

"I'll save you the trouble," Mark said. "Stay here. I think I know how we can find out her whole story right now."

CHAPTER TWELVE

Mark rode the elevator up to the ICU and took a seat in the waiting room beside the Marlboro Man, who was engrossed in an issue of *Modern Bride*. The man seemed very interested in an exhaustive report on the twelve awesome lip shades every bride needs to know.

"Excuse me," Mark said. "I was wondering if you could tell me how to make every day a great hair day?"

"Wear a sturdy hat," the man said, picking up the Stetson on the chair beside him. "That's my secret."

"How about letting me in on the ten great shortcuts to a new you?" Mark said.

"I don't know about that one, Dr. Sloan," the man said. "That's probably a question we should ask Rachel Swicord when she wakes up. I bet she probably has a couple good answers for that one."

Mark smiled. "The LA County medical examiner's office maintains a satellite morgue in this hospital. If I promise to have someone from security stay here and watch Rachel's room for you, would you mind coming down to the morgue with me?"

"That'd be fine," the man said.

* * *

Amanda and Steve were sitting at her desk, having a cup of coffee, when Mark returned with the big man wearing the Stetson. Steve immediately rose from his seat.

"I'm Steve Sloan," Steve said, extending his hand to the stranger. "My badge says LAPD. What does yours say?"

"United States Marshal," the man said, shaking Steve's hand with a strong grip. "The name's Tom Wade."

"How did you know he was a cop?" Amanda asked Steve.

"I looked at him," Steve said.

"Ma'am." Wade opened his jacket to show the badge and the gun clipped to his belt. "I'll be happy to show you my identification if you like."

"It's okay," Amanda said.

"I assume you're from Spokane," Steve said to the marshal.

Wade nodded and motioned to the corpse. "You need me to tell you about Deke?"

"We'd like you to tell us about Rachel Swicord," Mark replied. "You can start by explaining why you're sitting outside her room."

"I'm guarding my prisoner, Doctor," Wade said. "Rachel Swicord is a wanted fugitive."

"What did she do?" Mark asked.

"She killed a cop," Wade said.

Mark looked shocked. Wade studied Mark's face.

"Did you know her for some time, Dr. Sloan?"

"I didn't know her at all," Mark said.

"Then why do you seem so shaken?" Wade said.

Mark shrugged. "It's hard to believe a woman who could do that would also come up with a product like the Cuddle Bear."

"I've met men who'd slaughter children without blinking but would risk their lives to save a puppy from being hurt," Wade said. "There's no accounting for the criminal mind."

"How did the cop get killed?" Amanda asked.

"When Rachel was eighteen, that'd be eight years ago, she and her boyfriend stole a car and went out on a joyride. Her boyfriend, Pike Wheeler, stopped at a convenience store and robbed the place while she remained in the vehicle and watched," Wade said. "About an hour later, they were pulled over by a sheriff's deputy. When the deputy exited his patrol car, Pike ran him over, killing the officer. Other deputies were alerted and a pursuit ensued. Her boyfriend lost control of his vehicle and plunged into the Spokane River. She swam to shore and was apprehended; her boyfriend was swept away, his body never recovered."

"Don't tell me she got off," Steve said.

Wade shook his head. "Rachel pled guilty and served five years in prison. She was paroled on good behavior as part of a court-mandated initiative to reduce overcrowding in our prisons. They figured society would prefer to put a cop killer back on the streets than have three inmates share a cell and a toilet."

"So why are you chasing her now?" Amanda said. "She didn't break out of prison, she was released."

"She was paroled, ma'am, not pardoned," Wade said. "Two days after she got out she disappeared. That was three years ago. I didn't have a single lead on her until I saw that wire photo in the local paper."

"You chase all parole violators this hard?" Steve said.

"Yes, I do." Wade nodded. "But I am relentless when the crime involves the death of a law enforcement officer. Deputy Barker left a wife and three kids."

"Any theories on why she tried to kill herself?" Mark asked.

"Guess she didn't want to share a cell and a toilet again," Wade replied. "As soon as she's up to it, I'm taking her back to Washington State to serve the remainder of her sentence."

"What about him?" Steve tilted his head towards Deke.

"I packed light," Wade said, "but I don't think I can fit a casket in my car."

"Aren't you interested in who killed him?" Steve said.

"I have plenty of other interests," Wade said.

"Ask him about the eighty-seven ways to make your wedding reception unique," Mark said. "Or ten things you didn't know about sequins."

"What do you know about Maurice Balcore?" Steve asked.

"He's a sadistic bastard," Wade said. "The Spokane police have been trying to nail him for ten years."

"You think he could have done this?" Steve gestured to Deke.

"I think he'd kill his own mother if he loaned her a dollar and she didn't pay him back six-fifty a week later," Wade said. "I'll be upstairs if I can be of any more help."

He tipped the brim of his hat to Amanda and walked out. Steve and Mark watched him go, then looked at one another.

"There's more to this story than he's telling," Mark said.

"I'm sure there is," Steve said. "But now you've found out what you wanted to know. There's no reason for you to be involved any longer. If you still want to help her, maybe you can find her a good lawyer."

"Do you really think she jumped out her window to avoid going back to jail?" Mark asked.

"Makes sense to me," Amanda said. "I didn't even like sharing a bathroom when I was married."

"You can ask Rachel about her reasons when she wakes up," Steve said to Mark. "I'm more interested in who killed her brother and you should be, too."

"Why me?" Mark asked.

"Because you got me into this," Steve said. "So you had better help me get out of it."

"Is there really a mystery?" Amanda asked. "The Spokane loan shark probably killed this guy."

"Deke would have had to owe an awful lot to Maurice Balcore to make it worthwhile to send muscle all the way down here to collect," Steve said. "And it didn't look to me like Deke and Darla were living large."

"Didn't you just hear what the marshal said?" Amanda replied.

"There's another fact that doesn't fit," Mark said. "Why would Balcore's bone-breaker confront Deke while he's breaking into his sister's house?"

"It was better than killing him in broad daylight right in the street," Steve suggested.

"Why kill him at all?" Mark said. "It doesn't get them their money back."

"It sends a message to people who don't pay their debts," Steve said. "You can run but you can't hide."

"Who's going to hear about it?" Mark said. "I doubt the murder of a junkie is going to make the news here, much less in another state."

"Balcore will spread the news," Steve said.

"Wait a minute," Amanda said. "Didn't you just get done saying you didn't believe a loan shark would send somebody all the way down here after Deke and Darla?"

"I'm talking myself into it," Steve said.

"You just want to get this case off your back and toss it to the cops in Spokane," Amanda said.

"The thought occurred to me," Steve said. "Maybe one of their homicide guys would like a trip to Southern California to work on his tan."

Mark frowned. "Something isn't right about this."

"Look at the bright side," Steve said. "Whatever the answer is, it's got to be easier to figure out than who killed Winston Brant and how they managed to do it."

"Nice segue," Amanda said, sliding Deke's body back into the freezer drawer and closing the door. "Shall I pull out the next corpse under discussion?"

"That won't be necessary," Mark said, then told Steve and Amanda about his conversations with Brant's wife, Dr. Sara Everden, and his secretary, Grace Wozniak.

Mark explained that each woman had a different take on Brant's mood and intentions the day before his death, but they both agreed that the new investors were destroying the company to satisfy their greed. He urged Steve to bring in a forensic accountant to look at possible financial irregularities at Brant Publications. If Brant did discover that Hemphill, Perrow, and Nyby were stealing money in some way, it would give each of them a strong motive for murder.

Steve reiterated his theory that perhaps all three men committed the murder together, which prompted Mark to share his notion that perhaps Justin Darbo, the skydiving instructor, deserved a hard look.

Mark shared a couple of his theories about how Darbo might have switched the skydiving videos or, perhaps, had been an unwilling pawn of the actual killer.

When Mark was finished, Steve and Amanda just stared at him.

"You really *are* tired," Steve said. "Those are the kinds of contrived explanations I usually come up with."

"Oh no, Steve, these are worse," Amanda said, shaking her head. "These sound like ideas Jesse would have come up with."

"I'm not sure how I should take this," Mark said.

"Take it as a hint," Steve said. "Go home and get some rest while I do some digging."

A nap sounded like an awfully good idea to Mark right now.

"I can do that," Mark said.

CHAPTER THIRTEEN

Lenore had a smoke while she idled in the line of cars waiting to pick up students at Hanford Hall, an expensive private
school on Coldwater Canyon, a few blocks north of Ventura
Boulevard.

Jesse parked across the street and around the corner,
knowing Susan's Toyota would stand out amidst the Range
Rovers, Mercedes, Hummers, and Escalades. Even Lenore's
Lexus was noticeably downscale amidst a parent population
who gladly paid seventeen thousand dollars a year for
kindergarten. He wondered how many houses Lenore had to
sell to pay for her kids to attend fifth and sixth grades.

"Did you ever stop to ask yourself why you're doing
this?" Susan asked. She sat in the passenger seat, finishing
up the last of her McDonald's French fries.

"I'm helping Mark," Jesse said. "Like I always do."

"This is different," she said. "He hasn't asked you to
check on a patient for him or run an investigative errand. He
doesn't even know you're here."

"He doesn't need to."

"Like what you did for him with Noah Dent," she said,
referring to the ex–Community General administrator who
left for reasons only Jesse and Susan knew.

"I also did it for you and for the hospital," Jesse said.

"But you still kept it from Mark," she said. "I don't get it."

"I'm a nice guy," Jesse said.

"That much I know," Susan said. "I'm curious about your motivation. Why do you have this sudden need to be Mark's guardian angel?"

"He's done a lot for me," Jesse said. "I'm just giving a little back."

"Here's how I see it." She washed her last French fry down with a sip of Dr Pepper. "You're still trying to earn his respect, even though you got it a long time ago. The only difference now is that you're doing it in the shadows."

"You're overanalyzing this," Jesse said.

"You work at the hospital with him. You help him solve crimes. You opened a restaurant with his son. And now you're doing secret favors for him," Susan said. "What do you want from him that you don't already have?"

"Nothing," he said irritably.

"You have a father of your own, Jesse."

"It's not a relationship I wish to pursue," Jesse said coldly.

"So instead you spend your time treating Mark as your father and hoping he'll treat you as his son."

"That's not what I'm doing," Jesse said. "I like snooping around. I like helping people. This isn't just for Mark. This is for Lenore, too."

"You don't even know Lenore."

"You're missing the point," Jesse said.

"And you're avoiding it," Susan said. "But that's okay, at least I've got you thinking about it."

"No, you don't."

"You're not thinking about it now?"

"No."

"Then what are you thinking about?" she asked.

" 'The Gamesters of Triskelion,' " he said.

"What is that?" she asked.

"An episode of the original *Star Trek*," Jesse replied. "I'm still trying to figure out why those three throbbing brains-in-a-jar who lived at the core of the planet bothered gambling their quatloos amongst each other on alien gladiator battles. What did they do with all the quatloos they won? Buy clothes, jewelry, fancy cars? They were brains-in-a-jar. It makes no sense."

Susan just stared at him. "You're hopeless."

At that moment, Lenore drove out of the private school with her kids in the backseat. Jesse waited for a few cars to pass, then followed her.

On her way home, Lenore stopped at the Ralph's Market at Coldwater and spent an hour buying groceries and twenty minutes browsing through the *National Examiner*, the *Globe*, and the *National Inquirer*. She unloaded her children and groceries at the house, then went back down to her real estate office, where she stopped briefly before leaving again to show another property, this one a house on stilts that clung precariously to the edge of the Hollywood Hills.

While she was showing the house, Jesse drove back to the real estate office and had Susan go in to get a sheet of Lenore's listings. Susan had to leave a callback number to get it, but that was fine. It was all part of the plan.

Jesse looked at the careful notes he and Susan had made of Lenore's activities. He decided another day of surveillance should be enough to learn her routine. After that, the games would begin.

He didn't ask himself why he was doing it. It didn't matter. He just knew it was going to be fun.

Mark was so tired when he got home, he had no doubt he'd fall asleep the instant his face hit the pillow. But that's not what happened.

Once again, his mind wouldn't let him go. He'd close his eyes, and Rachel's suicide attempt would replay itself again and again in his mind. Only there was one difference this time. When her body hit the tree limb and snapped it, she cartwheeled and became Winston Brant tumbling out of the sky, a knife in his chest.

Help me.

An instant before Winston hit the ground, Mark would awaken, his heart pounding, his eyelids heavy with fatigue, to see that only ten or fifteen minutes had passed.

He kept at it for a few more hours, struggling to sleep, before giving up. It was dark outside. Mark squirted some eyedrops into his bloodshot, stinging eyes, brushed his teeth, and shuffled into the kitchen. He stood in front of the beachfront windows for a moment, taking in the view, watching the moonlight ride the swells.

He could understand why Brant was still on his mind. It was a murder he couldn't solve. But why couldn't he get Rachel Swicord out of his head? He knew her story and it hardly made her sympathetic. Whatever mystery there might have been was gone. Steve was right; there wasn't anything he could do for her now. Her immediate future was clear. She was going back to Washington.

So why couldn't he let her go?

If there was one thing Mark had learned about himself over the years it was never to deny the pull of his subconscious. It didn't have to make rational or obvious sense. Sooner or later, if he kept plugging along, whatever was nagging at him would make itself clear. It always did. All it took was discovering one fact, or hearing one key comment, and everything would make sense.

So until then, he had to be true to himself. He had to keep on the Rachel Swicord case until he knew what it was that was unsettling him.

Steve wasn't going to like this much. Mark wasn't wild about it himself. But Mark didn't have a choice.

He glanced at his watch. It was a little after eight. Steve

would be home soon, hopefully with some more details on the Brant homicide.

Since there was nothing he could do for Rachel at the moment, Mark decided to concentrate on the Brant case. He stuck the skydiving video back in the TV and watched it a few more times, gleaning nothing new from the repeat viewings. So he decided to see what facts he could find on the World Wide Web.

Mark used any excuse to go on the Internet, where he could get instant access to facts on just about anything that intrigued him on virtually any subject imaginable.

When he was a boy, he used to love sitting in the library, indulging his insatiable curiosity, limited only by the number of books on the shelves. Now he had the equivalent of tens of thousands of libraries right in his own living room or anywhere else he happened to be. With his laptop computer and a wireless connection, he could be plugged into a limitless world of knowledge at all times. It was only through sheer willpower that Mark wasn't planted in front of his laptop day and night.

But this wasn't a casual journey through the uncharted worlds of knowledge and imagination. This was a search for specific information. It made it easier for him to control himself, stay focused, and not take interesting side trips through cyberspace. As Mark knew all too well, one embedded link led to another and then another and pretty soon he was exploring topics he'd never even thought about before.

Mark spent the next two hours learning everything he could about skydiving, storing dozens of Web pages on his hard drive and printing out a ream of information on his laser printer to share with Steve. He paid particular attention to the packing of the parachute and the mechanics of its release. By the time he was done, his eyes looked bloodred and felt like hot coals.

He doused the flames with more eyedrops, closed his eyes to let the medicine work, and thought about what he'd learned about skydiving.

A skydiver usually packs and checks his own chute. In Brant's case, Airventures handled that step. Once the skydiver suits up, his straps and rig are double-checked by another skydiver, a task which fell to Justin Darbo and his crew.

The skydivers then board a plane that flies to a height of ten to sixteen thousand feet, which gives each jumper a 120-mile-per-hour free fall that lasts from forty-five to seventy-five seconds.

That, Mark thought, was the kill window. A mere minute or less.

When the altimeter hits twenty-five hundred feet, the skydiver pulls his rip cord. If he fails to do so, an automatic activation device does it for him, usually at seven hundred and fifty feet.

Mark had always assumed pulling the rip cord released the parachute, also known as the large canopy. What he learned in his brief research was that the skydiver first deploys a smaller, foot-long chute called the drogue, which catches the wind and pulls out the bridle, a ten-foot-long piece of nylon attached to the main chute.

As the drogue pulls the bridle, it yanks out the main chute and the five sets of lines that connect it to the risers, a pair of thick straps which, in turn, attach everything to the skydiver's pack.

The parachutes Airventures used were ram-air canopies, rectangular expanses of lightweight, zero-porosity nylon divided by fabric ribs into five individual bands that arc when they're hit by the wind. Unlike the familiar round parachute, the ram-air canopy resembles a nylon wing, allowing the skydiver to glide to the ground at an angle instead of dropping straight down. It also gives the skydiver a lot more control over his descent.

Mark didn't see any step in the deployment of the chute that offered the opportunity for the simultaneous deployment of a knife into Brant's chest.

So he looked elsewhere in the process and found something that had intriguing possibilities for the aspiring murderer.

He focused his attention on the automatic activation device that releases the parachute if the skydiver is unable to due to unconsciousness, injury, or distraction. The device is a small computer that monitors the altitude and fires a tiny knife-shaped projectile that cuts the cord and releases the reserve chute.

If the device could automatically fire the equivalent of a bullet, Mark wondered what else it could be modified to do.

Now I'm thinking like Jesse, he thought.

But even if the automatic activation device *could* be modified to shoot out a hunting knife, Mark still didn't see how the weapon could end up buried to the hilt in Brant's chest without going through his back first.

He didn't feel on the verge of any great discoveries, so he decided to give up on it for the night, to let the facts he'd learned percolate with everything else in his subconscious.

Something was bound to come up. It always did.

Then again, he thought, one of these days he was bound to be outsmarted.

Perhaps that day had finally come.

He opened his eyes and dismissed the thought. It was too troubling.

His son would be home soon and he'd be hungry. Mark was hungry already. So until he had some new facts to crunch, he decided to apply his considerable skills and imagination to the task of making dinner.

At least that was something he could still manage.

Tom Wade knew how to have great skin on his wedding day, ten shortcuts to a fantastic bust, how to prepare the perfect Seder, and seven secret techniques to control underarm odor without using an antiperspirant.

Of all the things he'd learned in the three dozen magazines he'd read in the waiting room, only the last topic was useful for him. He hated antiperspirants.

But the time wasn't a complete waste. He figured he now possessed all the specialized knowledge he needed if he ever had to hold his own in conversation at a baby shower, a Tupperware party, or a gynecologist's office.

Certainly men had waited here for news of their loved ones in the ICU. Why didn't any of them leave their reading material behind? Would it be asking too much for one of them to donate a *Motor Trend* or *Sports Illustrated* to the pile on the coffee table?

At this point, well into his second night in the waiting room, Wade would have welcomed another issue of *Highlights for Children*. He was down to his last magazine, an issue of *Modern Maternity*, and not looking forward to the experience of reading it, when his cell phone trilled.

"Wade," he said.

The caller didn't say anything, didn't even breathe as far as Wade could tell, but he knew instinctively who it was. His throat constricted and he could feel the blood pulsing in his temples.

"I'm taking her back to prison," Wade said. "And then I'm coming after you."

"I'll kill anyone who gets between me and Rachel," the caller said, his voice like tires on gravel. "Even you."

The caller hung up. Wade kept listening for a moment to the dead air, wondering if he'd imagined the whole thing. But he knew he hadn't. He'd never had much of an imagination; it had always been one of his failings, though certainly not his worst.

His worst failing was still haunting him today.

Haunting.

That was exactly the right word. He'd felt the pain of that failure, personally and professionally, every hour of every day for the last eight years.

He dialed a senior official at the Department of Corrections, spoke with him for a few minutes, and then called a friend at the Department of Justice to expedite the necessary paperwork on an emergency basis.

The reckoning was coming.

CHAPTER FOURTEEN

Steve came home to find his father cooking in the kitchen, an apron around his neck, happily humming some indefinable tune.

"I thought you were going to get some sleep," Steve said, glancing at the messy kitchen.

The sink was filled with dirty dishes. The counters were covered with mixing bowls, an open can of chopped clams, scattered vegetables, bottles of cooking oils, shakers of seasonings, cups of flour, cubes of butter, a carton of eggs, and a bowl full of chocolate chips.

"I tried to sleep but couldn't," Mark said, chopping onions. "So I tried to do some thinking about the Brant case instead."

Steve ate a couple of chocolate chips and motioned to the mess. "I can see how well the thinking went."

"I decided to take my mind off things and cook us some comfort food," Mark said.

"I don't need comfort," Steve said. "I need clues."

"Tonight, we're having Malibu clam chowder."

"Malibu?"

"It's like Boston clam chowder, only with more vegetables thrown in," Mark said. "And for dessert, your favorite Chocolate Decadence à la Sloan."

"Why can't you sleep?" Steve asked.

"You're not thanking me for making Chocolate Decadence à la Sloan?"

"You haven't made it in two years," Steve said. "You were up making it at five thirty in the morning because you couldn't save a young boy with an inoperable brain tumor."

"I keep seeing Rachel in that window," Mark said. "I keep seeing the look on her face."

"The case is solved," Steve said. "There's nothing more you can do for her."

"I know that," Mark said.

"So why is it making you crazy?"

"I'm not crazy," Mark said. "I'm just tired. Otherwise, I am in top form."

"Is that why you just put two cups of chopped onions into your Chocolate Decadence à la Sloan?"

Mark looked into the pot of melted chocolate in disbelief. If he'd put the onions in the dessert, where did he put the walnuts?

He deduced the answer without looking. There was nothing he could do to save either dish now.

Mark took off his apron and tossed it on a barstool. "How do you feel about hamburgers?"

"I love 'em," Steve said.

"Great," Mark said, moving the pots with the chowder and the chocolate to the sink. "I know where we can find the best burgers in town."

"BBQ Bob's?" Steve said.

"Better," Mark said. "The Community General cafeteria."

Steve shook his head and sighed. "I'll drive."

On the way to the hospital, Steve briefed his father on what he'd found, an exhaustive explanation that covered the drive from the driveway to the street.

Justin Darbo had a record for marijuana possession, which was no surprise to Mark, and had no apparent connection to Brant of any kind, beyond teaching him how to skydive.

Dr. Sara Everden authorized the LAPD to bring in a forensic accountant to go through the company books, but Steve was sure lawyers representing Clifton Hemphill, Dean Perrow, and Virgil Nyby would fight it.

Steve pointed out several fast-food places and restaurants along the way, but Mark insisted none of the establishments could match the fine dining to be had at the hospital.

"Everybody knows hospital food is the best," Steve said. "I've heard of people hurting themselves just so they could enjoy the cuisine."

Mark didn't take the bait. He simply sat in the passenger seat, unconsciously pressing his right foot to the floor as if there was a gas pedal there.

When they arrived at the hospital, Mark went straight up to the ICU, as Steve knew he would. Mark was in such a hurry that he didn't even notice something that made Steve forget his appetite. United States Marshal Tom Wade wasn't sitting in the waiting area anymore.

By the time Steve caught up with his father in the ICU, he found out why.

Rachel Swicord was gone.

A thin man with tiny, round glasses stood at the foot of her empty bed, reviewing her chart while Mark angrily confronted him. The man was thirty years old and had obviously spent most of his adolescence picking at his face.

"Who are you and where is my patient?" Mark said.

"I'm Dr. Huntley Lipp," the man said, not bothering to lift his eyes from the chart. "And Miss Swicord is on her way to my hospital."

Steve flashed his badge. "Which is?"

Dr. Lipp was unimpressed. "The prison ward at County-USC Medical Center."

"You can't move her," Mark said.

"I can and I have," Dr. Lipp said, reaching into his jacket and handing Steve a folded sheet of paper. "This is a court order. She's on her way to the ambulance and so am I."

Lipp marched off towards the elevator, Mark and Steve charging alongside him.

"She's neurologically unstable," Mark said. "She's been in a waxing and waning coma for over twenty-four hours, which could be indicative of brain swelling or bleeding. Transporting her now could be highly risky."

"Her CT scans and MRIs show no evidence of swelling or bleeding," Dr. Lipp said, stepping into the elevator. "The changing levels of her comatose state could simply be due to her severe concussion."

Mark and Steve crowded into the elevator with him. "The swelling and bleeding are often delayed for hours or days after the injury and can occur very quickly. If she's not in a hospital, available for immediate surgery to relieve the pressure, she could die or suffer irreparable brain damage."

"Then we'd better get her to the prison ward as fast as possible," Dr. Lipp said. "Now I have an excuse to use the siren."

Mark glanced at Steve, who met his gaze. "The paperwork is all in order, Dad. She's Wade's prisoner. It's out of my hands."

"She's certainly in no condition to run away now. Even if she was conscious, she's got a broken leg, a broken arm, and her free arm is restrained. Rachel can't escape or hurt herself," Mark argued as the elevator arrived at the lobby. "What's the rush to take her to the prison ward?"

"You'll have to ask Marshal Wade that question," Dr. Lipp said, and strode out.

They didn't have to go far to find Wade and his prisoner,

who was being wheeled by two orderlies towards the waiting ambulance outside the ER.

Mark and Steve caught up to them quickly.

"Why are you doing this?" Mark demanded of Wade. "Couldn't you at least wait until she's conscious to put her behind bars?"

"She's a fugitive and a suicidal one at that," Wade said. "The best place for her to be is in jail. Safer for herself, safer for society."

"She's not a danger to anyone," Mark said. "Especially now."

"Tell that to Deputy Barker's widow," Wade said.

They stepped outside onto the brightly lit ambulance bay. The medical transport was backed up nearly to the ER entrance, the rear doors of the vehicle swung wide open. The orderlies were about to slide the gurney into the ambulance when Steve glanced towards the street. Later, he would ask himself what made him look. Was it instinct? Something he saw in his peripheral vision that only registered subconsciously? He'd never know and it didn't matter.

Steve saw a man with a gun, illuminated for an instant, the sweep of headlights from a passing car revealing him in a doorway.

"Gun!" Steve yelled, tackling his father and pulling out his own weapon in one smooth motion.

Bullets from the gunman's automatic weapon riddled the front of the ambulance, blowing out the tires, the vehicle slumping forward with a gasping hiss. The windows of the ER doors behind Wade exploded in a spray of glass, but he barely flinched. He stood squinting into the darkness. The orderlies screamed and dove to the ground, hands over their heads. Dr. Lipp threw his body over Rachel and wheeled her gurney behind the protection of the open ambulance doors.

Steve got off four rounds before he hit the ground. One of the shots found its target, spinning the gunman around on his feet. The gunman stumbled, recovered his balance, and ran off, lurching to one side.

Wade charged across the street, his Glock in his hand, while the gunshots were still echoing in the air. Steve scrambled to his feet and quickly chased after him.

Mark went immediately to the orderlies, who suffered only minor glass cuts. He turned to Dr. Lipp, who was in the process of checking Rachel for wounds.

"She's unhurt," Dr. Lipp said.

"Let's get her back to the ICU," Mark said, taking the gurney and wheeling it back inside. He wasn't waiting for an argument and he didn't get one.

Steve caught up with Wade on the other side of the block, behind the building Rachel jumped from the day before. Wade was standing in the middle of the empty street, gun at his side, peering into the darkness, car alarms wailing everywhere.

The gunman had disappeared.

"I think I got him," Steve said, catching his breath.

"You did," Wade said, pointing his gun at some drops of blood on the street.

"What do you know?" Steve said. "Ghosts bleed."

CHAPTER FIFTEEN

Captain Newman didn't appreciate being yanked out of bed and dragged into the station at five o'clock in the morning. He especially didn't appreciate it when Dr. Mark Sloan was the one responsible.

It was bad enough that Steve let his father yank him into a suicide investigation, which then became a murder inquiry, and now inexplicably had grown into a federal case of some kind involving the United States Marshals Service. How one man—namely Dr. Mark Sloan—could get so many people into so much trouble was beyond Newman's understanding. But Newman was determined not to let this mushroom into anything bigger.

Dr. Sloan, his son Steve, and Tom Wade were crowded into the LAPD captain's cramped little office, which was cramped even when nobody but Newman was in it. Newman was big and he was wide and he filled spaces. Even when he was standing in an empty field, it somehow felt smaller. He looked as if he'd been artlessly carved out of an unforgiving, and not particularly interesting, block of stone. That hard, blockish physicality applied to his personality as well.

"I haven't showered, I haven't had my morning coffee,

and I'm constipated," said Newman. "So you can imagine what kind of mood I'm in right now."

"I can give you something to clear your bowels," Mark said.

"You certainly can," Newman said. "You can stop meddling in my homicide cases."

"Technically, this isn't one of your homicide cases," Mark said.

Steve winced. Newman pinned Mark with a cold, constipated stare.

"It nearly became one, didn't it?" Newman turned to Steve. "What the hell is going on here? I want the airline version, not the director's cut."

"Marshal Wade is here chasing a dead man," Steve said, "and using Rebecca Jordan for bait."

"Rachel Swicord," Wade corrected.

"So Sloan has it right?" Newman asked.

Tom Wade nodded. "She was in a stolen car driven by her boyfriend Pike Wheeler. He killed a law enforcement officer and, in the subsequent chase, lost control of his vehicle and drove off a cliff into the river. Rachel went to jail, Pike was presumed dead."

"But not by you," Newman said.

"The body was never recovered. To me, that means alive until proven otherwise. I was the only one who held that view."

"You could have told us what you were really doing here," Steve said.

"I did," Wade replied. "I came to apprehend Rachel Swicord. My other pursuit was strictly personal and unofficial. I wasn't going to ask anyone to help me chase after a ghost."

"Only he's not a ghost now, is he?" Steve said.

"At least now we know why she broke her parole, came

here, and created a new identity," Mark said. "And we know why she wanted to die."

"We do?" Newman asked.

"She was running from the same ghost Wade was chasing," Mark said. "When the article about her and the Cuddle Bear went on the wire, she knew the marshal would come for her. And Pike, if he was alive, would come for her, too. Apparently, she couldn't live with either prospect."

"I don't see how this changes anything," Wade said. "Now that we know Pike is alive, and willing to kill, it's all the more reason to move her to a prison hospital."

"She's not going anywhere," Newman said. "We'll keep her under twenty-four-hour guard at Community General."

"That's a mistake," Wade said.

"I can't risk Pike taking shots at more civilians or this woman dying because of medical complications during the transfer," Newman said. "You should have told us about Pike. We're damned lucky nobody got killed tonight, no thanks to you. You're going back to Spokane on the first plane out in the morning."

"I don't work for you," Wade said.

"If you did, I'd fire you." Newman handed him a ticket. "This plane ticket is from the U.S. Marshals Service."

"What about Pike?" Wade said. "He's still loose, carrying a bullet."

"I'm sure we'll find him, or his body, very soon," Newman said.

"He's a fugitive," Wade said. "It's not a local matter."

"Which is why a U.S. Marshal from the LA office will be taking over for you and working closely with me," Newman said. "Have a nice flight."

Wade walked out without another word. He didn't even bother tipping his hat.

Mark and Steve had started to follow him out, when Newman cleared his throat.

"I'm not done with you two yet," Newman said. "Dr. Sloan, stay away from Rebecca Jordan or whatever the hell her name is. She didn't invite you to meddle in her life and neither did we."

Newman turned to Steve. "That goes double for you, Detective. Stay away from her, it's not your case. You're supposed to be working twenty-four seven on the Winston Brant murder, remember? What progress have you made?"

"I'm pursuing several avenues of investigation," Steve said, well aware of how lame and evasive it sounded.

The painstaking search of the drop zone didn't turn up any evidence, nothing unusual was found in Brant's parachute pack, and the LAPD's forensic accountant had only just begun digging into the financial records at Brant Publications. And Steve hadn't found any motive for skydiving instructor Justin Darbo or Brant's business partners Clifton Hemphill, Dean Perrow, and Virgil Nyby to want the daredevil publisher dead. But the most annoying thing was he still hadn't figured out how the murder was committed in the first place.

Newman snorted derisively. "I want to see progress, Detective, or you'll be applying your investigative skills to parking enforcement. The media can't stop talking about this case. It's the cover story in the *National Examiner*, for God's sake."

"What happens to Rachel Swicord now?" Mark asked, not only because he was very interested, but also because he was eager to change the subject and take the heat off his son.

"It's up to the Marshal's office," Newman replied.

"What about her brother Deke's murder?" Steve asked.

"I've reassigned it to Detective Rykus, who is working closely with the boys from the Spokane PD," Newman said. "Stay out of it. Do I make myself clear?"

"Yes, sir," Steve said.

"I still have a few questions—" Mark began, but Steve

pulled him out of Newman's office before he could finish whatever he was going to say.

"Are you trying to get me fired?" Steve asked, leading his father through the nearly empty squad room.

"The captain would be a much more pleasant person if he added some fiber to his diet," Mark said.

"I think it will take more than a few bowls of bran to lighten him up," Steve said. "You've got to drop this Rachel Swicord thing. It's over."

"Hardly," Mark said. "Marshal Wade is still not telling us the whole story."

"I know enough and so do you," Steve said. "It's no mystery anymore why Rachel jumped. What's left to know?"

"Whatever Tom Wade is holding back," Mark said. "Do you think he's going to stop looking for Pike just because Captain Newman handed him a plane ticket home?"

"I don't care," Steve said, stopping at his desk and sitting wearily in his chair. "We've got the Brant homicide to solve. That should be enough to occupy us both, don't you think?"

"I haven't forgotten about Winston Brant. But he's dead. There's nothing I can do to change that," Mark said. "When Rachel wakes up, everything that drove her to jump out that window will still be there."

"Did you really think you could solve all her troubles?" Steve said.

"I thought I might be able to change some things in her life and so when she woke up, she had some new choices she could make," Mark said. "Maybe give her some hope she didn't have before."

"She and her boyfriend are cop killers, that's something you can't change," Steve said. "I'm not feeling a lot of sympathy for her."

"Rachel tried to kill herself rather than face Pike," Mark said. "Doesn't that tell you something about the woman she is today?"

"Or she jumped because she didn't want to go back to jail."

"It makes a difference," Mark said.

"Not to me." Steve nodded towards his desk. "I've got a lot of reports to fill out about the shooting, so I'm probably gonna be stuck here for a few hours. I'll have a patrol car take you back to the hospital. You should get some sleep, Dad."

Mark nodded. "I'll wait outside."

He understood what Steve was feeling and why he wanted to quit. So he didn't tell his son he wouldn't be going home to sleep, though he was physically and mentally exhausted, his body craving the rest his mind was denying him.

There was too much to do and probably not much time left to do it.

The way Mark saw it, there was still one way he could help Rachel, and that was to make sure Pike was no longer a threat to her.

Maybe then she wouldn't want to choose death anymore. Maybe then Mark could sleep.

Pike was out there somewhere with Steve's bullet smoldering in his flesh. The killer would be desperately looking for a shady doctor who'd treat his gunshot wounds without reporting it to the police.

Mark would be looking, too.

Three mornings a week, Lenore Barber went to the Celebrity World Gym in Studio City to work out for an hour which, in her case, meant using the treadmill at the lowest possible setting while watching the *Today Show* on one of the dozen flat-screen TVs on the wall.

There were no celebrities at Celebrity World Gym, just plenty of people who wanted to be. The draw was CBS Radford, the only actual studio in Studio City, which was around the corner. Every producer, director, writer, and casting agent going to the lot passed the windows of the gym, so an hour on a Lifecycle facing Laurel Canyon traffic was like an audition. All it took was one bored gaze from a director stuck at the light on Ventura Boulevard and a star could be born.

But that wasn't the main reason why Lenore was there three days a week. Her treadmill didn't face the window. It faced the weight room, where she could gaze upon the sea of glistening male pecs.

This was her singles bar, only better. Here she got a full, unfettered look at the merchandise. There was no chance of getting tricked by dim light and alcohol into taking home what she thought was a Greek god and waking up the next morning beside the Pillsbury Doughboy.

But she knew deception was still possible even in the unforgiving light of the gym because she was practicing it herself. Her skimpy leotard was carefully cut to hide the scars of her lung cancer surgery and she wore a pricey wig to disguise her radiation baldness.

It was only in the locker room that she revealed herself, but even there she practiced as much discretion as possible. She slipped into the shower wrapped in a towel and emerged in one as well, dressing quickly behind the open door of her locker.

When Lenore slid open the shower curtain, she saw a woman standing at a locker, getting undressed, her muscular back to her. She was in her fifties, but clearly in great shape for a woman her age, which is why Lenore was unprepared for what she saw when the stranger turned around. Lenore barely stifled a gasp before it almost escaped from her lips.

The woman's breasts were gone; two long ragged scars curved down from her armpits and up to her sternum like hand-drawn smiles, the suture marks a crude approximation of teeth. She had no nipples. She looked like a Ken doll, only without the sharply defined pecs.

For a seemingly endless second, Lenore couldn't look away; it was too grotesquely compelling.

"You can stare, I don't mind," the woman said.

"I'm sorry," Lenore said, lowering her eyes and hurrying to her locker. "I didn't mean to."

"You couldn't help yourself," she said. "Same way I couldn't stop myself from looking at your scar."

"You've seen it?"

The woman nodded. "It's hard to miss."

Lenore's pneumonectomy scar was long, wrapping around from the right side of her chest to the outer edge of her shoulder blade. She dressed quickly, wishing the other woman would cover herself. Had the woman no shame?

"Was it the Big C?" the woman asked, approaching her.

"Not anymore," Lenore said. "They took it all out."

"Me too," the woman said, patting her chest. "When I was going through a pack or two a day, I thought I was just smoking cigarettes. I didn't realize I was actually smoking my breasts."

"Is there something I can help you with?" Lenore asked, nearly dressed and trying with all her will not to look at the woman's chest again.

"I'm all out of shampoo," the woman said. "Could you spare a squirt?"

Lenore handed her the bottle, slammed her locker shut, and left as fast as she could without appearing like she was fleeing.

She failed, at least as far as Jesse was concerned. He was sitting on a stool at the juice bar, and when Lenore raced past him to the parking lot, she looked as if she was being chased by a ravenous beast.

A few minutes after Lenore sped away in her Lexus, the woman she'd been talking to came out of the locker room wearing loose-fitting sweats and a relaxed smile. She joined Jesse at the juice bar.

"I hope this wasn't too uncomfortable for you, Mrs. Caldicott," Jesse said.

"Not at all, Dr. Travis. I made my peace with what happened to me and how I look a while ago," she said, then motioned to the locker room. "I'm sure I shook her up. Think it will make a difference?"

"This is just the beginning. I'm not done with her yet," Jesse said. "But no matter how things turn out, I appreciate your help."

"It's the kind of help I wish someone had given me," Mrs. Caldicott replied.

"Can I buy you a smoothie for your trouble?"

"The hell with that," she said. "I deserve a McMuffin."

CHAPTER SIXTEEN

Mark visited four doctors who were rumored in medical circles to be flexible about reporting requirements when it came to treating gunshot wounds, stabbings, drug overdoses, and other crime-related injuries.

One of the doctors worked out of his garage in Venice, where he repaired motorcycles and gang members side by side. Instead of a lab coat, he wore a tank top that showed off his shoulder tattoos of the caduceus, the two serpents entwined around a wing-tipped rod that is the symbol of the American medical profession, and a buxom nurse straddling a Harley, which was the symbol of his biker group.

On the drive across the San Fernando Valley to see doctor number five, Mark's eyes began to feel heavy and his mind seemed to float free of his body, like a picnic napkin caught by a breeze. The car drifted towards the center divider of the freeway, the left front tire bouncing off a chunk of lumber on the shoulder. It jerked him awake and gave his body a jolt of adrenaline. He wrenched the wheel too hard, swerved back into his lane and nearly into the one beside it, coming close to sideswiping a van.

The van driver honked, flipped Mark off, and sped away. Mark took a deep breath, then gripping the wheel hard, carefully worked his way across the four lanes of traffic and got off at the next exit that came up.

He'd nearly fallen asleep at the wheel.

How many times had he treated patients in the ER who had done the same thing? How many times had he treated the victims of those weary drivers?

It was stupid and irresponsible of him to get behind the wheel of a car when he was so tired. It was almost as deadly as driving drunk. He was a danger to himself and others.

Mark stopped at a grassy playground, parked under a tree, turned off the ignition, and settled back in his seat.

He had to sleep.

Forty-five minutes later, he was still wide awake. The creeping slumber that he was nearly powerless to resist on the freeway totally eluded him now.

Perhaps it was the surge of adrenaline from narrowly avoiding death.

Or, more likely, it was the motion of the car that lulled him into sleep. He remembered that when Steve was a baby, the only way he and his late wife Katherine could get him to nap was to take him on a drive. Five minutes on the road, and Steve would be out cold. But the moment they stopped driving, Steve would instantly awaken. So they had to keep driving. By the time Steve woke up, they'd often find themselves as far away as Palm Springs or Santa Barbara. It got so bad, they started keeping a packed overnight bag in the trunk.

It had been decades since Mark thought of that. They were pleasant memories.

He started the car and cautiously drove down the block to a Jack in the Box, getting himself a large coffee with extra sugar. Then he rolled down the windows, cranked up the radio to an ear-blistering volume, and headed out to visit the fifth doctor on his list. If Dr. Mandell Yorder couldn't lead him to Pike, Mark promised himself he'd go straight home and stay there until he'd had some sleep.

A few minutes later, his ears ringing, his hair windblown, and his body jittery with caffeine, he parked in front of the Panorama City outlet of the Family Doctor, a national chain of medical clinics located in shopping centers and malls.

This particular Family Doctor clinic was located next to a grocery store, a Korean restaurant, and a check-cashing service in a decaying, largely vacant, 1980s-era strip mall. Above the clinic, the sign showed an illustration of a home-spun, Norman Rockwell-esque country doctor with his stethoscope and medical bag, smiling warmly out at the parking lot. Beneath the doctor was the clinic's motto: FAST HEALTH FOR PEOPLE ON THE MOVE!

Mark finished his coffee, did his best to smooth down his wild hair, then got out of the car and went inside the clinic.

The waiting area was sterile and entirely synthetic. There were rubber plants, plastic furniture, mass-produced art-work, and a falsely perky nurse in an old-fashioned, sharply pressed uniform sitting behind a Formica counter. She had contact lenses, hair extensions, collagen lips, silicone breasts, and her skin coated with makeup that gave her a neoprene sheen.

Mark approached the counter and half expected to see a power cord running from the nurse's back to an outlet in the wall.

"May I help you?" she asked, radiating energy and cheer and an almost human voice.

"I'd like a triple coronary bypass to go," Mark said. The way he felt, he almost meant it. "And a large Pepsi."

Her smile didn't waver. "Do you have an appointment?"

Mark looked at the waiting area. He was the only patient.

"No," Mark said. "Is that a problem?"

She handed him a ream of paper. "Just fill out these forms and the doctor will be right with you."

"Actually, I'm not here for a medical examination," Mark said, handing the forms back to her.

"You should be, Mark."

It was a man's voice. Mark turned to see Dr. Mandell Yorder standing in the open doorway leading to one of the two exam rooms. He'd gained a potbelly, a goatee, and a defeated slouch in the years since Mark had seen him last. The doctor was thirty-two but easily looked ten or fifteen years older.

"You look terrible," Dr. Yorder said. "When was the last time you slept?"

"I suppose that's one of the reasons I'm here," Mark replied.

"Step into my office," Dr. Yorder said, ushering him into the exam room and closing the door.

The exam room was decorated with framed prints of kindly doctors treating smiling patients, making house calls, and handing lollipops to children.

Mark took a seat on the edge of the exam table. Dr. Yorder sat on a tiny stool on wheels, then, out of habit, leaned forward, resting his elbows on his knees. Now Mark knew how the doctor had developed his slouch.

"If you want sleeping pills, you've come a long way for a prescription you could probably get Jack to write for you."

"Dr. Stewart is in Colorado now," Mark said. "He's got his own practice."

"Of course he does," Dr. Yorder said. "Good for him. I got my own, too, as you can see. Well, not entirely my own. It's a franchise, but it's a real money machine, Mark. The wave of the future in medicine. If you're thinking of retiring, I could set you up with one of your own. We could go into it together. Maybe Jack would like to get in on it, too."

"I appreciate the offer," Mark said. "The truth is, Manny, I've heard rumors that you're the doctor to go to if you need discreet medical help, no questions asked. For instance, if someone had a bullet wound, they could come to you."

Ordinarily, Mark would have been more amiable and circumspect in his approach, but he just didn't have the energy.

"You got a bullet in you, Mark?" Dr. Yorder asked, his voice tight. "Or are you planning for the future?"

"Steve shot someone in the shoulder last night," Mark said. "I want to know if the man came to you."

"I'm not a cop, I'm a doctor," he said. "My job is to ease suffering, to heal people, not ask how they got hurt."

"Especially if they pay in cash."

Dr. Yorder got up, went to the door, and opened it. "Great to see you again, Mark. Be sure to stop by again in another five years."

Mark didn't move. "I remember the bright young resident you used to be, before you started prescribing more drugs for yourself than your patients. You would have lost your license if it wasn't for me testifying on your behalf."

"So this is payback?"

Mark shrugged.

Dr. Yorder closed the door. "Suppose I do help people regardless of the legalities. If I do, it's because they need help. It's because they are in pain. That's what doctors do."

"There are legal obligations," Mark said.

"In the ER, does it make a difference whether the patient is a criminal or not? No. What matters is saving lives. We aren't supposed to care how our patients got hurt, just relieve their suffering and make them well. Unlike you, most doctors aren't cops and don't pretend to be."

It was a weak rationalization, but Mark didn't have the time, energy, or inclination to argue with him about it.

"The man I'm looking for would have come in this morning, with a bullet in his shoulder," Mark said. "He tried to kill someone and, if you helped him get better, he will try again. If he succeeds, you'll be responsible for the murder."

Dr. Yorder took a seat on his stool and slouched forward again, suddenly looking wearier than Mark.

"I'm not saying I know who your guy is and I'm not saying I treated him, you got that? And I'm certainly not saying I took a bullet out of him about an hour ago."

If Mark hadn't dozed off at the wheel, if he hadn't stopped at the park to try and sleep, he could have caught Pike right here, having the bullet taken out of his shoulder. The fugitive would have been caught and a good deal of Rachel's problems solved.

But it didn't work out that way. Mark was late. And Pike was gone.

"If I did, though, I would have prescribed antibiotics and painkillers," Dr. Yorder continued. "Then I would have sent him to Sid's Drugs up the street. That's where I send everyone."

As Steve wrote up his report on the shooting, it was only natural that he thought about everything he'd learned about Rachel Swicord, aka Rebecca Jordan, and the events of the last day or so.

All the facts seemed to fit, especially after Lissy Dearborn, Rachel's roommate, came in and positively identified Pike off a mug shot as the man who attacked her in her apartment.

Steve was about to say hello to Lissy, but a stern look from Captain Newman kept him rooted to his desk. When the case was over, and Pike was in jail for murder, Steve decided he'd send her a coffee table, with a ribbon around it, and a note asking her to forgive him for momentarily giving her assailant the upper hand.

That ought to get him a date, he thought, and establish what a charming, romantic, lovable guy he was.

He was about to set the Swicord case aside and open up the thin murder book on the Winston Brant homicide, but

there was still something about Tom Wade's story that
nagged at Steve. He just didn't know what it was.

It was a feeling, that's all. Like indigestion, he thought.

Steve wanted to ignore it. In fact, he'd been ordered to.
But the feeling was there, tugging at his attention, refusing
to let go.

So he went on the Internet and looked for articles about
Pike's joyride, the murder of the sheriff's deputy, and
Rachel's trial.

Technically, he wasn't getting involved in the investigation again. It was just reading. Even so, he kept looking
guiltily over his shoulder, keeping a watch out in case Captain Newman strolled by and saw what was on his screen.

There was nothing in the articles that contradicted what
Marshal Tom Wade had told them. Rachel went to prison
and Pike Wheeler was presumed dead, swept away by the
river.

Then Steve realized there was one vital fact missing from
the articles.

Marshal Tom Wade.

Nowhere in the articles was his name ever mentioned.
Not that it should have been. After all, Wade's job was chasing and apprehending fugitives. There were no fugitives in
this case, at least not until Rachel was released and jumped
parole. As far as law enforcement authorities were concerned, Pike was dead.

So why was Wade so intent on finding Pike Wheeler
from the beginning? What was it about the case that drew
the marshal into it so early? Did he know the murdered
deputy or his family? Did he know Pike?

Steve wasn't going to find the answers on the Internet. Or
could he?

He cracked his knuckles, looked around, and began typ-
ing away. The Internet was truly a detective's best friend.

An hour or so later, Steve found the answer. It wasn't

hard. It was a matter of public record that hadn't been made public. Anybody who bothered to look could have found it. But nobody bothered because, until now, there wasn't a reason.

Steve made a call to Walla Walla, Washington, and talked to Estelle Wheeler, Pike's mother. She wasn't very happy to hear from an a LAPD detective. He told her that her son was alive and being pursued by the U.S. Marshals, Spokane police, and the LAPD. Mrs. Wheeler wasn't overjoyed by the news. In fact, she used some common profanity in some very uncommon ways. He was tempted to take notes on the vocabulary alone to use himself if the right occasion ever arose. Their conversation was short and unpleasant, but he was able to fill the gaps in the information he found on the Internet.

His next call was to Mark, but after a few rings, he got kicked into voice mail. Frustrated, Steve left a message and hung up.

Now came the hard part. Steve glanced at Captain Newman's office, took a deep breath, and went in to see him.

CHAPTER SEVENTEEN

If Mark hadn't been so tired, he might not have forgotten his cell phone in the car when he went into Sid's Drugs. Then he would have received Steve's call, and the events of the next few hours might have played out very differently.

Sid's Drugs was an uninviting little convenience store with iron bars over the windows and doors. The narrow, dimly lit aisles were overstuffed with cheap toys, picnic supplies, snack foods, soft drinks, yellowed paperbacks, out-of-date magazines, and in the very back, a pharmacy.

There wasn't a single customer in the store or, it seemed, a proprietor.

"Hello?" Mark said, raising his voice.

He heard a groan from behind the pharmacy counter. The groan was muffled and weak, not the kind of sound that came from someone in fine health. He rushed up to the counter and leaned over it to see a bloody and bruised Asian man, lying on the floor.

The injured, semiconscious man was in his fifties and had, judging by his wounds, been recently beaten. The cash register was open, the drawer cleaned out.

Mark reached into his pocket for his cell phone and was just realizing he'd left it in the car, when he felt something cold and metallic touch the base of his skull.

"Take your hand out of your pocket," a man's voice said. "Put both hands behind your head and turn around very slowly."

Mark did as he was told and saw a tall, unshaven man in his late twenties, with deep-set, intense eyes, a strong jaw, and chapped lips. He wore dirty jeans and a new dress shirt that was untucked and already damp with sweat. His left arm was in a sling and there was a bulge under his shirt from the bandages on his shoulder. There was also the outline of two prescription pill bottles in his breast pocket.

It was Pike, Mark was certain of that. There was something vaguely familiar about the man, though Mark didn't get a good look at him the night before and hadn't even seen a mug shot.

"You must be Pike," Mark said.

The man blinked, but if he was startled by being recognized by a stranger, he covered it quickly. "And you're dead unless you do exactly what I tell you. Stand completely still."

Pike cautiously parted the flaps of Mark's jacket with the tip of his gun to see if he was wearing a holster of any kind. Satisfied that Mark wasn't, Pike stepped back but kept his gun trained on him.

"I remember you, old man. I saw you at the hospital," Pike said. "What are you doing here?"

"Looking for you," Mark said.

"You thought you could take me?" Pike asked, a smile on his face.

I wasn't thinking at all, Mark thought. He shouldn't have been driving half asleep. He shouldn't have been looking for Pike alone. He shouldn't have gone to Sid's Drugs.

But Mark hadn't been expecting to find Pike himself; he was simply hoping to uncover a lead to where the fugitive might be hiding.

Then again, he had to admit, he probably would have followed that lead alone, too. It was all a big, dumb, dangerous mistake, one Mark hoped wouldn't cost him his life.

"Who are you?" Pike asked.

"Dr. Mark Sloan," he said. "Rachel is my patient. I saw her try to kill herself. I'd like to stop her from trying again."

"You still can," Pike said. "You're going to help me get her back."

"I don't think so," Mark said.

Pike aimed the gun at him. "Then maybe I should drop you right now."

Mark met his gaze. The next ten seconds passed slowly; each silent second felt like an hour. And with it, Mark's weariness grew. All he wanted was to go to sleep, wake up, and discover he wasn't standing in a dingy grocery store with a gun aimed at his forehead.

"Where's your car?" Pike asked.

To Mark, the question was a huge relief. It meant he wasn't going to get shot, at least not for the moment.

"It's right outside the door," Mark said.

"Let's go." Pike motioned to the door.

Mark glanced at the pharmacy, where he could still hear the proprietor groaning. "That man you beat up needs medical attention."

"You're gonna need embalming if you don't move your ass right now."

There was a cold firmness in Pike's voice that left little doubt that Mark would be shot if he argued. Mark reluctantly headed down the narrow aisle for the door, Pike right behind him, pressing his gun into the doctor's back.

The Starbucks on Ventura Boulevard in Studio City was filled with the usual mix of aspiring actors, aspiring screenwriters, aspiring directors, and at least one real estate agent aspiring to nothing more at the moment than a cup of Colombia Narino Supremo.

Lenore Barber finally reached the counter, got her coffee, and in her haste to leave, nearly collided with the man right behind her.

She froze for a moment, too startled to move. There was a deep depression in the man's face where half his jaw should have been. It looked as if his face had caved in and was sewn shut with a scrap of dried flesh.

From the neck down, he was muscular and trim, a physically fit man in his thirties. He was the kind of guy she'd ordinarily be attracted to, if his face was whole, that is.

"Got a cigarette?" he asked in a muffled voice.

"Sorry, no," she said, once again embarrassed at catching herself staring at someone with physical deformities.

Lenore quickly sidestepped past him and hurried out to her Lexus. The day was turning into a living freak show. She couldn't wait to get to the sanctuary of her real estate office.

Susan Hilliard, sitting at the window, flipped open her cell phone and called Jesse at Community General.

"She's on her way to the office," Susan said.

"Perfect," Jesse replied, checking the clock above the nurse's station. "She'll be right on time for her first showing."

"I wish I could see it," Susan said.

"So do I," Jesse replied, hanging up.

The man with the missing jaw brought two cups of coffee over to Susan's table and sat down.

"Maybe I should have said trick or treat," the man said. "At least I could have got some candy from her."

"You think we're being cruel to her, Dennis?" Susan asked, then added tentatively, "Or to you?"

"You are incapable of being cruel, Susan," Dennis said. "I'll always remember how you took care of me after my surgery and during the chemo. I appreciate it and so does my wife."

"Lenore looked at you like you were a monster," Susan said. "That couldn't have felt good."

He shrugged. "If I can prevent one person from going through what I did, then I don't mind a little embarrassment. Besides, I'll do anything for a good cup of coffee."

"Really?" Susan said teasingly. "I wish I knew that before you got married."

Dr. Mark Sloan was driving his Saab convertible very slowly down the street, Pike sitting beside him, jamming his gun into Mark's side.

"Speed up," Pike said. "I could walk faster than this."

But Mark was afraid to go any faster or to get on the freeway. He was gripping the wheel tightly, blinking hard, fighting a wave of fatigue that threatened to wash over him, putting him to sleep. He was aware enough, though, to appreciate the absurdity and gravity of the situation.

How could he possibly sleep with a wounded murderer pointing a loaded gun at him? Who could take a nap at a moment like this?

It wasn't a choice for Mark to make. His body was making the choice for him. Apparently, being scared to death wasn't enough to keep a man awake.

"This won't work," Mark said. "You've lost a lot of blood and I haven't slept in two days. This is a disaster waiting to happen."

"Only if you don't shut up and drive a little faster," Pike said.

"Do you have a plan?"

"I'm going to get Rachel out of that hospital," Pike said. "You're going to help me."

"She's in intensive care," Mark said. "She can't walk out even if she wanted to. And even if she could, she's probably under police guard."

"I'll deal with it," Pike said. "I'm good at improvising."

"Like you did in Spokane?" Mark asked. "I suppose when you stole that car, and held up that convenience store, you always planned to kill a deputy and drive off a cliff."

"Shut up," Pike said.

"You haven't thought this out very well," Mark said drowsily, slurring his words and weaving into the next lane. A passing car honked loudly at him.

"Pay attention to the road," Pike said.

"You drive," Mark replied.

"I can't drive and keep a gun on you at the same time," Pike said.

"Then let me pull over," Mark said. "I can take a nap and you can think about a better plan. I'll still be your prisoner when I wake up."

Pike jabbed Mark with the gun. "Drive."

"If I fall asleep at the wheel," Mark said, "we could both get killed, along with whoever is on the road with us."

"I bet it's hard to feel sleepy when you're in excruciating pain." Pike pressed the gun into Mark's thigh. "Would you like some? I can spare the bullet."

Pain was an approach Mark was already taking, biting his tongue to keep himself alert. But even that was rapidly losing its effectiveness.

"I'll pass," Mark said, keeping his eyes on the road.

Pike snorted derisively. "I thought the offer would help you focus. Let me know if you change your mind."

Mark decided the best way to stay awake might be to keep talking. "Assuming you could get Rachel out of the hospital somehow, what would you do then?"

"Take her somewhere where no one can keep us apart," Pike said.

"It's not going to be easy."

"I was chased by every cop in Washington State, Doc. I drove off a cliff into a river. I broke my ribs, my nose, I nearly drowned. I crawled out of that river and lived like an animal in the woods for months before riding the rails down to Oregon. Do you think *that* was easy?" Pike said. "I survived all this time without nobody knowing I was alive. You think that was easy, too?"

Mark blinked hard, concentrating on the road, on the row of parked cars on his right and the broken white line on his left.

"What kept me going was waiting for her," Pike said. "Because I knew she was waiting for me. She still is. I'll take Rachel somewhere the police will never find us."

"The police know you're alive now," Mark said. "You killed a law enforcement officer. They'll never stop chasing you. I guarantee Marshal Wade won't stop until justice is done."

Pike laughed ruefully. "Wade won't stop because he's my father."

CHAPTER EIGHTEEN

At first, Captain Newman was furious that Steve had ignored a direct order and kept poking into the Rachel Swicord case anyway. But then the captain listened to what Steve had found out and decided to let the insubordination slide, at least for the moment.

Steve had discovered, through some simple Internet snooping, that Pike Wheeler was Marshal Tom Wade's estranged son. When Pike was five years old, Wade's wife ran off with an insurance broker named Dave Wheeler and took her kid with her.

She divorced Wade and was granted sole custody of Pike. The Wheelers were married as soon as the divorce was final and moved to Walla Walla, a farming community four hours south of Spokane and adjacent to the penitentiary, where she worked as a guard.

Pike got into trouble with the law almost as soon as he was old enough to walk out the front door of his house on his own, starting with petty vandalism and theft when he was an adolescent and evolving into arson and armed robbery by his late teens. As Pike grew up, so did the severity of his crimes. Each time he was caught, Wade used his influence to get his son a lighter sentence. But it didn't help. Pike's rebellion only escalated.

Steve wasn't a shrink, but it was clear to him that Pike resented his father and yet, at the same time, was desperate for his attention. By committing crimes, he got back at his dad, and everything Wade stood for. He also got his dad to notice him in a big way. It worked so well, Pike couldn't stop repeating the strategy and raising the stakes each time.

Pike was eventually sent to a youth camp for juvenile offenders. But instead of reforming him, the experience toughened him. He came out even more violent than when he went in. Pike drifted up to Spokane, bringing his crime wave even closer to his dad.

"Damn," Captain Newman grumbled. "Pick Marshal Wade up, bring him in."

"I'll try," Steve said. "But if he finds his son before we do, I'm afraid of what might happen."

"You think he'd kill his own son?"

"I think his son might try to kill him," Steve said.

"Wade doesn't strike me as being slow on the draw," Captain Newman said.

"All it takes is one second of hesitation," Steve said. "And then Pike will have killed two lawmen."

The long, gray boulevard was blurring in front of Mark's eyes. He knew he was on Roscoe, heading west across the San Fernando Valley floor, but he'd forgotten which cross streets he'd passed. He wasn't certain anymore where he was going or how he intended to get there.

Wherever they were now, it was a bleak, endless stretch of identical, decaying apartment blocks and empty industrial warehouses, tall weeds rising from the cracked, empty parking lots that surrounded them.

Had he passed the San Diego Freeway yet? Had he passed Van Nuys Boulevard? Had he crossed Sepulveda Boulevard? Community General Hospital was in West LA, somewhere south of wherever Mark was, on the other side of the Santa Monica Mountains. It might as well have been in Brazil. It seemed impossibly far away. He grew wearier even thinking about it.

Even the revelation that Tom Wade was Pike's father wasn't enough to keep Mark awake. Now he knew why Pike looked familiar. He had Wade's penetrating gaze and sharp features.

"It's not too late to reconsider your plan," Mark said, his voice heavy with fatigue. His fear of being killed by Pike had long since been lulled to sleep. The rest of his mind and body were ready to do the same.

"You're right, I could kill you, take your car, and drive myself to Community General with my good hand," Pike said. "But you might come in handy at the hospital."

Every time Mark blinked, raising his eyelids was like lifting weights. He managed it but wondered how much longer he could resist. Minutes, at most.

"If you truly love Rachel," Mark said, "you will turn yourself in."

Pike shoved his gun hard into Mark's side, almost hard enough to break a rib. Mark winced at the unexpected pain but, in a strange way, he was grateful. It jolted him awake, if only for a few more seconds.

"Don't play Tom Wade with me," Pike said, then began mimicking his father. " 'There are laws, son. We all have to follow them. That includes you.' "

Pike shook his head with disgust. "The hell it does. I don't have to do nothing. Except take Rachel back."

Mark found himself straining to keep his eyes open again, despite the ache in his ribs. He considered asking Pike for another jab with the gun. Without meaning to, Mark did.

"What makes you think she wants you?" Mark said. "Rachel ran away from Spokane and changed her name so you wouldn't find her. She jumped out a window rather than be with you. Take the hint."

Pike smacked Mark on the side of the head with the edge of the gun. The blow. stunned him. Mark swerved hard, then back into his lane, his eyes wide open, his head pounding. For a moment, the creeping slumber was held back, the sting of the blow crawling over his face like ants.

"You wanna die?" Pike yelled. "Do you?"

"I'm trying to keep us both alive," Mark said, his words slurring. He wasn't sure whether it was the fatigue or the blow, though he didn't think Pike had hit him that hard. "Your plan is suicidal. And I'm falling asleep at the wheel."

"You're faking it," Pike said. "Rachel wants me. She's been calling out to me since the river swept us apart. We're gonna be together and you're going to make it happen."

"Please," Mark mumbled.

His eyes closed again and this time, Mark couldn't open them, not even when he heard Pike's terrified scream.

Steve sat at his desk, tapping his pencil on his knee, a very worried man.

He wasn't able to reach Wade at his hotel, at the U.S. Marshals' office, on his cell phone, or on his pager. Neither could anyone at the U.S. Marshals' office. Steve checked with the airline. Wade hadn't taken the flight to Spokane, which was no surprise.

What was Wade doing?

Steve knew the answer to that. The marshal was hunting down his son. But where? What leads did Wade have that Steve didn't know about?

A missing marshal chasing his cop-killer son somewhere in the city was reason enough for Steve to worry. But Steve had even more.

He couldn't find his father, either.

Steve tried reaching Mark at the beach house, at the hospital, and on his cell with no luck. It was possible that his father was at home, so deeply asleep after days without adequate rest that he didn't hear the phone ringing. Steve doubted it, but just to be sure, he called Jesse, who had a key to the beach house and gladly went out to Malibu to check up on Mark.

Jesse had called only a few moments ago. Mark wasn't there. And neither was his car.

Steve had a hunch Mark was out there looking for Pike, too. If his father and the marshal found Pike at the same time, Mark could get killed in the cross fire.

Somehow Steve had to find them both. Fast.

The city was a sprawling mass of tangled freeways and endless boulevards that was so big and so wide, it was impossible to know where Los Angeles ended and other Southern California cities began. Mark and Wade could be anywhere from Camarillo to Redlands, from Palmdale to Torrance.

Steve could electronically flag their credit or ATM cards, wait for a hit, then roll to wherever the cards were last used. He could call the phone company and attempt to monitor usage of their cell phones, find out who they were talking to, and then zero in on the location they were calling from. He could get their pictures and license plate numbers out to every cop, highway patrolman, and sheriff's deputy in Southern California and hope somebody spotted them.

But all of those approaches would take time and a lot of luck. He didn't think he had much of either to spare.

And then it hit Steve.

The license plates.

He didn't know where either his father or Tom Wade was, but he knew they had to have one thing in common if they were both searching Los Angeles for Pike.

They were both driving cars.

He wouldn't have to find them. They would tell him where they were.

Mark didn't dream because he wasn't asleep. Thankfully, he wasn't dead either. He'd been unconscious, but for how long, he didn't know.

When he opened his eyes, the first thing he was aware of was the air bag in his face. Then his mind began instinctively conducting its physical diagnostic, sending signals to every nerve in his body, asking for damage reports.

Within seconds, the messages came back in the form of pain, discomfort, and range of movement. The jagged, shooting pain in his left arm, and his inability to move it, told him it was broken. The bone hadn't broken through the skin, and the pain seemed to be radiating from his elbow. The pain was a good sign, too. The fact he could feel the agony in his arm, wiggle his fingers and toes, and lift his head told him he wasn't paralyzed.

Mark was breathing without difficulty and wasn't experiencing any chest pain, so the air bag had done its job. He didn't know how he broke his arm and didn't care. At least he wasn't seriously hurt.

He slowly leaned back in his seat, feeling dizzy and nauseous. Blood was streaming down his face from what felt like a superficial gash on his forehead. Through the shattered windshield, he could see his folded hood, smashed up against the side of an old Cadillac parked at the curb.

Mark glanced at the seat beside him. Pike was gone. The passenger side air bag had deployed and there was blood on the seat. Pike had either been injured in the crash or the impact opened up his gunshot wound. Either way, the man would be hurting.

He looked out the back window, afraid he'd see crumpled cars and bodies lying in the street in his wake. The only bodies he saw were a half dozen curious onlookers, most of them Latino, standing around the accident scene. There were no other dented cars. There were no corpses in the street.

Mark Sloan hadn't killed or injured anyone. He breathed an enormous sigh of relief.

Wide awake now, he used his right hand to hit the trunk release button, open the driver's side door, and pull himself out.

He rose shakily to his feet and a wave of nausea swept over him. A symptom, he supposed, of his concussion, or a mild case of shock. The smart thing to do, and what he would advise anyone in his situation, would be to remain still, relax, and wait for the ambulance.

But Mark couldn't do that.

He made eye contact with the closest person staring at him, a large Latina woman in her thirties with her black hair pulled into a tight ponytail, then staggered to his open trunk.

"I'm a doctor," Mark said to her as he stumbled along. "Is anybody hurt?"

"No, just you, senor," the woman said tentatively, speaking with a heavy accent. "You drove right into the parked cars. Are you drunk?"

"Just tired." Mark found the dust sham he used to clean his car. He opened his medical bag, took out a roll of Ace bandages and used it, with the dust sham as a splint, to fashion a crude sling and brace for his broken arm. As he did so, he continued asking the woman questions.

"There was another man in my car. Did anybody see where he went?"

She pointed to an abandoned, three-story apartment building across the street. The windows were boarded up with rotted plywood, the property ringed with a cyclone fence. A tattered cardboard sign was nailed to the front door, all the words faded except for one in big block letters: CONDEMNED.

"He went in there," she said. "So did the other man."

"Other man?" Mark asked, then noticed the Crown Victoria parked at an angle across the street, the driver's side door wide open, the engine still running.

"They both had guns," she said.

Mark dragged himself over to the car and looked inside. There was a Stetson on the passenger seat.

Tom Wade.

The marshal knew he wouldn't walk away from the case. So Wade followed Mark, counting on him to find the doctor who'd treated Pike. Mark had been too tired to notice the tail.

"Call the police," he said to the woman, giving her Steve's number. "Ask for Lieutenant Sloan. Tell him what happened here."

She nodded.

He walked over to the fence, found a hole cut into it, and stepped through to the other side.

CHAPTER NINETEEN

Steve notified LoJack and had the auto theft tracking devices activated on his father's Saab and Wade's rental car. Both signals came back from the same Panorama City location.

It surprised him.

Were they working together? Did Mark contact Wade or was it the other way around? Why would Mark join forces with the marshal whose ill-considered action almost got Rachel killed? Why did Mark keep his son in the dark? Was it because Mark was protecting Steve from getting reprimanded or fired?

That never stopped his father before. The more Steve thought about it, the stranger it all seemed.

Something wasn't right about this.

No, Steve corrected himself, *nothing* was right about this. He was about to send the patrol cars to his father's location, and then drive out there himself, when his cell phone rang.

It was a Latina woman, and when she was done telling him her story, Steve changed his plans.

He called the police dispatcher, gave them the map coordinates of Mark's car, and ordered them to send paramedics and any available officers in the vicinity to the scene. The officers were to be warned that a U.S. Marshal was at the location, pursuing a murder suspect who was to be considered armed and extremely dangerous. He also alerted them that an unarmed and injured civilian, Dr. Mark Sloan, might also be there.

Steve hung up and paced in front of his desk. It would take him forty-five minutes, at best, to reach the scene himself. By then, whatever was going to happen would be over, and his father could be dead. He couldn't wait that long. He had to get there immediately.

Acting on impulse, he called the LAPD helicopter unit and lied. He said Captain Newman wanted a chopper on deck for him, ready to go.

It was a lie that could get him knocked down a pay grade or, worse, thrown off the force. But Steve didn't care. He'd worry about the consequences later.

Now that Mark was closer to the building, he could see it wasn't merely abandoned. It was one of the forgotten ruins of the Northridge quake that should have been razed years ago. The building's decorative brick façade had fallen away, the individual bricks long since scavenged and put to use in the neighborhood as paving stones, chimneys, and doorstops. The entire structure listed to one side, the walls riddled with huge cracks. If he blew hard enough, he could bring the whole place down.

The safety of the building didn't matter. The immediate danger was the people inside, two men with guns who wanted to kill each other.

A lawman and a fugitive.

A father and a son.

There was a good chance that somebody was about to die.

It occurred to Mark that it might be him, but that was also something he couldn't think about now. Although he didn't have a plan, he knew he had to go in. He couldn't wait for the police to arrive.

He hurried into the building, clutching his broken arm to his chest with his right hand to steady it.

The air was hot, heavy, and reeked of urine and decay. Beer bottles, fast-food containers, and a soiled mattress cluttered the hallway. As dangerous as the building was, the risk of imminent collapse hadn't stopped people from partying inside anyway.

And who could blame them, Mark thought. It was so lovely.

Then he heard the footsteps above him and the creak of weight on the thin floorboards. But even if he hadn't, he could feel the presence of the two men upstairs, shadowing each other, moving in for the kill.

Mark moved quickly to the stairs.

The sun came through the cracked wall in bright slashes of light that carved up Marshal Tom Wade as he crept down the corridor, his gun drawn.

If you pull your gun, you better be ready to use it.

That's what he told the new marshals who trained under him. And when you shoot, he'd say to them, always shoot to kill.

He knew the rules. They'd saved his life countless times. Hesitation was fatal in his line of work.

But if it came right down to it, could he really shoot his own son? Could he take that necessary kill shot?

He's not your son anymore. That ended when he killed a cop. He deserves no more and no less than any other cop killer. He needs to pay.

It was what he'd been telling himself for years. But now that the reckoning had finally come, he felt the quiver of hesitation in his chest. It might as well have been a heart attack that he was feeling. It was just as lethal in a situation like this.

"It's time to quit, Pike," Wade shouted. "It's time to come home with me."

Home?

Pike would have laughed if he wasn't afraid it would give his position away. When had he ever had a home with Wade? What the hell was home anyway?

He moved through one apartment after another, slinking through doorways and sliding between the exposed framing in the rotted walls. The floors were strewn with water-damaged drywall, broken glass, and rat droppings. The pain in his shoulder was excruciating. His shirt was soaked with blood. Flies buzzed incessantly around him, as if testing to see if he was already dead.

The rooms seemed to be getting smaller, the ceilings lower. Even the air felt heavier, harder to suck in. Everything was closing in on him. He had to get out of here.

Where was the river this time?

There was a crash behind him. Terrified, he whirled around and fired without thinking, blasting a hole in the wall. It looked as if a cannonball had gone through it instead of a bullet.

Tom Wade, who'd been silently tracking movement on the other side of the wall, also whirled around at the sound of the crash, but he was too disciplined to fire.

Whatever it was, or whoever it was, it wasn't Pike. The gunshot told him where Pike was, in one of the apartments to his left.

Wade slipped into the nearest apartment and flattened himself against the wall, waiting. That's when he saw the drops of fresh blood on the floor and the footprints in the plaster dust. He followed the trail to his prey.

* * *

The crash they both heard was Mark Sloan, falling through a step in the staircase. The wood beneath his feet disintegrated under his weight and he fell through as if a trapdoor had opened underneath him.

As he fell through the ragged opening, he wasn't even aware of himself reaching desperately for something to grab on to with his right hand.

But he did.

And now he dangled by one arm above the first floor, splintered wood standing up like spikes below him, his right hand holding the next step on the stairway.

His left arm was broken; there was no way he could pull himself up with it. He'd need to think of another way to do it before he lost his grip.

There was only one thing he could do.

Grimacing, Mark swung himself, planting his foot against the wall. Between his hand on the step and the pressure of his foot against the wall, he managed to pin his body in place. Now he was able to work his way into a roughly horizontal position and roll his body up onto the next step. He prayed that the step would hold his weight.

It did.

Wincing in pain, he managed to crawl up to the next step, and then the one after that, until he found himself peering over the landing, just in time to see a man's shadow slip into one of the open apartments.

Mark rose shakily into a standing position and shuffled towards the apartment. He didn't have a strategy. Every muscle in his body ached and his broken arm pulsed with pain. He wouldn't be a very formidable adversary. All he knew was that he had to do *something*. He had to talk them both back from the precipice.

"It's time to pay for what you've done," Wade shouted

from somewhere near Mark, perhaps separated by only a wall or two.

Pike responded with two gunshots, the wall exploding over Mark's head. He fell forward, slamming his broken arm against the floor, his startled cry of agony muffled by the echo of the gunshots.

"I don't have to pay for nothing," Pike screamed back. "They're your laws, not mine."

Mark rose slowly, cradling his wounded arm, and followed the sound of Pike's voice.

Pike felt Wade behind him, the hairs on his neck standing up, goose bumps rising on his flesh. He turned around slowly, tightening his grip on his gun, which he held at his side.

Tom Wade stood framed in a doorway, his gun aimed squarely at his son.

"Drop the gun, Pike," Wade said evenly.

Pike sneered at his father. "Drop yours."

"You can't win this," Wade said. "There's no way out except through me. We can both leave here alive or we can both be carried out dead. Your call."

"You can't shoot me." Pike laughed, shaking his head. "But I got no problem dropping you."

Mark stepped in from an adjoining room, finding himself between the two men, though not in their line of fire. Neither Wade nor Pike shifted their gaze to him.

"Nobody has to die today," Mark said carefully. "You can both lay down your guns. The police will be here any moment."

"The law is already here," Wade said.

"You're a joke," Pike said.

Mark could see something change in Pike. His face became as rigid and set as his father's, his eyes as focused.

Pike deliberately and fearlessly raised his gun.

Wade was stoic, his gun held steady. If Pike were anybody else, Mark knew that Wade would already have planted a bullet between his eyes.

But Pike wasn't anybody else.

That's when Mark noticed something had changed in Tom Wade, too. The lawman was frozen. He looked like a mannequin of a U.S. Marshal posed in the perfect shooting stance.

But he wasn't shooting.

Wade should have fired before Pike could bring his gun up. Any other cop in his position would have.

But he didn't.

In the second that passed, Mark realized Wade either wasn't going to shoot or he was going to wait until Pike could get a shot off, too.

It was suicide. For both of them.

Pike grinned, taking careful aim at his father. He wasn't going to need a river after all.

Mark couldn't let himself become a spectator at another suicide. Not after Lenore. Not after Rachel.

"No!" he yelled, as loudly as he could, railing against all the stupid, pointless, unnecessary sacrifices of life he'd seen today, yesterday, and so many days before. It was wrong, and he couldn't abide it any longer.

His furious, guttural cry seemed to startle Pike, who whirled on Mark, pointing his gun at him. There was a gunshot.

Mark flinched, closing his eyes for an instant. When he opened them again, Pike was still facing him, with an astonished expression and a smoking hole in the center of his forehead.

Pike fell forward, dead long before he hit the floor, the gun skittering out of his lifeless grasp.

Wade stared at his own gun in shock, as if it was a living thing that had acted on its own. He didn't know if Pike was going to shoot Mark or not. Pike probably didn't know either. But the lawman in Wade couldn't take that chance. Reflexes honed by years of experience acted for him. He might have hesitated where his own life was concerned, but not someone else's.

He fired. And now his son was dead, at his father's hand. The realization hit Tom Wade like a gut punch.

The marshal dropped to his knees, staring at his son's body.

Suddenly the whole building began to shake violently around them, though Wade seemed oblivious. Plaster dust rained down from the ceiling. Cracks opened in the walls. A heavy, rhythmic rumbling filled Mark's ears.

Earthquake.

Mark steeled himself for the inevitable. Any second now, the condemned heap would collapse on them. Of all the miserable, unbelievable luck . . .

Then Mark realized he wasn't hearing the subterranean roar of a ground-splitting tremblor. It was a helicopter.

Relieved, and suddenly exhausted, Mark leaned his back against the wall and allowed himself to slide slowly to the floor.

The police were here, not that it made much difference now. Pike couldn't get any deader.

Mark glanced at Wade, still on his knees beside Pike's body. Their eyes met.

"He's my son," Wade said.

Mark nodded and closed his eyes. He'd never felt so tired.

CHAPTER TWENTY

Mulholland Vista Estates, high in the hills south of Ventura Boulevard in Reseda, was a gated community of million-and-a-half-dollar tract-home mansions with backyards the size of a parking space. The mansions were so close to one another, neighbors could swap jars of Grey Poupon with each other through their kitchen windows.

The $750-a-month association fee paid for the lush tropical landscaping and the round-the-clock security at their ornate million-dollar gate, which couldn't stop the neighborhood from being besieged by rattlesnakes, coyotes, and mountain lions that came down from the mountains to feast on gourmet table scraps and tasty French poodles.

But none of that made the community any less desirable for people too poor to live in Beverly Hills, Malibu, or Brentwood, but still rich enough to want people to know it. A McMansion at Mulholland Vista Estates was just the way to do it.

The African American couple who were waiting for Lenore Barber when she drove up fit the buyer profile for a home in Mulholland Vista Estates perfectly. Mr. and Mrs. Guy Hanks were young, good-looking, and were sitting in a brand-new, BMW 7 Series. He was an executive in the rubber and plastics industry and she, as far as Lenore knew, was simply his stunning trophy wife.

Mrs. Hanks was more than that. She was an adjunct county medical examiner at Community General, but despite all the time Lenore spent at the hospital, she hadn't met Dr. Amanda Bentley. At least not yet. She would if she didn't stop smoking soon.

Amanda was the first one out of the car, striding towards Lenore with her hand out and a bright smile on her face.

"You must be Lenore," Amanda said. "We can't wait to see this house."

"I can't wait to show it to you, Mrs. Hanks," Lenore said.

"I'd like you to meet my husband, Guy," Amanda said, motioning behind the realtor.

Lenore turned to greet Guy Hanks and caught her breath. He was a tall man with a carefully trimmed mustache and beard, rimless glasses, and a smile as bright and enthusiastic as Amanda's. But his most distinguishing feature was the ragged scar across his throat and the hole in his neck, right below his Adam's apple. A tube was sticking out of the hole, held in place with a plastic strap so it wouldn't slip into his trachea.

He grinned, offered one hand to Lenore and, with the other, placed a finger over his tracheotomy hole so he could speak.

Lenore almost screamed.

"Amanda told me there's a screening room," Guy said with a weak, raspy voice. "I've always dreamed of having one."

Lenore shook his hand limply, unable to stop staring at the hole in his neck. The entire day was one horror after another. It was as if God was trying to send her a message. She was seriously considering getting back in her car, speeding home and barricading herself behind the door.

"It's a hole—" she began, then mortified by her slip, corrected herself in stride. "—entire theater with enough seats for you and a dozen of your closest friends to enjoy the latest Hollywood blockbuster. You'll never want to leave the house."

If he was aware of her mistake, he didn't show it.

"Magnificent," Guy said with excitement. "Let's see it."

He hurried towards the house like a kid eager to be the first through the gates at Disneyland.

Lenore wasn't paying attention, still remembering her last thought.

It was as if God was trying to send her a message.

Amanda shook her head in mock frustration at her mock husband.

"You'd think we were in the market for a movie theater instead of a house," Amanda said. "But I suppose he deserves it after what he's been through."

"What happened?" Lenore asked. In her heart, she already knew the answer, but she still had to hear it.

"Throat cancer," Amanda said. "I probably should have warned you about his permanent tracheotomy. It can be a shock the first time you see it."

"I hardly noticed," Lenore said, hoping that Amanda couldn't see her hands shaking.

The ambulance drove off with Mark Sloan in the back and headed for the Community General in West Los Angeles. There were three other hospitals that were much closer to the accident scene, but Mark insisted on being taken to Community General and was willing to pay whatever extra charges were incurred as a result.

Steve stayed behind while the medical examiner, a guy with two chins more than necessary, examined and removed Pike's body. He would have preferred to accompany his father to the hospital, but Mark's injuries appeared minor and Captain Newman had just arrived. It wouldn't look good if the lead detective on the case fled when his boss arrived, though Steve might have done it anyway if the helicopter he'd appropriated hadn't left minutes before the captain's arrival.

Tom Wade was still there, too. He'd already given Steve his statement and was waiting for the marshals to show up, so he could repeat his statement for them. Less than an hour earlier, he'd gunned down his own son, but Steve saw nothing in Wade's stony expression that betrayed a hint of emotional turmoil. At some point, he'd even managed to put his Stetson on.

Captain Newman was barely out of his car when Wade strode up to him, cutting Steve off. Steve was in no hurry to talk to his boss, so he gladly stood to one side to let whatever was going to happen play itself out.

"I heard about what happened here, Marshal," Captain Newman said somberly. "I'm terribly sorry for your loss. I can't imagine what you must be feeling."

Wade gave a slight nod in acknowledgement. "I'll be taking Rachel Swicord back to Spokane now."

Newman glanced at Steve. This was news to Steve as well, so he said nothing.

"She's staying here," Newman said to Wade.

"She's not in any danger now," Wade said. "I've seen to that."

There was nothing cavalier about the marshal's remark; it was said as a statement of fact. Nevertheless, the captain seemed unsettled by it.

Newman cleared his throat. "That's not the issue."

"She's a fugitive cop killer who violated her parole," Wade said firmly. "There's a price to pay."

"She's paid it," Newman said. "I've been in discussions with the district attorney here and up in Spokane. We won't extradite her to Washington State and they aren't asking us to. The feeling is that she's been through enough."

"Enough?" Wade's face tightened. "She broke the law. That can't be ignored."

"Sure it can," Newman said. "Rachel Swicord served her time and walked out of prison a reformed woman."

"She was on parole," Wade said. "There was still time on her sentence."

"She created the Cuddle Bear, for God's sake, and had her picture taken with tons of bald cancer kids," Newman said. "We aren't sending the Cuddle Bear to prison."

Wade's face tightened even more, which Steve didn't think was possible, and he spoke through clenched teeth. "My son is dead because he broke the law. She's as guilty as he was."

"She's not responsible for what he did today," Steve said gently. "That was his choice."

Wade watched the medical examiner wheeling his son's body bag into the morgue wagon. "This isn't right."

The marshal walked away. The captain looked at the body bag, then back at Steve.

"It sure isn't," Newman said.

Guy Hanks drove up to the front of Community General to drop Amanda off.

"That really was a spectacular house," he said. "The screening room was incredible. It even had a marquee."

"It's a little out of our price range, dear," she said with a smile.

"Not mine," Guy said. "I'm the supervising producer of *Killer Autopsy*, the forty-fourth highest rated forensic drama on network television. Do you know the obscene amount of money I make?"

"I'm guessing it's more than I get as a technical consultant on your show."

"Only slightly," he said. "Did you see the wine cellar in that place? It's bigger than my master bedroom."

She studied him for a moment. "You're serious about this, aren't you?"

"I wasn't really in the market, but now that I've seen it, I can't get the place out of my head," he said. "I think I'm going to make an offer."

"Maybe you ought to wait a day or two."

"What if someone beats me to it?"

"What if the realtor wants your wife's signature on the papers?"

"Oh," he said.

"Oh," she said, then motioned to his throat. "I think you can take that off now."

"It felt so comfortable," he said. "I almost forgot it was there."

Guy carefully peeled the elaborate rubber appliance off his neck and tossed it onto the backseat.

"Our special effects makeup department is incredible," he said, scratching his throat and examining it in the rearview mirror.

"Thank you for your help," Amanda said. "I owe you one."

"Are you kidding? This sting of yours is gonna make a great episode of the show. Of course, I'm gonna have to tweak it a bit to make it a cutting-edge story of forensic investigation."

"Will the tweaks involve ninja assassins, Italian sports cars, and flamethrowers?"

"Couldn't hurt," he said.

"I'll be glad to provide whatever technical assistance I can." Amanda gave him a friendly kiss on the cheek and got out of the car. "Flamethrowers are a big part of my job."

"If they aren't," Guy said, "they should be."

She watched him drive off, then headed into the ER to deliver her report to Jesse before starting her shift.

The first person she saw was Steve, standing at a nurse's

station, finishing up a phone call. His badge was clipped to his belt and his face was tight. This was a man on the job, and in his line of work, that only meant one thing.

"You got a corpse waiting for me?" Amanda asked.

"As a matter of fact, I do," Steve said. "But there's no mystery involved. His name is Pike Wade and he was shot by his father."

"Not Marshal Wade," Amanda asked, hoping she was wrong.

"Afraid so," Steve said, and explained that Pike was Rachel Swicord's ex-boyfriend, the one who killed a deputy in Washington State and was presumed dead. Pike's mother remarried and he took his step-father's surname, Wheeler. "Pike drew his gun on Dad. The marshal was forced to shoot."

"Where's Marshal Wade now?" Amanda asked.

"Being debriefed by the Marshals Service. Then he's getting on a plane to Spokane. I'm guessing his career is over, though I can't imagine he'd want the job anymore after this anyway."

"What about Rachel?"

"She woke up this morning," Steve said. "She's already been interviewed by the Spokane cops and somebody from the Marshals Service. Last I heard, they're gonna let her walk on the parole violation. As far as they are concerned, she can go back to being Rebecca Jordan as if nothing ever happened."

"You think she can do that?" Amanda asked. "Just go back to her new life, the way it was before?"

Steve shrugged. "She won't be afraid anymore."

"You aren't even sure that's why she jumped," Amanda said.

"I don't think anybody's asked her that yet."

"Maybe somebody should," Amanda said. "I'm surprised Mark isn't up there doing that right now."

"He would if he could." Steve tipped his head towards the exam room behind him. "Dad was in a car accident. Broke his arm, cut his head, then got into the middle of the confrontation between the marshal and his son. Dad's going to be fine, but he's lucky to be alive."

"Is it okay if I see him?"

"You're the doctor," Steve said, then headed for the elevator.

"Where are you going?" she asked.

"To ask Rachel Swicord the big question," Steve said.

Amanda went into the exam room to find Mark lying on a gurney, his eyes closed, a bandage on his forehead. Jesse was putting the finishing touches on the bright blue cast on Mark's left arm.

"Lately, Mark spends more time here as a patient than he does as a doctor," Jesse said.

"How is he?"

"Asleep. Besides the broken arm, he's suffering from a mild concussion, exhaustion, and dehydration. I'm admitting him overnight. I want to make sure he sleeps and gets plenty of fluids."

Amanda stroked Mark's cheek, rough with stubble. She hated seeing him like this. "You ought to put him in restraints."

"I'm tempted, believe me," Jesse said.

"One of these days," Amanda said, "he's going to get himself killed."

"You're beginning to sound like Steve. Next thing you know, you'll be saying he should stick to medicine and stay out of homicide investigations."

"That wasn't what got him banged up this time," Amanda said. "He was trying to solve the problems that drove Rachel Swicord to jump out a window."

"So what do you suggest we do?" Jesse said. "Tell him to stop caring about other people?"

"Believe it or not, you can care about others and still go through life without having a gun pointed at you."

"Like you and me, for instance?"

Amanda and Jesse shared a look.

"You once talked about getting him a Kevlar vest for his birthday," she said.

"I was joking."

"Find out what they cost," she said, then after glancing at Mark again, had another thought. "Get yourself one, too."

CHAPTER TWENTY-ONE

"I'm not sure what I should call you." Steve stood at the foot of the woman's bed in the ICU. "Rachel or Rebecca."

"I suppose Rebecca, because it reminds me that I'm a different person today than I was yesterday," she said softly.

"Does this mean you won't be diving out the window again anytime soon?" Steve said. "Because that's what the woman you were yesterday thought was a good idea."

Rebecca looked away from him, watching her heartbeat on the EKG. "You're not a very nice person."

There was a huge stuffed bear in the only chair, which was beside her bed. Steve put the Cuddle Bear on the floor and sat down. From the look on her face, he could see she preferred the bear's company to his. Too bad.

"I want to know why you did it," he said.

"Did what?" she asked.

"Tried to kill yourself."

"What do you care?"

"I don't," Steve said. She turned and met his gaze. "My father saw you jump and he's spent the last two days trying to repair your life so you won't do it again."

Rebecca looked past him now, staring at the wall as she searched her memory. "The old doctor with the mustache."

"He's down in the ER with a broken arm," Steve said.

"He nearly got killed for you. I need to know he didn't do it for nothing."

Steve saw her squeeze the button attached to her IV, sending a shot of painkiller into her system, as if just the thought of answering his question caused her agony.

"I met Pike at a party," she said. "He had a way of smiling, of looking at you, of carrying himself, that was powerful, you know? Almost like a drug. I couldn't get enough of him; I surrendered completely to it."

Steve couldn't imagine what that was like. He'd never surrendered completely to anything.

"We partied for weeks. Sex, drugs, and rock and roll. Who knew it could be a way of life instead of just a saying? It was wild," she said. "One afternoon, he shows up at my place in that car. I knew it wasn't his, but he was grinning that grin. So it didn't matter. I got in."

"Was he grinning when you watched him rob that convenience store?"

"It was just this big joke, a prank. I was laughing. So was he. It was fun. It didn't feel like any of it was real. We were high, but we weren't on anything. It was amazing. I thought that had to be love." She met his eye. "Isn't it?"

Steve didn't know; he'd never felt anything like that about anyone. If it meant surrendering completely to feel that, he wasn't sure he ever would.

"I don't know," he said.

Rebecca studied him for a long moment, then took a deep breath and went on with her story, a little less reluctantly now, perhaps because Steve had, in his own way, volunteered something about himself.

"When the deputies started chasing us, it just made it seem even less real, like we were on some kind of amusement park ride," she said. "I couldn't stop shrieking and laughing and neither could he. I've never been in a car that was going so fast. The windows were rolled down, the wind was blasting in. It felt like we were flying. And then, the police car cut us off. Pike stopped the car. I was breathing so hard, I was light-headed. I saw the deputy get out and then Pike got this funny look on his face and floored it . . ."

Rebecca closed her eyes tight and her finger squeezed the trigger on the painkiller, but Steve doubted there was anything in the IV that could wipe away that memory.

"The deputy flew up into the windshield, his face was right in front of me," she whispered. "I could see his eyes, the fear and the pain, and then he slid off and I felt the car roll right over him."

She shook her head and looked at Steve. Tears were streaming down her cheeks.

"I woke up," she said. "I wasn't sleeping, but that's what it felt like, like waking up, from a dream into a nightmare. We were being chased again, only now it wasn't one cop car, it was like an army of them. I knew Pike wasn't going to stop this time, not for anything. But he didn't look scared at all. Pike was happy. 'We're always going to be together,' he said, and when he grinned, I almost believed him. And then we were in the air, falling towards the water."

Steve picked up a cup of water beside the bed, bent the straw, and lifted it to her lips. She took a long sip.

"He didn't lose control of the car," Steve said. "He went into the river on purpose."

"We were both supposed to die," she said. "And in a way, I did."

Steve set the cup down and remained standing, looking down at her.

"I was a teenager when I went into prison," Rebecca said. "When I came out, I was a woman, an entirely different person. I wanted a new life. I knew I'd never have one if I stayed in Washington. So I came here, to the sunshine."

Steve knew the rest. She reinvented herself as a toy designer. She created the Cuddle Bear. And then came the article, the photograph, and the unwanted publicity.

But there was still something missing.

"You didn't jump because you were afraid of being punished for a parole violation or that your junkie brother would show up," Steve said, looking her in the eye. "You knew Pike was alive."

"I always felt it, maybe because I didn't want to believe he was dead," she said. "A few days ago, a man broke into my apartment. He didn't know my roommate, Lissy, was there. She works nights, she was sleeping."

"I saw the meat cleaver she threw at him."

"Lissy described the intruder to me and I knew it was him, but I still didn't want to believe it," Rebecca said. "One morning, I looked out my window at work and saw him standing on the street."

"He was out there the day you jumped?"

"I saw that grin, and I could feel myself surrendering to it again. Just like that. One instant. And I was his. I knew I couldn't resist," she said. "There was only one way out."

Someone knocked on the door. Steve turned to see Tucker Mellish standing in the doorway, a pink bakery box in his hand.

"Is this a bad time?" Tucker asked.

Rebecca lit up immediately, a huge, relieved smile on her face. She looked at Steve, who nodded and stepped away from the bed. He'd found what he needed to know.

"It's the best time," Rebecca said. "Today happens to be the first day of the rest of my life."

"Then it's the perfect occasion for fresh Danish," Mellish said, lifting the lid on the box to reveal it was filled with fresh cinnamon rolls, bear claws, coffee cake, and glazed donuts. "Can I interest you in a bear claw, Steve?"

"No thanks, I'm on duty," Steve said, remembering his bear claw hangover.

"You two know each other?" Rebecca asked.

"We're in business together now," Mellish said. "I bake pastries for his restaurant."

"Amazing how much can change while you're sleeping," she said, glancing at Steve.

He smiled and walked out, pausing in the doorway to take a last glance at her. The gnomish baker was settling into the seat beside Rebecca's bed, offering the box of pastries to her, the Cuddle Bear on the floor next to him.

And that's when Steve noticed something familiar about the big stuffed animal. The dopey smile. The big wet eyes. The round body.

The Cuddle Bear bore an uncanny resemblance to Tucker Mellish.

Abel Marsh, the LAPD's forensic accountant, took a table at the back of BBQ Bob's and sat straight, facing the door. Marsh's badge was clipped to the front of his belt and he wore a gun, positioned so everyone could see it when they walked in, though Steve couldn't imagine a situation where he'd have to use it.

"Expecting trouble?" Steve asked, sliding into the booth opposite him.

"Question is," Marsh replied, "is trouble expecting me?"

Marsh wasn't joking. He'd honed his Clint Eastwood drawl so well, it stopped being an impersonation and came naturally to him, even if none of Eastwood's other mythic qualities did. Perhaps if Marsh wasn't so short and so pale, and if his hairline hadn't receded to the back of his head, he might have an easier time pulling off the effect.

Lots of the detectives, Steve included, liked to give Marsh a hard time, but the forensic accountant took it in stride. Marsh would remind them it was an accountant who brought down Al Capone. He'd say that the biggest heists today aren't being done in the dark by clever thieves but in the light of day by corporate CEOs and CFOs. He'd argue that in today's world it takes a new breed of cop, a certified public accountant with a badge, to enforce the law.

Maybe, Steve thought, Marsh was right. Very soon, the joke might be on him.

"Can I treat you to some dinner?" Steve asked. "Smokiest ribs in Southern California."

"No thanks," Marsh said. "A tall glass of ice water will be fine."

It seemed to Steve that Marsh wanted desperately to embody the steely presence of a man like Tom Wade. Perhaps if Marsh knew the price the marshal paid for living his life that way, the accountant might change his mind. Steve was tempted to tell him, but realized it would do no good. Marsh wouldn't understand, not unless Steve could find a way to express it in numbers.

Steve waved a waitress over, ordered a slice of banana cream pie for himself and a glass of ice water for his guest, then got down to business.

"Have you had a chance to study the finances at Brant Publications?" Steve asked.

"A little bit," Marsh said.

"How do the books look to you?"

"Like a gang rape," Marsh said.

Over three glasses of ice water, and with one break to go to the bathroom, Marsh explained to Steve how Brant's partners were plundering the company. The first thing Clifton Hemphill, Dean Perrow, and Virgil Nyby did was radically reshape the look and content of the magazine to jack up the circulation and increase ad revenues.

"That doesn't sound illegal to me," Steve said.

"The makeover was simply a smoke screen to explain the dramatic increase in their circulation," Marsh said. "It looked like the changes revitalized the magazine and attracted hundreds of thousands of new readers."

"What really happened?"

"Rampant fraud," Marsh said. "The partners created several shell companies that bought tens of thousands of bogus subscriptions at giveaway rates. They printed up thousands of copies that they reported as newsstand sales, but were secretly sold for cash directly to a paper recycling company and pulped. And in addition to those schemes, they simply lied, making up whatever numbers sounded good to them."

"What's the upside to throwing magazines out and buying subscriptions themselves?"

"The real money doesn't come from subscribers, but from advertising, and the price of page space is based on circulation numbers," Marsh said. "The higher the circulation, the higher the ad rates. The higher the ad rates, the higher the revenues. The higher the revenues, the more the magazine is worth. The higher the value of the magazine, the more money they can borrow against it."

"The partners were taking out loans?"

"In the tens of millions of dollars," Marsh said. "Some of which they used to buy their new headquarters building at a grossly inflated price from an offshore, dummy corporation owned by Hemphill, who constructed the office tower in the first place. I'll bet my badge Perrow and Nyby got big cash payoffs that coincided with the purchase of the property."

The fraud didn't end there. From what Marsh could tell, they were siphoning off even more money by purchasing expensive drive-time ads on Virgil Nyby's radio stations, which actually broadcast less than half of the spots. The stations, however, used those sales figures, and contracts with Brant Publications for future ad time, to jack up their own bottom line to investors.

Steve was astonished, not only by the widespread fraud, but that Abel Marsh uncovered it so quickly.

"They must be pretty lousy crooks if you found out so much already." Steve saw the look on Marsh's face and quickly qualified his statement. "Not that I doubt your accounting skills."

"No offense taken," Marsh said. "I had an advantage I don't ordinarily have. Turns out Winston Brant had been quietly going through the books himself for months and left detailed notes. His secretary, Grace Wozniak, gave me access to his computer and I hacked his encrypted files."

"You know how to hack?"

"I do what has to be done," Marsh said, chewing an ice cube. "I'm sure there's more to find. I can smell the stink. I just haven't dug deep enough yet. We could arrest 'em now on a slew of charges."

"Not until I get one, or all of 'em, for murder," Steve said. "Keep this and whatever else you find between us for now. I don't want Hemphill, Perrow, and Nyby figuring out how much we know yet. If all else fails, maybe I can use the threat of jail time on financial crimes as leverage."

"For what?"

"To get one of them to point a finger at whoever killed Winston Brant."

Marsh nodded, finished his fourth glass of ice water, and walked out. Steve stayed in the booth, picking at the crumbs of his piecrust.

If the three partners found out that Brant had discovered their fraud, and that he was going to reveal it at the shareholders' meeting, then they had good reason to want him dead.

Now Steve had the evidence to prove motive and, since they were all on the plane together, opportunity as well. What he didn't have was the slightest idea how Winston Brant was stabbed to death in midair.

And without that, he had nothing.

CHAPTER TWENTY-TWO

Dr. Mark Sloan had seen the sun rise through hospital room windows many times over the years, but never as a patient.

The view from the bed was quite a bit different.

He didn't know how long he'd slept, but he felt completely rested for the first time in days, despite the discomforts of the IV feeding fluid into his veins, the Foley catheter emptying his bladder, and the hard cast supporting his broken left arm.

As brilliant as the sunrise was, when he looked out the window, he saw last night's dream playing out in front of his eyes again.

Rachel Swicord sat on the window ledge. Only she wasn't Rachel any more. She was Lenore Barber, and she looked at Mark defiantly, as if daring him to stop her. Lenore threw herself out the window, a wild grin on her face, and plummeted to the street below.

Her body spun and she became Winston Brant, and then the dream slowed, as if he'd been watching a DVD, paused the image, and then advanced the picture frame by frame. Brant looked at the knife in his chest. When Brant lifted his head, his face was speckled with blood and he stared right at Mark. There was no shock on Brant's face, no pleading in his eyes, only grim acceptance of his unavoidable fate. And then the dream sped up again and Brant hit the pavement, which was odd to Mark, since Rachel had landed on a car.

But now, in the bright light of morning, the inaccuracy didn't matter to Mark. It wasn't Rachel falling anyway; it was Winston Brant. Besides, it was a dream. Brant could have landed in a bowl of whipped cream. So what difference did it make?

It always struck Mark as odd how, even asleep, he was often observing himself observing the dream, reminding himself it wasn't real and yet still trying to apply some kind of logic to it all.

Mark pressed the call button and, within a few moments, a nurse came in. She was a slender African American in her mid-twenties, with a surprisingly energetic spring to her step for such an early hour. Mark didn't recognize her and felt bad about it. Nobody expected him to know every nurse in the hospital, but as Chief of Internal Medicine, he prided himself on trying.

"How are you feeling this morning?" she asked.

"Fine and dandy." Mark glanced at her name tag. "Nurse Ademu-John, I'd appreciate it if you'd take me off the IV and remove the Foley catheter."

She grinned at him. "I'm sure you would, but you'll have to wait until the doctor sees you."

"I am a doctor," Mark said. "In fact, I'm the Chief of Internal Medicine at this hospital."

"I know," the nurse said. "I was warned about you."

"Warned?"

"That you'd try to check yourself out before Dr. Travis came to see you. I was told to call security if there was a problem."

"You're joking," Mark said.

"But I won't need security." Her cheery expression suddenly turned implacable. "If you take those tubes out of your body I will pin you down in that bed myself and shove them back in."

"Shove?" Mark stammered.

She put her hands on his bed railing and leaned in close. "Do I make myself clear, Dr. Sloan?"

Mark nodded vigorously.

"Good." She stood up straight, her bright demeanor immediately returning at full wattage. "Dr. Travis will be in to see you in a few hours. Would you like some breakfast?"

He was afraid of what she would do if he said no. "Yes, that would be lovely."

The nurse left and returned a few moments later with cold scrambled eggs, cold bacon, and frozen sausage. No one would ever accuse him of receiving preferential treatment.

He forced himself to eat the food rather than face the possibility that she might *shove* it down his throat if he didn't. After breakfast, he tried to pass the time by watching television, but that effort lasted a full ten minutes.

There was no way he was going to lie in that bed until Jesse showed up.

As long as he was in the hospital, Mark decided, he might as well do his job. He got out of bed and, barefoot and wearing only his hospital gown, he headed off to check on his patients, wheeling his IV stand and urine bag beside him.

It felt strange to Steve to be alone in the beach house. During the night Mark spent as a patient in Community General Hospital, their Malibu beach house seemed twice as big and full of shadows. Steve turned on all the lights, locked the doors, and kept the television tuned to CNN. He wasn't interested in watching the news. But the constant commentary helped him feel less lonely and drowned out the odd creaks and groans of the house, which sounded disturbingly like someone creeping around in the darkness. He made sure his gun, taser, and asp baton were within easy reach.

In the gray dawn of morning, putting on his sweats, Steve was embarrassed at the memory, only a few hours old. He was a grown man. A police officer. He carried a loaded weapon. What should have scared him was not being alone in the empty house, but what would happen to his career if he didn't make some progress soon on the Winston Brant investigation.

Steve had spent most of the night going over the murder book on Brant's homicide. He reread his interviews with all the suspects and witnesses. He studied the crime scene photos and Amanda's detailed autopsy. He watched the video of Brant's dive again and again and again. He scrutinized the schematics of the airplane and even took apart a parachute pack the skydiving school had loaned to him. And the only thing he learned was that he didn't know anything, which didn't bode well for his homicide investigation.

Clifton Hemphill, Dean Perrow, and Virgil Nyby all had motives to want Winston Brant dead. But they couldn't have stabbed him in the airplane, not with the skydiving instructor and the crew on board. And even if they did, the LAPD techs would have found traces of blood in the aircraft. But that was all irrelevant anyway. Steve knew Brant was alive when he jumped out of the plane; the video that the skydiving instructor shot proved that. Even if the video didn't, the blood spatter pattern on the parachute clearly showed that Brant was stabbed while falling through the air.

So how the hell was it done?

Around two a.m., with no better understanding of how the crime was committed than he had before, Steve gave up and went to bed.

Now, after four hours of fitful sleep, Steve trudged upstairs and for a moment was disappointed to see that all his files, notes, schematics, and videotapes were exactly where he'd left them. If this had been an ordinary morning, he would have found his father in the midst of it all, eager to offer his theories and deductions. Or Steve would have found all the files neatly arranged, covered with little yellow Post-it notes with Mark's questions and observations. And he would have found his breakfast prepared, fresh squeezed orange juice in the fridge, and a stack of hotcakes kept warm for him in the oven.

But this morning there were no brilliant deductions, no Post-it notes or pancakes waiting for him, only the evidence of his fruitless labors the night before.

Steve crossed the house as quickly as he could, trying to ignore the files and papers, and went outside for his morning jog on the sand.

The beach was fogged in and empty, exactly how he liked it. He jogged along the berm, just out of reach of the surf, keeping a steady pace, scaring flocks of seagulls into flight. The exercise cleared his head, got his blood pumping, and revitalized him.

Steve returned to the house with a renewed vigor and determination to break the case. He might not have the key clue yet, but he felt confident he'd be able to play the suspects against one another until one of them betrayed the others. That confidence lasted right up until the moment he picked up the *Los Angeles Times* from the front step and read the headline on the front page.

At ten a.m. sharp, Dr. Jesse Travis stood at the foot of Mark's empty bed and called for the nurse. She arrived a moment later.

Jesse pointed to the bed where Mark Sloan was supposed to be. "I thought I told you not to let Dr. Sloan leave this hospital."

"He's still here." Nurse Ademu-John put her hands on her hips.

"Where?"

She nodded towards the ceiling. "On the fourth floor, doing his rounds. Still hooked to his IV and Foley."

Jesse stared at her. "You let him go to work?"

"You said to keep him in the hospital and hooked up," Nurse Ademu-John replied. "You didn't say anything about him seeing his patients."

Jesse stood there in disbelief. He couldn't imagine how Mark could do that. "I hope he remembered to tie his gown."

There was an amused grunt from the patient in the bed beside Mark's. Jesse looked at him.

"Afraid not," the man said.

Jesse hurried out of the room and ran up the stairs to the fourth floor. He emerged breathless from the stairwell and heard Mark's voice coming from one of the rooms.

"You're coming along just fine, Mr. Ardner," Mark said. "The surgeon tells me your hiatal herniorraphy was a complete success. I'll have the nurse come in with a warm compress to relieve your incisional discomfort."

Jesse was following his voice when Mark suddenly emerged from a room down the hall and unintentionally mooned him.

"Mark." Jesse rushed up to his side. "Do you really think it's a good idea to be visiting patients?"

"It's comforting for them to see a familiar face," Mark said.

"They're seeing a lot more than that." Jesse tied up Mark's gown, covering up his naked backside.

Mark glanced over his shoulder. "I thought I felt a draft."

"How are you feeling this morning?" Jesse steered Mark into the first empty room he could find and closed the door.

"Like my old self again," Mark said. "Not that I ever feel old, of course."

"You're making up for it by aging me pretty fast." Jesse

helped Mark over to one of the beds, unhooked him from the IV and removed the Foley catheter.

"Does this mean you're releasing me?"

"Do I have a say in this?"

"Just make sure you let Nurse Ademu-John know you've let me go," Mark said. "She scares me."

"Not enough, apparently," Jesse said. "On the way back down to your room, there's someone I'd like you to meet."

They took the elevator to the third floor and Jesse led Mark to one of the private recovery rooms. Jesse motioned to the open door.

"She's made an amazing recovery," Jesse said. "We're releasing her tomorrow."

Mark peered inside and saw Rebecca Jordan sitting up in her bed, surrounded by bright flowers and pink pastry boxes. The enormous Cuddle Bear was propped up in a chair on one side of her bed and in a chair on the other side sat a plump little man wearing suspenders, reading aloud from an old leather-bound book in his lap.

" ' "Our talk has been like a declaration of love," said Kolya. "That's not ridiculous, is it?" Alyosha smiled brightly. "Not at all ridiculous." ' "

Tucker Mellish himself smiled brightly, and was about to go on reading, when Rebecca noticed Mark in the doorway.

"You're the man in the window," Rebecca said.

And she reminded him of the woman who jumped. But looking at her face, seeing the gleam in her eyes, he knew he was mistaken. She wasn't that woman. Not anymore. Hopefully, she never would be again.

"I'm glad to see you're feeling better," Mark said.

"No small thanks to you."

"It's Dr. Travis you should be thanking. He's a fine doctor who took very good care of you."

She shook her head. "You know what I'm talking about,

Dr. Sloan. I heard what you did for me. You gave me my life back. I don't know how I'll ever repay you."

Mark glanced at the book in Mellish's lap and recited a line from memory. "'How good life is when one does something good and just.'"

"Hey, we just read that part," Mellish said. "You want to stay, have a pastry, and find out who killed old Karamazov?"

"I already know whodunit," Mark said, grinning. "I'll see you around."

"Wait." Mellish grabbed a box of pastries and shoved them into Mark's hands. "You deserve something sweet."

"Thank you." Mark turned to go and Mellish started reading again, his voice carrying out the door and into the corridor.

"'"And if it were ridiculous, it wouldn't matter, because it's a good thing."'"

Instead of leading Mark back to the elevator, Jesse tipped his head towards the end of the hall. "There's another stop I'd like to make."

They walked down the long hall, crossing out of the patient recovery wing into the treatment center, which housed various physical therapy units and psychological counseling programs.

Jesse stopped at the glass doors leading to the Smoking Cessation Center. "Take a look."

Mark did, and was stunned to see Lenore Barber among the circle of patients sitting in chairs and talking to the bearded counselor.

"I don't believe it," Mark said. "What could have possibly changed her mind?"

"You don't realize how persuasive you can be," Jesse said.

Mark eyed him suspiciously. "How did you know she was here?"

"The important thing is, she's here." Jesse headed for the elevator.

"The way you're leading me around in this gown, it's like I'm Scrooge and you're one of the ghosts of Christmas past, showing me where my mistakes will lead."

"Difference is, I'm not showing you the horrors ahead but the tragedies you prevented," Jesse said. "These are two people who won't try to kill themselves again. They're willing to fight for their lives now."

The elevator arrived and Jesse stepped inside. But Mark stood where he was, staring into space, completely oblivious to the world around him.

Any other doctor would have assumed Mark was experiencing a medical problem, that he was on the verge of collapsing. Jesse made no move to help. He wasn't worried. If anything, he felt a jolt of adrenaline.

Jesse knew what the look on Mark Sloan's face meant. A thousand seemingly unrelated facts were coming together in Mark's mind to form an undeniable truth, a picture of absolute clarity where before there had been confusion.

"What do you know?" Jesse asked him.

Mark grinned. He wouldn't be having last night's dream ever again.

"I know how Winston Brant was killed," Mark said. "And I know who did it."

CHAPTER TWENTY-THREE

Mark showered in the doctors' locker room, a trash bag cinched tight around the cast on his left arm to protect it from getting wet. He got dressed in fresh clothes, carefully maneuvering his broken arm through the sleeve of his shirt, then hurried to meet Steve, Amanda, and Jesse in the morgue. It wasn't the most pleasant or comfortable place in the hospital to have a discussion, but at least they would be assured of privacy.

There wasn't any real reason for Jesse to be there, but inviting him was the only way he'd stop nagging Mark to explain who killed Winston Brant. In return, Mark made Jesse promise not to reveal to Steve that he'd solved the case.

Besides, Mark felt that Jesse had earned a little special consideration. He knew Jesse was responsible for Lenore Barber's sudden change of heart and he was grateful for it. He also knew that whatever Jesse had done, it was motivated more out of concern for Mark than for his stubborn patient.

When Mark strode into the morgue, Steve had the front page of the *Los Angeles Times* spread out on one of the autopsy tables and both Amanda and Jesse were reading over his shoulder.

"Why do you look so grim?" Mark asked his son.

"Before Winston Brant was murdered, he discovered his three fellow board members were plundering the company. Our forensic accountant gave me the facts last night." Steve swatted the paper. "Now somebody has leaked everything to the *Times*. Not only have they printed everything we know, but also a whole bunch of stuff we haven't got yet."

Steve outlined for his father what he knew about Clifton Hemphill, Dean Perrow, and Virgil Nyby's illegal activities and what he'd just learned from reading the paper. According to anonymous sources, the three men pumped their ill-gotten gains into a South Africa–based dummy corporation, which then loaned the money back to Brant Publications with considerable interest.

"They were loaning the company the money they stole, and getting paid interest for it." Jesse whistled. "You've got to admire their chutzpah."

"It's all falling down around them now," Amanda said. "Brant's stock price is going to plummet and the Securities and Exchange Commission is launching an investigation. The whole company could crumble."

"Right along with my homicide investigation," Steve lamented.

"Don't worry, it won't have any impact on the case," said Mark, watching Jesse squirming in his seat.

"Of course it will," Steve said. "Now our three suspects know what we have on them. I won't be able to use the information as leverage to turn them against one another and flush out the killer."

"Trust me, you don't need it," Mark said.

"Getting one of them to crack may be our only hope of solving this murder," Steve said. "It's an impossible crime."

"It certainly is," Mark said.

Jesse couldn't contain himself any longer. "But you told

me this morning that you knew who murdered Winston Brant and how they pulled it off."

Steve and Amanda stared at Mark.

"You figured it out?" Amanda said.

"And you already told Jesse?" Steve said.

"I know how Winston Brant was killed, but I haven't told anybody yet," Mark said. "But the solution is so simple, I don't know how we missed it."

Now Jesse was staring at Mark, too. "You're telling us there's a *simple* way to stab a guy in midair without being seen or leaving a single trace of evidence?"

"There can't be," Steve said. "I went over everything last night. I examined the video, the autopsy report, the schematics of the plane. I even took apart a parachute pack. I didn't see anything that could explain what happened."

"But you've already explained it," Mark said.

"I have?" Steve asked, confused.

"You said it's an impossible crime."

"It is," Steve said.

Mark shrugged. "Then it didn't happen."

"Excuse me?" Steve said.

"It didn't happen," Mark repeated.

Amanda gestured to the morgue freezer. "I've got Winston Brant's corpse right here."

Steve looked at Jesse. "I thought you said Dad had a *minor* concussion. Does this sound minor to you?"

"Hold on." Mark held up his hands. "What I mean is, nobody murdered Winston Brant."

"Since when is a knife in the chest natural causes?" Steve asked.

"I didn't say he died of natural causes, I said he wasn't murdered," Mark said. "Winston Brant killed himself."

That was what his subconscious mind had been trying to tell him for days, robbing him of sleep. That was why when he dreamed of Rebecca Jordan leaping out her window, she morphed into Lenore Barber and Winston Brant before she landed. Because in his mind, Rebecca Jordan, Lenore Barber, and Winston Brant were all the same.

They all wanted to die.

He didn't make the connection until he saw Lenore Barber in the smoking cessation workshop.

Mark resolved to pay a lot more attention to his dreams from now on.

"Captain Newman will never buy that it's suicide. He'll think I'm stumped and that I'm taking the easy way out," Steve said. "There's no suicide note, no evidence whatsoever that Winston Brant killed himself."

"Brant *is* the evidence," Mark said. "The only way he could have jumped out of an airplane at ten thousand feet and been stabbed to death on the way down is if he did it to himself. That's what the parachute pack, witness statements, airplane schematics, and videotapes prove without a doubt."

"It's not enough," Steve said.

"If what you're saying is true," Jesse said to Mark, "why didn't Brant leave a suicide note?"

"I don't know," Mark said. "But even without a note, suicide is going to be a lot easier for us to prove than murder."

"We may already have some evidence," Amanda said. "When I did the autopsy, I found therapeutic amounts of Prozac in his system. You don't take an antidepressant if you're feeling great about life."

Mark nodded. "It fits with something Grace Wozniak, Brant's secretary, told me. She said Brant lost his spirit over the last few months, that he didn't seem to care about anything anymore."

"The guy had everything," Jesse said. "What did he have to be depressed about?"

Amanda pointed to the article on the front page of the *Los Angeles Times*. "You mean besides all of this?"

"So what? Brant was going to expose their evil deeds at

the stockholders' meeting anyway, wasn't he?" Jesse said. "They'd go to prison and he'd get his company back."

"In ruins," Steve said. "It would have been a pretty empty victory."

"But a victory nonetheless. Brant was a man who liked a good fight," Mark said. "His wife says that's why he insisted everyone call him 'Win' instead of Winston."

"So why not wait to kill himself until after he exposed those three jerks?" Jesse asked. "Why kill himself at all?"

"Good point," Amanda said.

Jesse looked at her in surprise. "Really? You think so?"

"You had to make one eventually," Amanda said.

"I'm certain that Winston Brant killed himself," Mark said. "Why he chose to do it *when* he did and *how* he did, I don't know."

Dr. Sara Everden's medical practice was in a European-style cottage on the East Coast Highway, conveniently located across from the Newport Beach Country Club and within walking distance of the neighborhood Bentley dealership.

She ran a family practice, which in Newport Beach meant that her waiting room was occupied by well-heeled retirees in cardigan sweaters, middle-aged men in golf attire, socialite women in tennis outfits, and gleaming-toothed children in private school uniforms.

The clinic was decorated with French antiques and maritime art, so it felt less like a doctor's office than it did the front room of a physician's home in a seaside village in France, circa 1904.

Sara met with Mark and Steve in her office, which was dominated by a faux brick fireplace, the mantelpiece covered with family photos of herself, Winston, and their kids engaged in outdoor activities against the backdrop of various exotic locales. Skiing in Switzerland. Fishing in Cabo

San Lucas. Snorkeling in Tahiti. In all the pictures, Winston Brant looked fit, tough, and proud. It wasn't the face of a suicidal man, but Mark knew not to read too much into what a person showed of himself to a camera. Photos could barely be trusted to capture the obvious, much less reveal a person's inner life.

Sara was shocked to see Mark's broken arm and bandaged forehead, and after some polite small talk about his car accident and recovery, she took a seat behind her uncluttered, carefully organized desk and pinned Steve with her gaze.

"Detective Sloan, you said on the phone that you'd concluded your investigation."

Mark and Steve sat in leather chairs across from her. Mark couldn't help noticing how much more comfortable these chairs were than the ones in her living room.

"I thought that was a little vague," she added. "Does this mean you know who killed my husband?"

"We do," Steve said.

She took a deep breath and let it out slowly. "Have you made an arrest?"

"No," he replied.

She cocked an eyebrow. "Why not?"

"Because there's nobody to arrest." Steve cleared his throat and shifted in his seat. "I'm sorry to have to tell you this, Dr. Everden. Your husband killed himself."

"No, I don't believe it," she said. "He wouldn't do that."

"We're closing our homicide investigation," Steve said. "I wanted you to hear it from me, face to face."

"You're just giving up because it's too hard," she said, glaring at him. "That's the truth, isn't it?"

Steve turned to his dad, as if to say, *I told you so.* Her comment simply confirmed his fears about the reaction he could expect from his superiors at the LAPD.

Sara also turned her attention to Mark, almost daring him

to say what she knew he would. "Do you think Win killed himself, too?"

Mark nodded. "I'm sorry, Sara."

She shook her head in disappointment as if scolding two misbehaving children. "You can't seriously believe that Win jumped out of a plane and stabbed himself. It's unthinkable."

"But not impossible," Mark said. "Which is what murdering him that way would be."

"Please, Mark, you can't let them get away with murder. There has to be a way to prove what they did," she said. "Win deserves justice. So do our children."

"I know how much you want to blame somebody for his death, especially those who made his last few months so difficult," he said. "But suicide is the only logical explanation for what happened. The evidence backs it up."

"What evidence?" she asked.

Mark carefully walked her through it, point by point, in exhaustive detail. The blood spatter pattern on Brant's chute proved he was definitely stabbed after he jumped out of the plane. The skydiving instructor's videotape proved that no one got close enough to Brant to kill him. And the forensic examination of Brant's parachute proved that it hadn't been booby-trapped in some clever way to plunge a knife into his chest.

"And we know from you and his secretary that your husband was despondent about what was happening to his magazine."

"Win wasn't despondent, he was angry," she said. "There's a difference."

"He was taking antidepressants, perhaps for some time," Steve said. "It certainly appears that he was a deeply troubled man, apparently more than anyone knew, even those closest to him."

Her eyes flashed with anger. For an instant, Sara looked

as if she might leap across the desk and throttle Steve. But that moment passed, leaving behind a flush on her cheeks.

"My husband climbed cliffs with his bare hands, Detective. He swam with sharks. He rode in a balloon halfway across the globe. Those are not feats achieved by a man hobbled by sadness, doubt, or despair. Win was a relentlessly driven man who didn't let any obstacle get in his way. That drive, that unflagging self-confidence, took enormous strength, physically and emotionally. But he was human, and as much as he hated to admit it, he couldn't constantly sustain that drive. He had his occasional down days."

Sara looked past the Sloans to the family photos on her mantelpiece. "When you live at peak emotional and physical levels, those rare but inevitable depressions can be extreme. Occasionally, he needed my help. But my husband was, above all else, a fighter, a competitor, and a winner. He was always preparing for the next bigger, tougher challenge. It's what he lived for."

"Until he found an obstacle he couldn't overcome," Mark said.

"Like what?" she said.

Mark shrugged. "I don't know."

"How about the ruination of *Thrill Seeker* magazine and Brant Publications at the hands of his major investors?" Steve asked.

"Didn't you read the paper this morning, Detective?" she asked. "He would have beaten them."

"But at what price? To the public, your husband and *Thrill Seeker* were one and the same, like Hugh Hefner and *Playboy*," Steve said. "The magazine would have been destroyed by the scandal. Maybe he couldn't live with that."

"How dare you presume to know what my husband felt about anything," she said. "You didn't know him at all."

"No, we didn't," Mark said sadly. "But we know how he ended his life."

CHAPTER TWENTY-FOUR

Mark and Steve didn't say anything until they were outside and walking to the car.

"That's it for me, case closed," Steve sighed. "It's no longer a homicide investigation. Cops with calculators will take over now."

"You sound disappointed," Mark said.

"I wish it was a murder."

"Because you disliked Brant's partners? Or because you feel bad for Brant's family?"

"Because I feel cheated," Steve said. "I was looking forward to you figuring out how it was done."

"I did," Mark said.

"Yeah, but it doesn't feel quite the same, or as satisfying, without you laying out the clues and exposing a murderer."

"Not every homicide investigation ends that way."

"It does when you're around," Steve said. "I'm almost embarrassed to admit this, but there was a moment back in Dr. Everden's office when I thought you were going to surprise me by revealing she killed him."

"It's a suicide, Steve," Mark said. "And even if for argument's sake we say it wasn't, Sara was on the ground with her kids and the families of the other skydivers when Brant was killed. She couldn't have stabbed him."

"I know. I was telling you what I felt, I didn't say it was logical or rational." Steve opened the passenger door for his father, then walked around and got into the driver's seat. Once they were both in the car and buckled up, Steve started the ignition and caught his dad looking at him curiously.

"What?" Steve asked.

"Why did you think I was going to accuse Sara of murder?"

"I suppose it was the way you spoke to her and what you said. There was a wariness about it," Steve said. "It was like you were playing her."

"Remind me never to play poker with you."

Steve looked incredulously at his dad. "You *do* think she killed her husband."

"Of course not," Mark said. "Winston Brant's death was absolutely, positively, unquestionably a suicide."

Steve nodded and was about to pull into traffic, when Mark spoke again.

"But she was lying."

The car came to a jolting halt, its nose out in traffic, as Steve stomped on the brake. He abruptly shifted the car into reverse, backed sharply into the parking space again, and turned to face his father.

"Lied about what?" Steve asked calmly.

"She knew his death was a suicide," Mark said. "I think she knew it all along, despite everything she said today."

"She may have guessed, but that's not a crime," Steve said. "Unless she was hiding a suicide note so she could get her hands on the life insurance settlement."

"Sara doesn't need money," Mark said. "She's already an extremely wealthy woman."

"She is now," Steve said.

"She didn't kill her husband for his money," Mark said. "Winston Brant killed himself."

"So you keep saying," Steve said. "If you're convinced

that's what happened, and that she isn't trying to swindle the insurance company, what difference does it make whether she knew it or not?"

"It doesn't," Mark said. "But I don't think Brant killed himself because he couldn't live with the downfall of his magazine."

"Then why?"

Mark shook his head. "I wish I knew."

"Are you going to keep poking around?"

"It's none of my business," Mark said.

Steve stared at his father, dumbfounded. "This from the same man who just spent days investigating an *attempted* suicide?"

"I'd only be hurting the family to satisfy my own curiosity."

"That never stopped you before," Steve said.

"I could tell myself I was serving a greater purpose, seeing that justice is served or, in Rebecca's case, preventing a death. That's not the situation this time," Mark said. "I'll just have to accept the fact that some mysteries in life will never be solved."

Steve doubted his father could do that any more than he could surrender himself completely to someone, but he thought it was nice that Mark was willing to try.

Maybe, Steve thought, he'd try to overcome his nature, too, which reminded him that he ought to give Lissy Dearborn a call. There was no reason he couldn't date her now.

But first, he'd have to buy a coffee table and a big red ribbon to tie around it.

Steve dropped Mark off at the beach house and went in to headquarters, where investigators from the Securities and Exchange Commission and the FBI were already huddled in the conference room with Abel Marsh, going over Brant's financial records.

He popped his head into the conference room long enough to introduce himself and confirm he wasn't needed, then went to his desk to work on his report. It took him three hours to write up everything and deliver it to Captain Newman, who took only fifteen minutes to scan it and wave Steve back into his cramped office.

To Steve's surprise, the captain accepted without question his conclusion that Brant committed suicide and seemed pleased the Feds could run with it on their own.

Steve was turning to leave Newman's office, astonished that he'd come through the meeting unscathed, when the captain asked him if he knew how much it cost, per hour, to operate a helicopter. Perhaps, he added, Steve would like an LAPD chopper to pick him up at home from now on and save him the stress of dealing with traffic.

Steve assumed these were rhetorical questions, kept his mouth shut, and turned to face a verbal lashing. He was smart enough not to interrupt, and certainly not to argue that he'd only appropriated the helicopter because he feared for his father's life. He knew that defense wouldn't score him any sympathy from Newman. Black-and-whites were on their way to the scene and, in fact, arrived at the same time as the chopper. If anything, the captain would attack him for letting personal matters affect his judgment.

So he kept quiet, nodded his head often, and apologized for his mistake. Without getting an argument, the captain seemed unable to muster up any more abuse so, in frustration, he simply ordered Steve to get out.

All in all, Steve figured this was one for the win column and called it a day.

BBQ Bob's was packed for dinner that night, so Mark had to take a stool at the counter. Thanks to Dr. Atkins and the low-carb carnivore craze, Dr. Travis was kept busy, taking orders and bussing tables, until Mark was nearly finished with his ribs.

Jesse took a break, drawing himself a Coke and leaning against the bar while Mark picked at his ribs and told him about what happened in Sara Everden's office. Mark also passed along the sentiments Steve shared afterwards in the car.

"I wasn't even there, and I feel cheated, too," Jesse said.

"So do I," Mark replied.

"You do?" Jesse set down his glass and poked at the crushed ice with his straw.

"Somehow it feels incomplete," Mark said. "You have any idea how hard it is to eat spareribs with one hand?"

"You're changing the subject." Jesse lifted his glass and took a mouthful of sweet, slushy crushed ice.

"I know," Mark said.

"Why?"

"Because I'm embarrassed. I've got barbeque sauce all over myself."

"That's not what you're embarrassed about," Jesse said, embarrassed himself because he was talking through a mouthful of ice.

"I'm saying I could use a napkin." Mark raised his sauce-smeared face up to Jesse.

Jesse picked up a napkin and wiped Mark's chin.

"Could you get my mustache, too?"

He did.

"Thanks," Mark said.

It seemed strangely intimate, this polite favor he'd just done for Mark. No more so than dressing a wound, pulling out an IV or a Foley catheter, and yet somehow it was.

"Where's Steve?" Mark asked. "Isn't he supposed to be helping you out around here?"

"He called a couple hours ago, said something about having to buy a coffee table."

"We've got a coffee table."

"There's some big sale at Ikea that ends tonight," Jesse said. "He didn't want to miss it."

"If we had to get a coffee table, it wouldn't be one that we've got to snap together," Mark said.

Jesse took another mouthful of ice, then ditched the glass in the dish bucket under the counter. "I haven't forgotten my question, Mark. What are you embarrassed about?"

"My own selfishness."

"I've never known you to be selfish," Jesse said. "In fact, your selflessness has nearly gotten you killed on a number of occasions. Yesterday comes to mind."

"Sara Everden lost her husband, her kids lost a father, and the worst thing is, it didn't have to happen." Mark pushed his plate away. "Why would I want to add to their pain?"

"Who says you do?" Jesse wondered what it was about a bar that made people open up to whoever was behind it. It couldn't be alcohol, because they only served beer and wine, and Mark wasn't drinking any. Maybe it had something to do with sitting alone, on a stool, because until the other day in the doctors' lounge, Mark never talked to him like this.

"Because that's what I'm bound to cause them if I go ahead and do what I can't seem to stop myself from doing," Mark said.

"Doing what?" Jesse knew the answer, but he wanted to hear Mark say it.

"I want to know why Brant killed himself and there's no reason I have to know," Mark said. "None at all."

"Why does there need to be a reason?" There was also something about a bar that made the person standing behind it wiser than he usually was, or so it seemed to Jesse at that moment.

"To justify me asking questions, poking at open wounds, prying into people's personal lives."

Jesse shrugged. "I'd like to know."

"Know what?"

"Why Winston Brant killed himself." Jesse cleared Mark's plate and stuck it in the dish bucket. "I bet his kids would like to know, too. Even his wife."

"They might not appreciate me asking right now."

"So don't ask them," Jesse said.

"Now that you mention it, there is someone else I could talk to," Mark said. "You've become a bad influence."

"I learned from the best," Jesse said.

CHAPTER TWENTY-FIVE

When Mark got home, he found Steve sitting on the living room floor, assembling a coffee table using tiny L-shaped, hexagonal Allen wrenches to drive in special screws that had matching hexagonal sockets.

The vaguely art-deco table was made of particleboard with a fake wood veneer and came in about twenty separate pieces, cut to fit with predrilled holes.

"What's the table for?" Mark asked.

"It's an invitation for a date," Steve said. "I'm sending it to Rebecca's roommate, Lissy Dearborn."

"Nowadays you have to give a woman a coffee table when you ask her for a date?"

"It's sort of an inside joke."

"I see," Mark said, though he didn't understand at all. "So are you still feeling cheated at the way the Brant case turned out?"

"I'm getting over it," Steve said, eyeing his father suspiciously. "Why?"

"Does the press know the homicide investigation is closed and that Brant's death was a suicide?"

"Not yet," Steve said. "The department won't make an official announcement until tomorrow afternoon. There's still time for you to figure out it was a murder."

"It wasn't," Mark said.

"Damn," Steve said.

"I'd still like to know why Brant killed himself," Mark said. "There's one person besides his wife who might be able to tell me."

"Grace Wozniak," Steve said. "His secretary."

"She knew him all his life," Mark said. "I'd like to ask her a few questions tomorrow morning."

"Go ahead," Steve said.

"I think it might go better with you there," Mark said.

Steve gave his father a knowing look. "To give her the impression that there's still an active police investigation and by answering your questions, she's answering mine."

"I can't be held responsible for any assumptions she might make because you happen to be standing there."

"I can," Steve said.

"Does that mean you won't come?" Mark asked.

"I wouldn't miss it."

"Why is that?"

Steve smiled. "Because you wouldn't keep asking questions if you weren't onto something."

"I'm not onto anything," Mark said.

"You will be," Steve said.

For the first time in days, Mark didn't dream of Rebecca Jordan throwing herself out a window, but he slept fitfully that night. He couldn't find a comfortable sleeping position with his rigid left arm and managed to whack himself twice in the head with the hard cast.

He got up before Steve, picked up the morning paper, and saw that the Brant case had made the front page for a second day in a row. The scandal caused the value of Brant Publications stock to plummet. Shares that formerly traded at nearly three dollars fell to a mere fifty cents.

There was a brief mention in the article that the homicide

investigation into Winston Brant's death was ongoing and that police officials remained "tight-lipped" on the details.

Steve emerged showered and shaved at seven thirty, intending to casually read the paper over a cup of coffee and a light breakfast. But he could feel Mark staring at him, radiating his eagerness to get going.

So within twenty minutes, Steve read the story on Brant, swallowed a cup of coffee, and arranged for a messenger service to pick up and deliver the coffee table to Lissy. By eight o'clock they were headed for Orange County, driving through a McDonald's on the way for McMuffins and coffee.

The rush hour traffic on the southbound 405 freeway moved at speeds barely above idle. It took them nearly two hours to make the drive south to Newport Beach. When they arrived, the Brant Publications building was ringed with television news vans. Steve's arrival in one of the LAPD's unmarked Ford Crown Victoria sedans didn't go unnoticed by the reporters, who quickly crowded his vehicle. It made Steve wonder who the department thought it was fooling by calling the cars "unmarked"; they were every bit as obvious as a black-and-white patrol unit.

Steve gave no comment to the reporters and hustled himself and his father into the building. They were met in the lobby almost immediately by Detective Abel Marsh, who emerged from a conference room packed with SEC investigators and FBI agents sifting through stacks of financial records.

"I thought this was a federal production now," Steve said to Marsh.

"It is. I've been assigned as department liaison to the federal agencies investigating Brant's books. What are you doing here?"

"Cleaning up a few details," Steve said.

"On a suicide?"

"Have you met my father?" Steve said, clumsily changing the subject. "Dad, this is Abel Marsh, the LAPD's top forensic accountant."

"Pleased to meet you." Mark offered his hand. "Dr. Mark Sloan."

Marsh gave him a firm handshake. "I count myself among your admirers, Doctor. We ought to sit down and talk shop sometime."

"Shop?"

"Forensics," Marsh said. "You deal with the relation between medical facts and murder. I do the same thing, only with numbers. We aren't that much different, you and I."

"Except I can't balance my checkbook," Mark said.

"And I can't reattach a severed thumb, though I tried once."

"Who hasn't?" Steve said. "Anything new come up in your investigation?"

Marsh scowled and ushered them across the lobby, out of earshot of the agents in the conference room. "They're closing me out. I'm basically just fetching coffee. But I picked up some interesting chatter on the street."

"What street?" Steve asked.

"Wall Street," Marsh replied, lowering his voice. "Brant's wife is gobbling up the devalued shares of this company for pennies apiece. And she's got the leverage now to get Perrow and his gang to sell her their stake in Brant Publications for pocket change. Way things are going, what's left of this magazine will belong to the Brant family again once this is all over. Looks like there's a happy ending after all."

Steve and Mark went upstairs and found Grace Wozniak still manning her post outside Winston Brant's office, though most of the file cabinets were gone. About the only thing left standing was her stuffed dog Starchy, which she was carefully grooming with a brush. She greeted the Sloans with a pleasant smile.

"I'm surprised you're still here," Mark said. "Isn't your job done?"

"Protecting Win's interests is even more important now than ever before," she said. "And I want to be here if the investigators need any help."

"Does that include reporters from the *Los Angeles Times*?" Steve asked.

Grace chewed on her lip as she considered her response, then came to a decision, setting her dog brush aside and looking Steve directly in the eye. "If you're asking if I was their anonymous source, the answer is yes."

"Did you ever consider that telling the *Times* all about the financial games going on here could damage our investigation?"

The color suddenly drained from Grace's face. "No, of course not. I never thought of that. I just wanted to expose what those bastards did to him, to this company."

"What was the hurry?" Steve said. "It all would have come out."

"Don't be so sure," she said. "Dean Perrow is a major fund-raiser for the mayor and Virgil Nyby has a media empire in this town. Between them, they wield enough power to make sure what they did to this magazine is buried with Win's body."

"Then why didn't you tell me or Steve about Brant's secret files to begin with?" Mark asked.

"I didn't know about them," Grace said. "When you came here, you said you'd heard from Sara that Win was planning on fighting back, that he was going to make a major announcement at the shareholders' meeting. It made me curious. What was his announcement going to be? Was that what he'd been killed for? After you left, I went into his computer and found his hidden, encrypted files. It didn't take me long to figure out his password and open up the files."

"Detective Marsh said he had to hack into them," Steve said.

"He did. I showed him the hidden files, but I didn't tell him the password. I didn't want him to know that I'd already looked at them."

"Thanks to your leak," Mark said, "Brant stock is nearly valueless now."

"Serves those bastards right," she said.

"Including all the rank-and-file Brant employees who own stock?" Steve asked.

"They're hurting now," Grace said. "But it will bounce back under Sara's leadership."

"You knew Sara would buy back the stock?" Mark asked.

Grace nodded. "She was absolutely devoted to her husband. She knows what this magazine meant to him. He would have wanted the family to control the magazine again. Going public was the biggest mistake he ever made. He lost more than his magazine. He lost his soul."

"It must have torn him up, seeing the evidence of what they'd done and knowing what it would cost him to expose their crimes," Steve said. "He had to know the scandal could destroy him and the magazine too."

She nodded. "He managed to hide his pain from everyone, but I could see it."

"His wife saw it, too," Mark said. "She was treating him with Prozac."

Grace looked surprised. "Win didn't believe in taking any drugs except for necessary antibiotics and vaccines. He believed that taking anything else was a sign of physical, mental, and moral weakness. He had a phrase for it: 'abdicating command of your own body.'"

"Then he must have changed his views, because he abdicated in a big way," Steve said. "Brant killed himself."

Grace jerked back, her eyes wide, her mouth agape. *"What?"*

"He wasn't murdered," Mark said. "He jumped out of that plane and stabbed himself."

"Win wouldn't do that," Grace said.

"I guess you didn't know him as well as you thought," Steve said. "Isn't it possible he killed himself rather than face the scandal?"

"He wouldn't have given those bastards the satisfaction," she said. "Then they really would have beaten him."

"Then what would he have killed himself for?" Mark asked.

"Nothing," she said, then seemed to change her mind. "Unless it was for a greater good."

"You mean like throwing himself on a live grenade to save his platoon," Mark said. "Or cutting his rope to save the other climbers on the line."

"His death would have meaning, it could stand as a victory," Grace said. "I can't believe he died this way. I didn't see the slightest hint that he was thinking of ending his own life."

"You didn't see it," Steve said. "Maybe Sara did."

"What difference does it make now?" Grace said. "He's dead."

"If she knew he was suicidal and hid it from us, she could be guilty of fraud," Steve said.

"You can't be serious," Grace said. "She's just lost her husband. How can you even consider tormenting her like that?"

"She was in line for a huge life insurance settlement, which gave her a couple million reasons not to reveal he was suicidal and to encourage us to believe he was murdered," Steve said. "That's a criminal act."

Grace looked more shocked now than she did before. "Oh my God, you're right. He *did* kill himself."

Mark stared at her, trying to understand her sudden change of heart. "Why do you believe it now when you didn't two minutes ago?"

"Because of what he just said." Grace wagged a finger at Steve. "Win was afraid you'd do this, that you'd go after Sara."

"What are you talking about?" Steve asked.

She got up and walked across the outer office to a painting of a whaling ship on stormy seas and lifted it away from the wall to reveal a safe.

Grace quickly spun the combination, opened the safe, and pulled out a sealed envelope.

"I found this in the safe yesterday. There was a note for me from Win attached to it, instructing me to give the envelope to the police if Sara was ever in trouble." Her hand trembled. "I didn't understand what the hell he meant. Now I do."

She handed the envelope to Steve. Mark stood beside Steve and looked over his shoulder. The envelope was sealed with wax and notarized, signed by Winston Brant and the notary on the morning of Brant's death.

Steve took a letter opener from Grace's desk and carefully slit the top of the envelope, then used a rubber glove from his pocket to remove the folded paper inside. It was a handwritten letter from Winston Brant that began with four simple words:

I killed myself today.

CHAPTER TWENTY-SIX

I killed myself today.

The alternative was succumbing to my disease—betrayed by the rapid and unstoppable deterioration of my flesh, wasting away until I became a helpless prisoner of my own useless body. My last days would have been a waking nightmare.

Instead, I saw how I could spare myself and my family the slow, unbearable torture of my certain demise. I saw how my death could be used to vanquish my enemies and assure my loved ones of a happy and prosperous future.

I decided to leap out of an airplane and stab myself in the heart before I reached the ground. I wanted my last moments to be filled with the exhilaration of life, floating above the earth, the wind and the sun in my face.

But there were other considerations as well.

I wanted to die in an extraordinary way that would draw enormous attention to me and, more importantly, the three men on the airplane. I believed the intense scrutiny by the media and law enforcement would reveal the crimes committed by those men for all to see. I hoped the ensuing scandal would remove those parasites from the company, lower the stock price, and allow my family to assume control of the magazine that was, in so many ways, an extension of myself.

If you are reading this, then I have failed and my loving wife Sara has become entangled in my vengeful machinations. For that I am deeply sorry . . . and solely responsible. She had no part in this whatsoever. Nobody knew what I intended to do.

Suicide was my choice, one I made alone in the solitude of my own hopelessness and as an act of fury at the cruel unfairness of my affliction. Perhaps I failed to save my company, but I surely conquered my fate, forging my own destiny instead of blithely accepting the horrific one chosen for me.

I face my death satisfied that I died as I lived . . . on my own terms.

Winston Brant

Sara Everden was quiet for a long time after she read the note, then she handed it back across her desk to Steve, who sat beside Mark in the same chairs they'd been in that morning.

"He had ALS," she said.

"What's that?" Steve asked.

"Amyotrophic lateral sclerosis, commonly known as Lou Gehrig's disease," Mark said. "It's an incurable disease of the nerve cells of the spinal cord that results in the gradual loss of muscle function."

"It starts in the extremities and then becomes more insidious, until you can't speak, swallow, or breathe," she said. "The mind, however, stays sharp, trapped in a body that no longer functions. It's like being buried alive."

It was a horrible death for anyone but especially for a man who prized his physicality as much as Winston Brant. There was only one way Brant could overcome this obstacle, Mark thought, and he took it.

Steve glared at Sara. "When were you going to tell us this?"

"Never," she said.

Her unapologetic reply only made Steve angrier. "When did he tell you he was going to kill himself?"

"He didn't, though I suppose I probably should have realized he'd never allow himself to die this way."

Mark glanced at Steve, shaking his head slightly, signaling him to back off. If Steve continued attacking her, she'd shut up and throw them out before they got the details Mark wanted.

"When did he find out he had ALS?" Mark asked softly, trying to be as nonconfrontational as possible.

"Only a few weeks ago." Sara sighed heavily. "Win was feeling weak and lethargic. He tried to hide it from everyone, even me. As if a wife wouldn't notice, especially one who practices medicine. He denied anything was wrong, of course, but finally he agreed to see a doctor, as long as it was me and nobody knew about it."

"Why was he so concerned about anyone knowing he was seeing a doctor?" Mark asked.

"His reputation was based on his strength, his physical abilities," she said. "He didn't want anyone to suspect for a moment that he experienced weakness of any kind."

"Didn't he realize he was human?" Mark said.

"You wouldn't believe how many times I tried to remind him of that," she said. "I don't think he finally accepted it until the moment he decided to kill himself."

She opened a drawer in her desk, pulled out a file, and opened it in front of her. "I suspected a thyroid condition, something simple and easily treatable. But then the blood work came back."

Sara handed Mark the lab results. He took them with his free hand and studied them intently.

"The tests show elevated levels of creatine phosphokinase and aldolase," Mark said, which he then clarified for Steve's benefit. "They're enzymes in the muscles. As muscles lose mass, the enzymes enter the bloodstream. It doesn't specifically indicate ALS, though the results are certainly troubling for a man of his physical fitness."

"So I did a battery of tests." Sara slid more pages in front of Mark to review as she talked. "Including a muscle biopsy, a spinal tap, and an MRI."

Mark studied the stack of test results and, after a time, nodded grimly. "It's pretty conclusive."

"I still didn't want to believe it," Sara said. "But Lisa Klink and Morgan Gendel confirmed my fears."

Mark only knew Dr. Klink, a top rheumatologist at UCLA Medical Center, from listening to her fascinating talks on antiphospholipid antibody syndrome at medical conventions. But he knew Dr. Gendel well, a highly respected neurologist Mark personally recruited five years ago to join the Community General staff.

"Telling Win he had ALS was the hardest thing I've ever had to do," she said, her voice barely a whisper, tears welling in her eyes at the memory.

"Did anyone else besides you and his doctors know?" Mark said.

She shook her head, the motion spilling her tears. "He was adamant about that. Not even our kids knew. He was afraid of what it would do to the company if word got out. Someone with an incurable, muscle-wasting disease is hardly a winning image for a magazine that celebrates a man's ability to exceed his physical limitations. Circulation could fall drastically. And even if he'd only told the board, it would have been just the excuse they needed to push him out completely."

Mark could imagine what Brant saw in his limited future. If he'd let the disease take its course, he would have watched helplessly while his body and his life's work deteriorated around him. Every day truly would have been a waking nightmare for him. Brant knew he only had a short time before his symptoms became obvious and he lost the ability to do anything for himself. It made sense that he would use those precious weeks for one last, decisive victory, to give his death meaning and purpose.

"You've lied to us every time we've seen you," Steve said. "Do you really expect us to believe you didn't know what he was going to do?"

"I don't care what you believe," Sara said, giving Steve an icy stare. "Win committed suicide, so you have no official standing. His health was a private matter and I'm under no obligation to share anything with you. I did so as a courtesy, which you have abused. We're finished now. Tomorrow I'm burying my husband and we're going on with our lives."

She gathered up the papers, placed her husband's medical file back in her desk, and slammed the drawer shut.

Mark and Steve got up from their seats.

"I need to take this note from your husband," Steve said. "I'll get it back to you in a few days."

That was Steve's good-bye. He went directly to the door without looking back.

Mark lingered for a moment, reached across her desk, and gently took Sara's hand. He could feel her hand shaking, ever so slightly.

"I apologize if anything we've said or done today has upset you," Mark said. "I can't imagine what you've had to endure over the last few weeks. The last thing I want to do is add to your pain."

"I appreciate it, Mark," Sara said.

"If there is anything I can do to help you or your family, please don't hesitate to call."

He let go of her hand, gave her his warmest smile, and left the office.

* * *

Steve was waiting for Mark outside, leaning against the car, his arms crossed over his chest, his cheeks red with anger.

"Why didn't Amanda discover Brant had ALS when she did her autopsy?"

"If he was in the earliest stages of the disease, the muscle wasting wouldn't be immediately noticeable," Mark said. "And she wasn't looking for indications of anything like ALS in his blood work. Unless the disease was further along, it's just not something that would arise in the course of a routine autopsy."

"The guy was stabbed after jumping out of an airplane," Steve said. "There's nothing routine about that."

"There is if you're looking at the immediate cause of death, not the circumstances surrounding it," Mark said. "From Amanda's view, the cause of death wasn't a big mystery."

"Well, there's no mystery left anymore. We know how Brant was killed and why it happened," Steve said. "Satisfied now?"

Mark frowned. "Not really."

"You got the answers you wanted. Everything makes sense. What could possibly be bothering you now?"

"I don't know," Mark said. "Why don't we start with what's bothering *you*."

"I'm fine," Steve said.

"You're furious."

"I just hate being lied to," Steve said. "If I could throw her in jail for that, I would. She wasted a lot of our time for nothing."

"If wasting a person's time was a criminal offense, I could be sent to prison for life."

"Why did she lie to us?" Steve said. "That's what I still want to know."

"Because she wanted to preserve her husband's memory

as an icon of physical adventurism and masculinity," Mark said.

"While she buys up Brant Publications stock, which suddenly costs as much per share as a Krispy Kreme donut. Those aren't the actions of a grieving widow."

"One could argue that everything she's done has been on her husband's behalf," Mark said. "That even now she's fighting for, and protecting, what was important to him."

Steve gave his father a skeptical look. "'One could argue'?"

"Yes," Mark said. "One could."

"But not you."

"Not me," Mark said.

Steve smiled. "Now we're talking."

On the drive back to Los Angeles, Steve got two calls on his cell phone.

The first call was from Lissy Dearborn, thanking him for the coffee table and agreeing to go out to dinner with him the next night. She was taking some time off to help care for Rebecca, who would be returning home today and wasn't able to get around on her own with a leg and an arm in casts. Lissy told Steve that Tucker Mellish had sent over enough pastries to fill a bakery. Steve was already eager to see her, but the lure of fresh bear claws only made the prospect more tempting.

The second call was from Captain Newman, assigning Steve to a homicide investigation. Two homeless men got into a knife fight over a bag of Cheetos, leaving one of the combatants dead. There was no mystery who the killer was or how the murder was committed, so Mark didn't try to come up with an excuse to accompany Steve to the scene and his son didn't invite him.

Steve dropped Mark off at Community General and went directly to the crime scene. Mark went directly to his office, where he spent the next few hours catching up on the enormous stack of paperwork that had accumulated over the last several days.

He tried to concentrate on his work, but his thoughts kept wandering back and forth over his numerous conversations with Sara Everden, sampling bits and pieces seemingly at random.

Something wasn't fitting into place. He could feel it, almost like an itch, but couldn't identify it.

This persistent mental glitch was particularly irritating since, as far as Mark could tell, all the mysteries surrounding Brant's death were solved.

There was no doubt that Winston Brant killed himself and if there had been, the notarized suicide letter he'd left for Grace Wozniak removed any question. The letter not only confirmed how he died, but why. The few details Brant left out were neatly filled in by the test results in his medical file. Brant had an incurable, muscle-wasting disease. Rather than let the disease take its course, he concocted an attention-getting way of killing himself that would demand intense scrutiny and expose the criminal activities within his company.

And for the most part, his scheme worked. The police investigated, the financial misdealings were revealed, and the stock price of Brant Publications fell so low, his family was able to buy back control of the company.

There were no more questions left unanswered. All the facts were there and they fit together perfectly.

Except they didn't.

Where, or why, they didn't, Mark couldn't say. But the feeling that he was missing something wouldn't subside.

Or was it simply hunger?

Mark suddenly realized how long it had been since he'd eaten, and he was starving. He gave up on his paperwork and went down to the cafeteria for a late lunch.

While standing in line, waiting to pay for his macaroni and cheese, small Caesar salad, and slice of strawberry cheesecake, Mark spotted Dr. Morgan Gendel sitting at a table by himself, reading the newspaper and eating his last few bites of chocolate cake.

Mark picked up his tray and headed over to Dr. Gendel's table. "Mind if I join you?"

"Of course not, Mark." Dr. Gendel swept the newspapers off the table and set them on one of the empty chairs. "Sit down. It's good to see you."

Dr. Gendel was in his late forties with premature flecks of gray in his hair, which he tried to hide with a buzz cut. He was recently divorced, his ring finger still white where he'd worn his wedding band for fifteen years.

"What happened to you?" Dr. Gendel asked, his eyes drifting with concern from the bandage on Mark's head to the cast on his left arm.

"I was in a little car accident," Mark said, starting to eat. "I'm fine, it's my car that's in intensive care."

"Can it be saved?" Dr. Gendel asked.

"I hope not," Mark said, between mouthfuls of macaroni and cheese. "There are a lot of nice convertibles on the market these days."

"You don't have to tell me about it," Dr. Gendel said. "What do you think I bought myself as soon as the divorce was final? Didn't you notice the new SL in my parking space?"

"Does that mean your life is settling down?" Mark asked, sampling the salad. He couldn't remember the last time he was so hungry.

Dr. Gendel nodded. "Jerrilyn and I are getting along better now that we're divorced than we did over the last couple years. My daughter is handling it great and we see each other every weekend. It's the dating scene that's been hell."

"Has it changed a lot since you were single?"

"I'm rusty," Dr. Gendel said. "Besides, when I try asking women out, they look at my ring finger, see that white band, and think I'm some sleazy married guy cheating on his wife. I think I'm going to have to hold off on dating until my finger gets tan."

"Have you tried offering them a coffee table?"

Dr. Gendel gave Mark a bewildered look. "No, I can't say that ever occurred to me. Does it work?"

"It seems to," Mark said, then tipped his head towards the newspaper. "Did you read the story about the scandal at Brant Publications?"

"Yeah," Dr. Gendel said. "It's amazing how many ways there are to steal money."

"I understand Winston Brant was your patient," Mark said.

Dr. Gendel was surprised. "How did you know that?"

"I've been consulting with the police on the Brant homicide investigation," Mark said. "He wasn't murdered. Brant killed himself and I think you know why."

"I do?" Dr. Gendel said.

"I know Brant had ALS," Mark replied. "Sara told me they came to you."

"I suppose if Dr. Everden told you, then I'm not breaking any confidences talking about it now," Dr. Gendel sighed. "It's so sad. The truth is, a med student could have looked at the elevated muscle enzymes and the MRI film and made the same diagnosis I did. The areas on each side of the brain near the ventricles were intensely white on the MRI, clearly indicating high signal intensity in the corticospinal tracts."

"I wouldn't have wanted to tell a man like Winston Brant what he was facing."

"Neither would I," Dr. Gendel said.

Mark felt his pulse quicken. He dropped his fork and pushed aside his plate, his appetite immediately forgotten. "You didn't give him your diagnosis?"

"I never met him," Dr. Gendel said. "I spoke to Dr. Everden on the phone, she told me his symptoms, and then sent over his blood work, spinal fluid analysis, and the MRI for me to review."

"So you never even spoke to him," Mark said. "You looked everything over and called her back with your findings."

"I sent over a written opinion, too," Dr. Gendel said. "But I think I was just confirming what she already knew."

"I'm certain you were." Mark slid the cheesecake over to Dr. Gendel. "Thanks, you've been a big help."

"With what?" Dr. Gendel asked, but Mark was already out of his seat and on his way.

Dr. Gendel shrugged, picked up a fork, and started to eat his second dessert.

CHAPTER TWENTY-SEVEN

When Mark rushed into the morgue, Amanda was in the middle of performing an autopsy on a man who fell off his roof while replacing shingles and impaled himself on his wrought iron fence.

"I need your help, Amanda," he said, huffing out each word between deep breaths.

Amanda looked up from the chest wound she was measuring. "It looks like what you need is oxygen. You better sit down. Did you run over here from someplace?"

"Up the stairs," Mark said, taking a seat at her desk. "From the cafeteria."

"What's the big rush?"

"Winston Brant."

"He's not going to get any deader," Amanda said.

"He had ALS," Mark said, his breathing becoming regular.

She cocked an eyebrow. "I didn't see any signs when I opened him up. Are you sure?"

"No, I'm not," Mark said. "That's why I'd like you to do a muscle biopsy and examine his spinal tissues."

"I can't," she said.

"Of course, I understand," Mark said, gesturing towards the body on the table. "You've got a lot of other work without revisiting a suicide. I can prepare the samples here myself."

"That's not it," Amanda said. "Brant's body isn't here anymore. I released it to the family this morning. The mortuary came and picked him up hours ago."

Mark's throat went dry. He suddenly remembered the way Sara's hand was shaking when he held it. Was it from anger or fear?

He bolted up from his seat. "Drop what you're doing. We have to get that body back right away."

"You're going to need a search warrant," Amanda said.

"That's Steve's problem," Mark said.

Amanda draped a sheet over the corpse in front of her. "Let's go."

While Amanda drove the fifty miles south to Newport Beach, Mark worked his cell phone.

First Mark called Steve and told him about his conversation with Dr. Gendel.

"I think Winston Brant was completely healthy and was tricked into believing he had ALS by his wife."

"How?" Steve asked.

"The Prozac," Mark said. "He probably had no idea he was taking it. Maybe she spiked his food with it or told him it was vitamins. How she did it doesn't matter. I believe it was the pills that made him feel weak and listless."

"She examined him, ran the tests, and faked the results," Steve said.

"Or she used results from other patients and told him they were his."

"I can see how she fooled her husband," Steve said. "But how did she con the other doctors?"

"They never saw Brant themselves," Mark said. "They based their opinions solely on the test results."

"If you're right, that means she drove him to suicide."

"It's murder," Mark said. "Only she used blood tests and an MRI as her weapons."

"Can you prove any of this?"

"Not without Winston Brant's body," Mark said.

"I'll talk to a judge," Steve said. "If I can get a warrant, I'll meet you at the mortuary."

Next, Mark tracked Jesse down at BBQ Bob's and asked him to do some research on Dr. Everden and the patients she'd treated over the last few years.

"What are you looking for exactly?" Jesse asked.

"Any patients of hers who suffered from ALS."

"I'm glad to oblige," Jesse said. "But I'm not sure I can get what you need without bending some of the rules governing the confidentiality of medical records."

"Do what you have to do," Mark said. "But don't put your career at risk doing it."

"Good advice," Jesse said. "I'll make a deal with you. I'll follow it if you do."

It was a deal Mark couldn't make. And Jesse knew it.

Mark fidgeted nervously in his seat for the next hour as they inched slowly along the traffic-clogged freeway to the wealthy Orange County enclave.

The Richonen Brothers Mortuary looked more like a resort hotel than a funeral home, the low-lying glass-and-stone building surrounded by lush green grass and enormous burbling fountains.

Amanda had barely brought the morgue van to a stop in front when Mark jumped out and hurried inside. She caught up to him quickly, joining him in the immense entry, which was bathed in sunlight by a huge skylight.

"Slow down, Mark. You're not going to get anywhere without me," she said.

It was true. Mark was merely an anxious man with a bandaged face and an arm in a sling. Amanda had all the authority and she was displaying it to full effect. Her Los Angeles County Medical Examiner ID was clipped to her bright blue Windbreaker, which had the county insignia on the chest and the words MEDICAL EXAMINER stenciled in big yellow letters on the back.

They were met almost immediately by a somber young man in a perfectly tailored suit. Mark figured somber was at the top of the list of qualities required for the job.

"Who are you?" Amanda asked, taking charge.

"Emil Richonen, the funeral director," he said in carefully enunciated English. "How may I help you?"

"I'm Dr. Amanda Bentley from the LA County medical examiner's office and this is Dr. Mark Sloan, homicide consultant with the LAPD. We need Winston Brant's body back."

"I'm afraid that's not possible," Richonen said carefully.

"The search warrant is on the way," Amanda said.

"That's irrelevant," Richonen said. "He's being cremated."

"Now?" Mark said in dismay.

"The body was placed in the cremation chamber fifteen minutes ago," the funeral director said.

"I'm sorry, Mark," Amanda said.

Mark did some quick mental calculations. The body would be wrapped in plastic and cremated in a casket. Depending on the type of casket and the size, weight, and body fat of the corpse, he knew the incineration could take as long as an hour and a half. Once the cremator door closed, a giant blowtorch aimed at the head of the casket would spit out a stream of flame. The coffin would ignite first, then collapse in on the corpse, burning it from the outside in. The spinal cord would be the last portion of the body touched by fire.

They might not be too late.

"Take us there now," Mark said.

"Surely you're not serious," Richonen said, glancing at

Amanda for support. For a moment, she looked like she agreed with him, but then her expression changed.

"You heard the man," Amanda said. "Move your ass."

Richonen led them through the casket showroom, behind a door, and down a set of stairs to the basement, which was dominated by a giant, square, stainless steel cremator, a long conveyor belt leading to the mouth.

A mortuary worker stood nearby, keeping a watchful eye on the computer display mounted on a podium, monitoring the temperature, the indicator reading fourteen hundred degrees Fahrenheit. He was a heavyset man in his thirties, with a nose that had been broken so many times it was nearly flat.

"Shut it down and get the body out of there," Mark said.

"We can't do that," the flat-nosed man protested.

Amanda shoved her ID in his face. "Do it."

The worker looked to Richonen for approval. Richonen nodded reluctantly. Cursing to himself, the worker hit a series of switches, powering down the gas incinerator.

"Stand back," the worker said. "That coffin is going to come out spewing hellfire."

Amanda glanced at the wall beside the cremator, found the fire extinguisher, and held it steady, ready for action.

"Here it comes," the worker said, pressing a button.

The metal mouth of the cremator slid open automatically to reveal the coffin inside, enveloped in flames. The heat immediately drove Amanda, Mark, and Richonen back towards the stairs.

"I'll push it to you from the back of the cremator," the worker yelled. "Douse the fire or this whole room could go up in flames."

The flat-nosed man scrambled to the rear of the cremator, put on a pair of protective goggles, then picked up a long-handled rake. He opened the back door of the cremation chamber and, wincing against the intense heat and the flying embers, pushed the rake against the head of the coffin, easing the box forward.

As the coffin slid towards Amanda at the opening of the cremator, she sprayed it with foam, dousing the flames.

The coffin, devoured by fire, disintegrated into glowing embers, revealing the smoking, black corpse inside. The room immediately filled with black smoke and the putrid smell of burning flesh.

"You better hope that warrant gets here, Dr. Bentley," Richonen said evenly, holding a monogrammed silk handkerchief to his face. "Or that is what your career will smell like."

Amanda sprayed everything again, making certain the fire was dead. The foam smothered the smoke and most of the smell that came with it. She dropped the extinguisher, put on a pair of heavy gloves she found nearby, then grabbed Brant's foam-covered corpse by the ankles and pulled him swiftly onto the conveyor belt.

Mark grimaced against the smell and leaned over the body, studying it.

"What do you think?" Amanda asked. "Is he too far gone?"

"We won't know until we cut him open."

That's when Mark heard someone coming down the stairs. He turned to see Steve standing on the steps, surveying the scene in front of him in disbelief.

"Hey, Steve," Mark said. "Glad you could make it."

Steve shook his head. "You can't do anything the easy way, can you, Dad?"

"Do you have the search warrant?" Amanda asked.

"Hardly matters at this point, does it?" Steve said, tipping his head towards the smoking, charred corpse on the conveyor.

"It does to me," Richonen said. "I need to know who is going to pay for this outrage."

Steve produced a paper from inside his jacket, much to Mark and Amanda's relief. "Send the bill to the friendly citizens of Los Angeles County."

Mark and Amanda wore protective goggles, surgical masks, rubber gloves, and blue scrubs. They stood on either side of Winston Brant's charred corpse, which was laid out facedown on a stainless steel autopsy table in the Community General morgue.

The corpse had cooled considerably in the chilled cabin of the morgue van on the ride back to West Los Angeles. Any resemblance the body once bore to Winston Brant was gone.

It hardly looked human anymore.

"Are we all set?" Amanda asked.

Mark nodded.

Amanda took a scalpel and expertly cut through the burnt flesh to expose a section of the spinal column.

Mark peered over her shoulder and examined the scorched spinal column, looking for the least damaged section.

The spinal cord itself was a rubbery white strand about the thickness of a finger. The collection of nerves ran up through the canal in the center of the vertebrae. Nerves branched off from the cord every inch or so, passing through other openings in the vertebrae and out to the rest of the body.

Mark pointed to a portion of the spine near the shoulder. "This area looks like it came through relatively unscathed, all things considered."

Amanda picked up a pair of scissors and cut away some nerves from the spinal cord around the area Mark had chosen. "This is a first for me."

"You've never tried to extract a spinal tissue sample from an incinerated corpse?"

"Have you?" She used a scalpel to slice between two vertebrae, cutting a section of the spinal cord at the same time.

"Not lately," he said, holding out a sterile specimen pan.

With a pair of tweezers, she removed the inch-long piece of severed cord and placed it in Mark's specimen pan.

"This is a real long shot," she said. "You know that, don't you?"

"I know," Mark said. "But it's a chance worth taking."

He set the pan on the counter, picked up the tissue sample, and carefully washed it in the sink.

When the tissue sample was clean, Mark set it on a slide and cut off an eighth-of-an-inch section, which he placed in a tiny metal container that resembled the perforated side of a garlic press.

Mark wrapped the remaining section of spinal cord in polythene, put it back in the pan, and handed it to Amanda, who placed it in her microbiology safety cabinet in case they needed it for future testing.

He slid the metal container with the sample into a machine that would bathe the tissue in formalin and then seal it in wax to make it easier to cut into micro-thin slices for analysis.

It would be twelve hours before the process, known as "fixing" the specimen, was complete and he could continue with the testing.

There was nothing more Mark could do now.

He knew the next twelve hours of waiting and uncertainty would pass with excruciating slowness. But he took some solace in knowing that the night would be even longer for Sara Everden, who surely had guessed why he wanted her husband's body and what he must be doing.

CHAPTER TWENTY-EIGHT

Mark was wrong about one thing. He hardly noticed the time go by at all.

He'd accumulated a considerable sleep debt over the last few days and he paid it off that night. After a light dinner at home, he went to bed and passed out the instant his head hit the pillow. He slept dreamlessly and even managed not to club himself with his cast.

The phone rang at seven a.m., waking him from his deep sleep. It was Amanda, calling from the pathology lab. She'd processed and examined Brant's spinal tissue.

Using a microtome, she'd sliced the tissue into very thin, translucent sections. She stained the slices with hematoxylin and eosin, put them on slides, and studied them under a microscope.

"What did you see?" Mark asked.

"It's what I *didn't* see." She took a deep breath. "No degeneration or scarring of the lateral spinal nerve tracts."

"Thank you, Amanda." Mark hung up, put on his bathrobe, and walked into the kitchen, where he found Steve dressed and waiting, badge and gun already clipped to his belt.

"Winston Brant was a perfectly healthy man," Mark said. "He killed himself for nothing."

"Oh, it was for something," Steve said. "Let's ask Sara Everden what it was, shall we?"

Mark frowned and glanced at his watch. "Guess we're in for another Egg McMuffin breakfast and a long drive to Newport Beach."

Steve shook his head. "We're going out for a leisurely breakfast someplace on the water. I'll send a black-and-white to pick her up. She can sit in traffic for hours. That's only the beginning of the punishment she deserves."

The harsh light of the interrogation room wasn't kind to Dr. Sara Everden. It wasn't kind to anyone. The hateful snarl on her face as she sat across the table from Mark and Steve didn't help her appearance much either.

"This is an outrage," Sara hissed. "My lawyer will be here any minute."

"I hope he's good, because you're going to need him," Steve said. "You're charged with violating penal code sections 148.5, 205, 401, and 487. You know what all those numbers add up to? Thirty years in prison, minimum. Considering the heinous nature and depraved indifference of your crimes, it might take the jury as long as ten minutes to reach their guilty verdict."

"I haven't committed any crime," Sara said.

"You made your husband believe he was suffering from ALS," Mark said.

"What was I supposed to do?" Sara said. "Lie to him? He had the right to know he was dying."

"Before your husband's body was fully incinerated, we were able to remove him from the cremator and recover a sample of his spinal tissues for testing," Mark said.

"You violated my husband's body for some twisted experiment?" she said. "You're a sick man with no respect for the dead or their families."

"Aren't you interested in what we found?" he asked.

"I want my husband to be able to rest in peace," she said.

"There was no sign of ALS whatsoever," Mark said. "He was completely healthy."

Her face went pale and she swallowed hard.

"Oh my God. My poor, sweet Win." Her chin quivered; her eyes filled with tears.

"Spare us the fake tears," Steve said. "We're in a budget crunch here. I have to pay for the Kleenex out of my own pocket."

She glowered at him. "You should be going after the doctors who misdiagnosed my husband instead of dragging *me* out of my house in handcuffs. It's their incompetence that killed my husband."

"The doctors gave you accurate opinions based on the test results you gave them," Mark said. "The problem is, none of those test results were your husband's."

Mark opened the file in front of him and held up what looked like a full-color x-ray of a skull.

"This is an MRI taken from one of your patients, Mr. Theodore Trucott, two years ago. He was diagnosed with ALS and died last summer."

He removed another film from the file and held it up beside the other one.

"This is the MRI supposedly taken from your husband a few weeks ago."

Mark held the two films side by side for a moment, then put one over the other. The images were a perfect match.

"Mr. Trucott's blood work and muscle biopsy are also identical to your husband's, though the names, dates, and labs have been changed," Mark said.

Sara didn't bother to look at the films. She stared past both men defiantly, fixing her eyes on her own reflection in the mirror behind them.

"The least you could have done was cherry-pick test results from the files of more than one of your patients," Steve said. "But then again, you never expected anyone to check up on you. Your husband wasn't going to tell anyone he had the disease and you sure as hell weren't going to."

"The whole con would have worked, except for one thing," Mark said. "You didn't count on your husband leaving behind a letter to defend you. If he hadn't been so worried about your well-being, we never would have known that he thought he had an incurable disease. You could have cremated his body and, with it, the only way to prove your crimes."

Sara shifted her gaze to Mark, who met her look of intense hatred without flinching.

"If you want to cry now," Steve said, "I'll be glad to supply the Kleenex."

Sara's cheeks flushed with rage. Her whole body began to shake. "I told Win not to take the company public, but he wouldn't listen to me. He invited those bastards in. And while he was off climbing mountains, he let those parasites take our money and our future."

"So you came up with a way to get back the company and all the wealth that came with it," Steve said. "And punish your husband for his unforgivable mistake at the same time."

"I was protecting my family," she said, slamming her fist on the table. "We would have lost our house, the yacht, the condo in Cabo, everything."

"Instead, your children lost their father," Mark said. "And now they're going to lose you, too."

Jesse watched the ruination of Sara Everden from behind the mirror in the observation room. He wanted to applaud, and he might have, too, if Captain Newman wasn't standing beside him, looking mean.

"Don't you love the way Mark does that?" Jesse asked. "Just once, I wish I could look a murderer in the eye and unpeel the lies, one by one, the way Mark does. How about you?"

The captain regarded Jesse as if he'd caught him urinating in public.

"Who are you again?" Captain Newman asked.

"Dr. Jesse Travis, I work with Mark. I'm the one who hunted down the Trucott medical records for him. You might say I made the case."

The captain walked past Jesse and out the door of the observation room without saying another word. They emerged to see Steve clapping his father enthusiastically on the back.

"*Now* I'm satisfied," Steve said with a grin, which evaporated when he saw the stern look on the captain's face.

Captain Newman approached Mark. "You actually interrupted a cremation and pulled the burning body out of the flames?"

"It's not something I recommend doing too often," Mark said affably.

"I would hope not," the captain replied, then walked back to the squad room, shaking his head.

Steve turned to his dad. "The fact the captain didn't chew us out is his way of saying how much he appreciates the good work we did."

"Then I'm flattered," Mark said.

"What does it mean when the captain looks at you like you're a cockroach?" Jesse asked.

"It's his way of saying he thinks you're a cockroach," Steve said. "You mind giving Dad a ride home?"

"No problem," Jesse said. "What've you got going?"

"A dinner date," Steve said.

"With who?" Jesse asked.

"Lissy Dearborn," Steve said. "Rebecca Jordan's roommate."

Mark glanced at his watch. "It's not even noon."

"Lissy works nights," Steve said. "So for her, it's almost dinnertime."

"Have a nice evening," Mark said. "Afternoon. Whatever."

"It's too soon for whatever," Steve said. "Maybe by the third or fourth date."

"That falls under the category of more than I want to know," Mark said.

"Not me," Jesse said. "I want all the details, in writing if possible."

Steve headed for the squad room, while Mark and Jesse started down the corridor in the opposite direction.

"How did Steve get a date with Rebecca's roommate?" Jesse asked.

"He got her a coffee table," Mark said.

Jesse thought about that for a moment. "Good thing he didn't get her a couch. They'd have to get married."

Steve arrived outside Lissy Dearborn's apartment in Culver City ten minutes early. He thought about driving around the block a few times or simply sitting in his car and listening to the radio until the appointed time. But he thought of her rugged humor, the meat cleaver in the wall, and the fresh bear claws, and couldn't wait.

He strode into her courtyard and thought about the day he had planned for them, beginning with grilled fish in a restaurant overlooking the beach, followed by a long walk along the water, and if she wasn't too tired, a movie in Santa Monica.

But he wasn't sticking to any preconceived plan. He'd let things play out naturally. Maybe they wouldn't leave the restaurant. Maybe they'd walk for miles. Maybe they'd drive to Las Vegas, play a few hands of blackjack, and drive back into the Los Angeles basin as the sun was rising on a new day.

Steve was so busy fantasizing about the day ahead, he didn't notice the front door of Lissy's apartment was ajar until he was standing right in front of it.

He knocked on the door. "Lissy? It's me, Steve."

The door swung inward enough for him to see the edge of the new coffee table he'd sent her.

He knocked again. "I know I'm a bit early, but I thought it was better than being a bit late."

Steve was chastising himself over the lame remark when the door crept inward even more and revealed two bare feet of someone lying on the floor. His heart skipped a beat and he felt a terrible sense of déjà vu, remembering how he first met Lissy, kicking open her door and finding her in a violent struggle with an intruder.

He pushed open the door and saw Lissy lying facedown on the carpet, groaning softly. He rushed inside, crouched beside her, and gently turned her over. She was unconscious, a gash under her right eye, the skin just beginning to swell underneath it, as if she'd just taken a punch.

Just taken . . .

The realization was beginning to sink in when Steve sensed the motion behind him. He was starting to whirl around, reaching for his gun, when the kick caught him in the side, knocking the wind out of him and sending him sprawling.

Before he could recover, the boot caught him in the face, rolling him over. Fighting for air and consciousness, Steve struggled to his knees, looking up just as Tom Wade brought the coffee table crashing down on his back.

One thought went through Steve's mind as the coffee table splintered apart and the blackness overtook his consciousness:

It's a good thing I can't afford nice furniture.

CHAPTER TWENTY-NINE

By the time Dr. Mark Sloan emerged from the monthly staff meeting, it was well after two p.m. His broken arm was aching and his stomach was growling.

He ambled over to the cafeteria and decided to reward himself with a pie doubleheader: chicken potpie for lunch and chocolate cream pie for dessert, and a milk shake to wash it down with.

It wasn't the healthiest lunch, but it quenched his appetite and made him forget all about how much his arm hurt. Eating chicken potpie, even a bad one like the cafeteria served, always evoked pleasant memories of his boyhood. His mother often made potpies for Mark because she knew she could get away with feeding him anything that way. Calling a meal a pie made it a treat, no matter how many vegetables were inside. They had beef potpie, chicken potpie, garden potpie, and his mother's favorite catchall, leftovers potpie.

Now, whenever Mark ate a potpie, he felt soothed, relaxed, even loved. It was amazing the medicinal and psychological healing powers one simple entrée could have, Mark thought. He devoured his pie, drank half his milk shake and, feeling renewed, went back to his office to finish up the paperwork he'd left behind yesterday.

Before getting started, however, he checked his voice

mail. There was only one call, from Dr. Mandel Yorder, the physician who treated Pike at the Family Doctor clinic in Panorama City. In consideration of the help Dr. Yorder gave him, Mark didn't mention the doctor's name in his statement to the police. It was a necessary omission, but one that bothered Mark anyway. He hated leaving a crooked doctor on the street.

"I gave the guy you sent over what he asked for," Dr. Yorder said on the recording. "But now I'm wondering what you were really after. Is it me? We need to talk."

Mark had no idea what Dr. Yorder was talking about, so he gave him a call. The phone was answered by a woman's voice. He couldn't tell whether it came from a machine or an actual human being but, as he recalled, he had the same problem when he met the receptionist face to face.

She took his name and Dr. Yorder picked up almost immediately.

"Is anyone else listening in on this call?" Dr. Yorder asked.

"Not that I'm aware of," Mark said.

There was a pause. "Interesting choice of words, Mark. Is that a legal disclaimer cleared by the district attorney's office so they can use this recording in court?"

"I am not recording this call nor is any law enforcement agency that I know of, okay? Now what is bothering you?"

"Ever since your friend left here this morning, I've been going over the whole thing in my mind. I started thinking, what if it was some kind of setup? If it is, I want to state now, for the record, that he walked in saying you sent him for syringes and a vial of Versed. You're a doctor, I granted the request as a professional courtesy. I would never have given them to him otherwise. So if you sent him for any other purpose, it's entrapment."

Mark felt goose bumps rise on his skin. He could think of only one person who knew he'd been to see Dr. Yorder.

"This man who wanted the sedatives," Mark asked, "did he look like he'd just stepped out of a John Wayne movie?"

Dr. Yorder breathed a sigh of relief. "So you *did* send the guy. I was worried there for a minute. Where did you find this guy, at a rodeo someplace?"

"How much Versed did you give him?"

"Ten cc's, just like you asked," Dr. Yorder said. "I don't get you, Mark. You're too good to give him the stuff yourself but you don't mind sending him to me for it. Interesting ethics you've got there."

"I didn't send him, Manny."

Dr. Yorder caught his breath. "Then how did he know about me? How did he know to use your name? And how come you're able to describe him?"

"He followed me when I visited you the other day and must have improvised the rest," Mark said. "He's a United States Marshal."

"Oh my God."

"Don't worry," Mark said. "It's not you he's after."

"Then who?"

The question raised another shiver on Mark's skin. He could think of only one person Tom Wade could still want and why he'd need a sedative.

Mark hung up on Dr. Yorder, leaving his question in the air, and quickly dialed Steve's cell phone.

There was no answer. After five rings, he got kicked into Steve's voice mail. Mark left a message, asking Steve to call him right away, and hung up.

Mark turned to his computer, pulled up Rebecca Jordan's admission information on screen, found her home phone number, and gave her a call.

He let the line ring twenty times. There was no answer, not even from a machine.

Something was very wrong. He could feel it.

Rebecca Jordan was in danger. And so was his son.

He reached for the phone again to call the police, then stopped himself. What would he tell them? That he couldn't reach Rebecca and Steve on the phone? That he had a feeling there was trouble?

The police wouldn't help him. Mark was on his own.

He jotted down Rebecca's address and hurried out, feeling an overwhelming sense of dread.

Mark borrowed Jesse's car and drove with one arm to Rebecca Jordan's apartment in Culver City, using surface streets to avoid the gridlocked freeway. It was the longest half hour of his life. The dread that had hung over him since leaving the hospital became blood-chilling fear when he saw Steve's car parked in front of the apartment building.

There could be a hundred harmless explanations why Steve's car was still there, but Mark knew none of them applied.

There was violence in the air.

Mark parked in a red zone, ran into the courtyard, and started looking for Rebecca's apartment. His eyes were immediately drawn to the one open door in the building. As he approached, he recognized the splintered pieces of the coffee table on the floor.

"Steve!" he yelled, bursting into the apartment.

His son was on his knees, still too dizzy to stand, rubbing the back of his head.

"I'm okay," Steve said. "Check on her."

Lissy was getting groggily to her feet as well and, like Steve, was more concerned about someone else's well-being than her own.

"Is Rebecca okay?" Lissy said weakly. "She's all alone in her room."

Mark scrambled down the hallway, past one empty bedroom to the other, where he saw Cuddle Bear in a chair facing an unmade bed, pillows propped up against the head-board.

Rebecca was gone. As he knew she would be.

She wouldn't have been able to leave on her own with her broken arm and leg. His eyes searched the room. It only took him a moment to find what he was looking for. On the floor beside the bed was an empty syringe.

Mark took a handkerchief from his pocket, picked up the syringe, and placed it on the nightstand to prevent someone from stepping on it and to preserve any fingerprints.

He went to the kitchen, took two ice packs from the freezer, and brought them to the living room, where he found Steve helping Lissy onto the couch. Her cheek was swollen and bruised.

"Rebecca is gone," Mark said, handing ice packs to both Steve and Lissy. "Tom Wade has her."

"He's the one who walloped me with the coffee table," Steve said. "How did you know Wade would be here?"

Mark told Steve about the phone call from Dr. Yorder and the details of their conversation, though he left the doctor's name out of it. He also shared his theory that Wade sedated Rebecca so he could carry her out of the apartment without a struggle.

"Is he really a United States Marshal?" Lissy asked, holding the ice pack to her cheek.

"How did you know he was a marshal?" Steve asked.

"He showed me his badge, right before he decked me. One of these days, it would be nice to see you without getting the crap beaten out of me first."

Steve smiled. "You're one tough lady."

"And you're my knight in shining Levis," she said.

"Wade didn't make any effort to hide his identity," Steve said, turning to his dad. "In fact, he made sure she knew who he was before he attacked her. Surely he knew she'd tell the authorities his name."

"He's an honest man," Mark said.

"Who punches a civilian, clobbers a cop, and kidnaps a woman." Steve picked up his gun off the floor and put it in his holster. "Does he still think he's capturing a fugitive? Nobody is going to prosecute her, but now they sure as hell will be lining up to prosecute him. What is Tom Wade hoping to accomplish?"

It was a good question, one Mark had been thinking about since he got off the phone with Dr. Yorder.

"This isn't about the law or arresting Rebecca anymore," Mark said. "Wade wants justice."

"He's lost his mind," Steve said.

"He's lost his son," Mark said.

"But Rebecca didn't kill him," Steve said. "Wade did."

"It all goes back to the murder of the sheriff's deputy in Spokane. Rebecca and Pike were both in the car that ran him over," Mark said. "That's the event that ultimately led to the moment when Wade shot Pike. If she isn't held responsible in some way, then there's only one person left for Wade to blame for his son's death."

"Himself," Steve said.

"I don't think he can live with that," Mark said.

"I don't care whether he can or not. The way I see it, he's a kidnapper now, armed and dangerous." Steve took out his cell phone and started dialing. "I'm putting out an APB and alerting the FBI."

While Steve made the call, Mark examined Lissy's bruise and made sure she was comfortable. He didn't see any reason to call an ambulance, or any indication that her injuries merited a visit to the hospital. She was relieved to hear that. There was a big deductible on her medical insurance and she was going to need the money to buy new furniture.

Steve hung up the phone and came over to them.

"The APB is going out now, along with Wade's picture and the make and license number of his rental car, though he's probably switched cars or plates by now," Steve said. "I can't figure out what he's doing. He could be anywhere."

Mark thought about everything he'd learned about Rebecca Jordan since she leaped out of her office window. He thought about Wade's unwavering belief in justice and his son Pike's rebellion against it. And he thought about the number of syringes Wade took and the amount of sedative in a vial of Versed.

When he put those facts together, it all made sense.

"I know where he's going," Mark said.

CHAPTER THIRTY

Tom Wade knew how to run without leaving tracks, physically or electronically. He knew how to blend into a sea of faces and become invisible. He knew how to survive without an identity.

And he knew none of it mattered. Because he knew the ultimate truth no fugitive was willing to accept:

Everybody leaves a trail.

He'd been a hunter too long. In the end, the pursuer always had the advantage.

They were out there, chasing him even now, but he wasn't worried. By the time they found him, his job would be done.

Justice would be served.

Wade was driving a Toyota Camry, the best-selling car in America. There were hundreds of thousands on the road. It was blank, unremarkable, and to the casual observer almost identical to a dozen other Japanese and Korean sedans. The LoJack had been deactivated, the rental car stickers removed, the license plates changed. No one would notice the car or its driver.

He took an indirect route to where he was going, adding hours to what already would have been a twenty-hour drive, but he didn't care. It was a necessary precaution.

Every four hours, he got off the freeway or whatever road he was on, found a secluded spot, and changed his license plates. He chose from among the collection he stole before leaving LA or, if opportunity allowed, swapped them with a car parked wherever he'd stopped. Wade also used the time to relieve himself, change his clothes, alter his appearance, and tend to Rebecca. He gave her food or water and, if she was getting too clear-headed, another sedative.

Wade filled up the gas tank only when he was certain his prisoner was unconscious, covering her up with a blanket in the backseat before going to pay the attendant in cash.

There was no need to get food; he brought all the sandwiches, potato chips, water, and Coca-Cola that he needed.

Wade drove straight through without sleep. He was afraid to close his eyes. Afraid of what he'd see.

But he saw it anyway.

At night, Pike stood just beyond the reach of his headlights, smoke curling from the bullet hole in his skull. During the day, Pike's body lay in the shimmering waves of heat rising from the asphalt, blood pooling underneath him.

Pike haunted him as he had for the last eight years. But it was different now. This time, Wade knew for certain that Pike was dead. Because he'd executed Pike himself.

His son robbed a convenience store and killed a sheriff's deputy. He faked his own death and ran from the law. But it was futile. Nobody can run from the law.

You can't run from me.

It was Wade's sworn duty to see that justice was served. He'd built his life around that obligation. And Tom Wade always got the job done.

There was still one more thing to do, one last reckoning, and then it would be over.

Hour after hour passed, his mind completely blank, a single gunshot ringing incessantly in his ears for thirteen hundred miles. The world around him became a dizzying, carousel blur of passing cars and changing landscape, moonlight and sunshine.

He didn't hear Rebecca whimpering. He didn't hear his own sobs.

His attention finally focused on something familiar, the Great Northern Clock Tower rising over Riverfront Park and the Spokane Falls in the heart of the city.

The clock struck high noon. It felt right.

Soon he was driving along the same sunbaked road his son sped down eight years before in a stolen Chevy. It was a dead part of town now, lined with boarded-up storefronts and abandoned gas stations, weeds poking up through the cracked asphalt.

He passed the convenience store that Pike held up all those years ago. It was a falafel stand now. People died and lives were changed because of events that happened there, but it didn't show. Nothing marked the place. Nobody would ever know.

A few miles later, he passed the spot where the deputy was run over. Someone had made a simple white cross and staked it into the dirt along the roadside. The cross was rotted and cracked, the paint peeling. Several dried, long-dead bouquets of flowers lay in front of it. Someone kept coming back. Someone didn't want anyone to forget that blood once soaked this ground.

Not far ahead, the road curved towards the river and the roiling rapids of fate. Everything would come full circle. Justice would be done.

But when he rounded that corner, Tom Wade saw a line of police cars blocking the road, providing cover for the dozens of officers aiming their weapons at him.

He slowed to a stop twenty-five yards from the police barricade and glanced in his rearview mirror to see squad cars peeling out from hiding behind the storefronts he'd passed, coming together to block his retreat.

But Tom Wade had no intention of retreating. It was never an option, not once in his life.

He kept his left hand on the wheel and with his right, slid his gun out from under the newspaper that covered it on the passenger seat.

Dr. Mark Sloan stepped out from behind the barricade and walked slowly towards Wade's car.

Twenty-four hours earlier, it was decided, for the sake of public safety, to let Tom Wade make his journey to Spokane. It was Mark's opinion, and one shared by the U.S. Marshals' office, that Wade wouldn't harm Rebecca until he got to his destination.

There was some discussion among the various law enforcement entities, who'd gathered in an immense conference room at LAPD headquarters, about mounting an interstate dragnet for Tom Wade. But the authorities feared that stopping Wade along the way could put Rebecca in jeopardy and lead to innocent civilians getting hurt, either in a high-speed car chase or in the cross fire of a shoot-out.

They were reasonably certain where Wade was going. They knew it was a location they could control. And they knew that they'd have a day to prepare. It seemed like waiting for him there was the safest and most effective alternative.

Mark and Steve flew up to Spokane to work with the local authorities and set up the roadblock.

Meanwhile, the law enforcement agencies in California, Oregon, and Washington quietly searched for Wade along the major highways. The officers had strict orders to keep their distance if he was spotted, to do nothing that might spook him and provoke a confrontation. But if the right opportunity came up, like finding him sleeping in his car at a rest stop, the U.S. Marshals wanted to take it.

But Wade was good. He wasn't spotted until he hit

Spokane on Interstate 395 and then he was closely tracked overhead by two choppers.

Now the moment had arrived. Wade had returned to the river.

There was a lot of debate over whether Mark Sloan or a trained hostage negotiator or Wade's long-time supervisor should approach the renegade marshal. In the end, it was decided that Mark would appear the least threatening and, having been at the scene of Pike's death, the most likely to talk Wade down. The only person who was still against the idea was Steve.

Mark gave a lot of thought to what he was going to say to Wade, incorporating the unsolicited advice he'd received during the night from three police shrinks, one FBI psychologist, and four different hostage negotiators.

But as Mark approached the car and saw the weariness and sadness on Wade's face, he ditched all his rehearsed lines and decided to go with whatever felt right at the moment.

Wade lowered his driver's side window and Mark stepped up to it, glancing into the backseat to see Rebecca under a blanket, half-conscious, groaning softly. She looked fine for a woman who'd spent the last twenty-four hours under moderate sedation.

"You look tired, Marshal," Mark said.

"I am." Wade's gaze drifted past Mark to the river, just beyond the edge of the roadblock. "Right down to my bones."

Only a few days ago, Wade gunned down his own son. Mark couldn't imagine the pain that Wade was feeling and the corrosive effect it was having on his mind. It didn't matter whether it had been the right thing to do or not. No man should have to do what Wade had done.

"How would you like to handle this?" Mark asked softly.

"I'd like you to step back behind those police cars and let justice take its course."

Mark tipped his head towards Rebecca. "We both know she was tried, convicted, and sent to prison. She's done her time, Marshal."

"She broke her parole," Wade said.

Mark chose his words carefully. "I don't think you took her into custody and brought her all the way back here for a parole violation."

"They murdered a deputy and drove into the river," Wade said. "They both should have died that day. Now Pike has paid for his crime with his life. So should she."

"You're a United States Marshal," Mark said.

Wade nodded.

"You've stood for the law all your life," Mark said. "You do this, and you will commit the same crime as your son. You do this and your life will stand for murder. How will that serve justice? What will your son have died for then?"

Wade took a deep breath and let it out slowly.

Mark saw a change in Wade, an even deeper weariness showing itself in his lined face. The ruggedness and authority that Wade naturally radiated seemed to fade away, leaving him weak. It was as if Wade had aged five years in the time it took to exhale.

Below the dash, out of sight of the police officers behind the roadblock, Wade aimed his gun squarely at Mark's chest.

"Tell your son to drop his weapons and approach my vehicle," Wade said. "Tell him I have a gun on you."

Mark did as he was told.

Steve made a show of laying his gun on the ground and removing his Kevlar vest to prove he had no hidden weapons. Then, with his arms held loosely at his sides, he walked slowly up to the car, keeping his eyes on Wade the whole time.

"The back door is unlocked, Lieutenant," Wade said. "You may take the prisoner."

Steve looked into the car and saw the gun leveled at Mark.

"What about my father?" Steve asked.

"I'd like him to stay here with me for a little while," Wade said. "He'll be fine as long as nobody shoots me."

Mark nodded at his son. "It's okay."

Steve opened the back door, put his arms under Rebecca, and gently lifted her up. He carried her back towards the police line and the waiting ambulance beyond it.

Mark watched Steve go, then turned to Wade, who was no longer holding a gun in his hand. Instead, Wade held his badge.

"All my life, I served the law," Wade said. "Even when it meant taking my son's life."

"You didn't take his life," Mark said. "He threw it away."

Wade shook his head. "You're a father, Dr. Sloan. You know as well as I do that a son is a reflection of the man who raised him. I made Pike the man he became, so I'm ultimately responsible for the mistakes he made."

He tossed Mark his badge.

Mark caught it and saw a familiar look in Wade's eyes. He'd seen it once before, when Rebecca Jordan met his gaze from the window of her office.

Before Mark could say anything, Wade floored the gas pedal and sped off towards the roadblock.

The officers scrambled for safety, one or two managing to fire off an errant shot as they fled, shattering Wade's windshield.

But Wade kept coming.

He smashed his way between two police cruisers and then flew off the embankment, his car flipping over in midair before dropping upside down into the roiling waters of the river below.

Mark ran to the edge of the embankment just as the water surged over the car and swallowed it up in its inexorable current.

Whatever secrets his tormentor wanted to know, Mark was ready to reveal—his ATM codes, his e-mail password, his bank account numbers, anything. If only the torture would end.

Of course, they didn't call it torture. The politically correct term was "physical therapy." And they didn't call the sadistic practitioners of this evil art tormentors but "therapists."

The pain shooting through Mark's arm didn't feel like therapy to him. It felt like his arm was breaking all over again.

"Okay, let's count to three," said Paul, holding Mark's left arm against his chest. The ponytailed therapist gently bent the arm towards Mark's shoulder.

Mark, lying on a table, curled in pain.

"One Mississippi, two Mississippi—" Paul began.

"Couldn't you pick a different state?" Mark said through gritted teeth. "Like Ohio? Or Iowa?"

"—three Mississippi," Paul finished, releasing Mark's arm. The pain immediately subsided. "The flexion is definitely improving, Dr. Sloan."

Mark relaxed, his arm throbbing, his body damp with sweat in his shorts and T-shirt. "Are you sure this is good for me?"

"Absolutely, it's the best medicine," Paul said. "In a few more weeks, you'll be able to sign up for the Olympic arm wrestling team."

"You enjoy this way too much," Mark said. "Admit it, you like watching a doctor, a member of the senior staff, squirming in pain."

"If it hurts, you know we're doing some good," Paul said.

"That's the dumbest thing I ever heard." Mark knew that Paul was right, that the stretching exercises were necessary, but he didn't have to like it.

Mark was in the midst of an intense physical therapy regime to regain the range of motion he'd lost in his left arm after weeks in a cast.

"Ice that elbow up for twenty minutes and I'll see you tomorrow," Paul said.

"Can't wait," Mark groused.

He was on his way out of Community General's physical therapy unit when he nearly collided with Lenore Barber as she emerged from the smoking cessation workshop across the hall.

"Dr. Sloan," she said, offering him a big smile. "What a wonderful surprise."

"You look terrific, Lenore."

She'd gained some weight, but it was a good thing. It filled her out in a healthy way. Her skin seemed softer and her eyes radiated with energy.

"I feel wonderful," she said. "I'm six weeks smoke free."

"That's fantastic," Mark said.

"Just looking at a cigarette repulses me now," she said, then glanced at her watch. "Yikes, I'm running late."

"You have a property to show?"

"My weekly Bible reading workshop, which reminds me, I have something for you." She rummaged around in her enormous purse and pulled out a Bible. "A small token of my appreciation."

"Thank you," Mark said, astonished.

She took his free hand and squeezed it. "God touched my life, Mark. He saved me."

"I can't tell you how happy I am for you," Mark said. He also couldn't tell her that it wasn't God who saved her from killing herself with cigarettes; it was Jesse Travis.

But as Mark watched Lenore hurry off, happy and

healthy, he wondered about what motivated Jesse to mount such an elaborate con to convince one person to do the right thing.

Mark glanced at the Bible in his hand and decided maybe Lenore was right after all.

Read on for a preview of
Dr. Sloan's next adventure

THE PAST TENSE

Coming from Signet in August 2005

Dr. Mark Sloan awoke that February morning to an empty house, feeling as if he hadn't slept at all.

He hadn't slept well the last few nights. It could have been the rain, which pummeled the house all night long. Maybe he wasn't accustomed to the sound anymore, the rainstorm coming after one of Southern California's prolonged droughts, which had left the hillsides brittle, dry and prone to wildfires.

Only a few days ago, the newspapers were full of dire warnings about the parched soil, about catastrophic crop failures and uncontrollable fires, about the desperate need to conserve water before Los Angeles withered away from thirst.

Now, after three days of rain, those concerns were gone. Instead, everyone was worried about the water-saturated soil, about deadly flash floods and gigantic landslides, sweeping power outages and gridlocked freeways. Sandbags were being handed out at fire houses across the county. TV stations were interrupting regular programming with live "Storm Watch" reports, as if the city were facing an imminent hurricane instead of a common rainstorm.

Sometimes, Mark wondered if what really worried people was having nothing to worry about.

It wasn't raining in the morning, though the dark clouds

remained, exhausted from the long night of thundering and pouring, gathering their strength before unleashing their mayhem again.

As Mark made himself coffee and looked out at the beach, covered with seaweed, driftwood, shells and trash churned up by the stormy seas, he realized he'd been sleeping poorly for a while now.

It started when he'd witnessed a woman leap out the window of her office building. She's survived, but the memory of that horrible moment tormented Mark's sleep until he discovered what drove her to suicide and then solved the problem for her.

But even after that, sleep still didn't come easy. He'd broken his arm in a car accident and had difficulty with his cast getting comfortable in bed. Once the cast was removed, his arm was sore for weeks, making it hard to get a good night's rest.

Perhaps it was age, he thought. As much as he hated to admit it, he wasn't a young man any more. He was in his late 60s. His days of eight hours of deep, uninterrupted sleep might be gone for good.

He took his coffee to the kitchen table and sat by himself, watching a flock of seagulls, circling over the sand, picking at the enormous clumps of seaweed. He listened to the crash of the waves, the squawk of the gulls, the settling of the house, and the wind-like *whoosh* of cars passing by on the Pacific Coast Highway.

He was acutely aware of the emptiness of his Malibu beach house, which seemed to double in size whenever his son Steve was away.

Steve lived on the first floor but, lately, had been spending more and more nights at his girlfriend Lissy's apartment.

Although his son's job as an LAPD homicide detective kept him busy and out of the house a lot, Steve's presence had been there even if he wasn't. If Mark didn't run into

Steve at night, or on his way out in the morning, there would always be signs that his son had been there. Dishes in the sink. Sandy tennis shoes on the deck. Case files on the coffee table. But lately, the house looked the same in the morning as it had the night before.

Maybe it wasn't the rain, or his arm, or his age, that was causing him to rest so uneasily, Mark thought. It's being alone.

He immediately rejected the idea. Loneliness couldn't be the problem. His life was full of people and activity. Between his work at the hospital, and consulting on homicide investigations for the LAPD, he had very little time alone. The more he thought about it, he realized he should be savoring the time to himself.

Or was that what he was afraid of?

Was all the work simply a way to avoid being alone?

Ridiculous.

Mark set his empty coffee cup aside. As a doctor, he knew the best prescription for what ailed him: a brisk walk on the beach, followed by a scalding shower and a big, healthy breakfast rich in fruit and fiber. Two hours from now, he'd feel rested and energized and ready to work. All this moping would be forgotten.

Until tomorrow morning, anyway.

He changed into an old pair of jeans, a faded sweat-jacket and his most comfortable pair of ragged tennis shoes and hurried down the steps from his second-floor deck to the beach below.

Mark paused on the bottom step and took a deep breath, luxuriating in the crisp, clean air, rich with the ocean mist. That was one of the great things about a storm, it washed the gunk out of the air. Of course, that meant the muck was dumped onto the streets, where it was swept into the gutters and out to sea, where—

He abruptly dropped that line of thought. He decided it

was better to just enjoy the fresh air than think about how it got that way.

The sand was pleasantly thick under his feet, soaked wet and pocked-marked by raindrops. He was dismayed by the amount of trash that had been washed ashore amidst the seaweed, driftwood and palm fronds. Styrofoam cups, fast food cartons, newspapers, candy wrappers, cigarette stubs, beer bottles . . .

It could be worse, he thought. A few years back, the morning surf littered the shoreline from Manhattan Beach to as far north as Ventura with thousands of used syringes that'd been illegally dumped into the sea.

As he worked his way around and over the obstacles in his path, his walk became more of a slog. Ahead of him, the seagulls picked and fluttered and fought over a pile of kelp resting above the berm. From the smell drifting his way on the ocean breeze, Mark guessed that the carcass of dead seal had washed ashore, tangled in the rubbery vines and tiny bladders.

As he got closer, he saw the hint of a fin and the silver glint of scales. It wasn't a seal after all, but rather some kind of large, dead fish.

Mark turned, and was about to continue on his walk, but curiosity got the better of him. No fish he'd ever seen had a tail fin quite so perfect or scales that shone so bright. He had to know what it was.

So he grimaced against the stench and crouched beside the mound of seaweed, scattering a thousand flies and infuriating the gulls, who continued to hover low over him, squawking their fury at his intrusion.

Using a stick of driftwood, he brushed away dozens of hungry sand crabs and carefully parted the strands of seaweed to get a better look. First he saw the long, graceful fin, tapering to a fan-tail at its point. Then, as he cleared more kelp, he saw mane of fiery red hair.

For a moment, he simply stared in disbelief.

It was a mermaid.

Her face was a ghostly pale, almost translucent. Her eyes were wide and green, her lips slightly parted, her slender throat slit from ear-to-ear.   •

It started to rain again just as the crime scene techs finished erecting the tent over the clump of seaweed where the woman's body had been found.

While she was being kept dry, scores of officers and forensic investigators were getting drenched as they moved slowly up and down the beach, looking for clues in a race with the rain and tide, both of which threatened to wash away any remaining evidence.

Dr. Amanda Bentley, the medical examiner, squatted beside the body, waving away the swarm of flies and sand crabs that stubbornly refused to give up their claim to the corpse.

"She isn't a mermaid. She's wearing a costume," Amanda said. "And those big openings on either side of her throat aren't gills."

"I figured that much out for myself," Mark said, studying the body.

The only reason that he was still allowed to be at the crime scene was that Dr. Amanda Bentley worked for him, too. She was staff pathologist at Community General Hospital, where her lab doubled as the adjunct county morgue. Amanda not only juggled two jobs, but she was also a single parent, raising a six-year-old son. And she did it all with seemingly boundless energy and enthusiasm. Mark couldn't figure out how she pulled it off.

"It's not going to be easy determining time of death," Amanda said. "But judging by the lividity, the shriveling of the skin, and the lack of bloating, I'd say she's been in the water no more than eight-to-ten hours. I'll know more after I get her on the table."

"This may come as a shock to you," a familiar voice said, "but I'm actually the homicide detective in charge of the investigation."

They turned to see Steve Sloan entering the tent, water dripping from his umbrella, his hair surprisingly dry. His badge was clipped to his belt.

"I know it's just a small technicality," Steve said, "but shouldn't you be saving your report for me?"

Amanda shrugged, tipping her head towards Mark. "He was here first."

"That's only because the body washed up in his front yard," Steve said.

"Isn't it your front yard, too?" she asked. "Come to think of it, weren't you wearing those same clothes yesterday when I saw you at the beheading?"

"Beheading?" Mark asked.

"Never mind," Steve said.

"This couple, married for thirty years, is sitting down to dinner," Amanda said. "The husband turns to his wife and says that the casserole she made for dinner is too salty. So his wife does the natural thing. She smacks her husband with a cast-iron frying pan, cuts off his head with an electric carving knife, and tosses it out the window."

"What happened to the casserole?" Mark asked.

"She's not one to waste food. She kept it and offered to serve it to us while we worked the crime scene," Amanda glanced at Steve. "I didn't think it was salty, did you?"

Steve shook his head.

Mark stared at his son in disbelief. "You *ate* the casserole?"

"It wasn't the casserole that killed the guy," Steve said.

"In a way it was," Amanda said.

"Could we please move on?" Steve said.

"You're right," Mark said. "Let stick to the point. Steve spent the night with his girlfriend."

Steve groaned.

"What girlfriend?" Amanda said. "He's never mentioned a girlfriend. Who is she?"

"Her name is Lissy," Mark said. "She used to work nights as a technical support operator until her job got outsourced to India. Now she's studying for her real estate license. He made her a coffee table. Not from scratch, of course. One of those snap-together things from Ikea."

"They don't just snap-together," Steve said. "There's fifty parts you've got to assemble with hundreds of special screws and inter-locking bolt-thingies using only this tiny little tool they give you that's impossible to get a good grip on . . ."

Mark and Amanda stared at him, making him feel self-conscious. He cleared his throat.

"Do you think we could discuss something else now?" Steve motioned to the body. "Like, for instance, this dead mermaid."

"She's not a mermaid," Mark said. "It's a costume."

"Thank you, Dad." Steve replied. "It's nice to know I won't have to go to Atlantis to interview suspects. What can you tell me, Amanda?"

"I'm not a forensics expert, but I'm certain this wasn't where she was killed."

"Because there are no signs that she bled out here?" Steve said. "The blood could have been washed away by the surf."

"It's not the lack of blood," Amanda said. "It's the body. She's covered with post-mortem scrapes and some deep, ragged gashes. She didn't get them from being splashed by the tide on a soft, sandy beach. This body was slammed against a rocky shoreline a few times before washing up here. I'd bet she was in the ocean most of the night."

Mark sighed. "Which means that, for the moment, the victim herself is the only evidence we have to work with to solve her murder."

"We?" Steve asked.

"She did wash up on my front yard," Mark said.

"That doesn't mean you've got the right to start investigating her murder."

"Of course it does," Mark said.

"I have the strangest feeling I've experienced this conversation before," Amanda said.

"Send that mermaid costume down to the crime lab as soon as you can, okay?" Steve said.

"Sure," Amanda said. "If you like, I can also finish your end of the argument for you. I think I know all the lines by heart. I can even tell you who wins."

"I know who wins," Steve said, leading his father out of the tent, putting his arm over his shoulder and sheltering him from the rain under his umbrella. They headed for the beach house.

"You've got some kind of luck, Dad."

"What do you mean?"

"A couple months ago, you walked in on a murder at the house next door. Now a corpse washes up on the beach, practically on your porch."

"*Our* porch," Mark corrected.

"If I was one of your neighbors," Steve said, "I'd move."

THE SERIES BASED ON THE HIT TV SHOW
BY
LEE GOLDBERG

DIAGNOSIS MURDER:
THE SILENT PARTNER

0-451-20959-1

Dr. Mark Sloan is assigned to the LAPD's "unsolved homicide" files. As he reopens one case on the murder of a woman whose killer currently sits on Death Row, Sloan learns that the wrong man was charged. And the real killer is still at large...

DIAGNOSIS MURDER:
THE DEATH MERCHANT

0-451-21130-8

A dream vacation in Hawaii turns into a nightmare for Dr. Mark Sloan and his son when a man they've befriended falls victim to a shark attack. And things go from bad to worse when Mark discovers the victim was already dead when the attack occured.

Also in this series:
DIAGNOSIS MURDER:
THE SHOOTING SCRIPT

0-451-21266-5

Available wherever books are sold or at
www.penguin.com